THE WEDDING CRASHER

A Sam Tate Mystery

by

Nikki Stern

Cover Design: Diana Ani Stokely at GRAFIX *to go*

445 Sayre Drive
Princeton, NJ 08540
rutheniapress@gmail.com

ISBN: 978-0-9995487-3-8

LCCN: 2019900017

Library of Congress Cataloging-in-Publication Data is on file with the Library of Congress.

Acknowledgements

A number of professionals lent their expertise concerning law enforcement practices in Tennessee. Thanks to Josh DeVine with the offices of the Tennessee Bureau of Investigation (TBI), staff at the Office of the Chief Medical Examiner, and Pickett County Sheriff's Office administrator Katy Smith. Of paramount assistance was Former FBI Special Agent Russell Gregory III, whose working knowledge of field office work in both Tennessee and Florida contributed greatly to my understanding of the complexities of law enforcement as practiced state by state.

Several editors contributed to the effort. Steve Axelrod's wisdom about writing dialogue proved invaluable. Katharine Sand's insightful encouragement prompted me to recast my central character as a far more flawed yet ultimately relatable heroine. Laura Dragonette was a dream copy editor. Jeanette DeMain, Martha Anderson, and Lezlie Bishop contributed their proofing skills. Diana Ani Stokely provided creative design. The cover image is courtesy of Alison Ellis at Floral Artistry.

As always, infinite gratitude goes to my friend and sibling Deborah for her all-around talents and encouragement. To her and the other readers and followers who have expressed unwavering confidence in my ability to tell a tale and spin a story, I promise to keep writing.

SPRING

"Love many things, for therein lies the true strength, and whosoever loves much performs much, and can accomplish much, and what is done in love is done well."

~ Vincent van Gogh

Chapter 1

The dead woman lay in the clearing like a macabre version of Sleeping Beauty. She wore a modest, long-sleeved ivory gown, set off by luminescent pearl drop earrings and a matching necklace that almost hid the dried blood around her throat. Her head rested on a satin pillow, her silky walnut hair spread behind her like a fan. The right hand held a bouquet of wilted flowers and rested on her chest underneath the left, absent the fourth finger. The ring finger.

Sheriff Sam Tate stood to one side of the grim tableau, arms folded, and took it all in: the victim; the tall white-haired man who knelt by the body; the deputy who walked the scene in throwaway boots, snapping pictures; the pale young man in running gear sitting on a rock, head almost to his knees; the uniformed officer who squatted beside him.

Sam had dressed in her standard uniform of pressed black slacks and a spotless white shirt. A shaft of early-morning sun bounced off the polished badge at her left breast pocket. On her right wrist, she wore a utilitarian watch. Three small studs twinkled along one earlobe, her single visible concession to a rebellious streak. She'd pulled her unruly dark locks into a tight braid. Ray-Bans shielded her green eyes, though not the line that formed between her brows.

One of the victim's low-heeled white pumps had dropped off to reveal a slim ankle in hosiery. Stockings, not pantyhose, held up by an old-fashioned garter. Sam didn't need to look.

He's back.

She lifted her eyes to the stately trees that hovered over the victim. *Quercus alba*. White oak, sturdy, long-lived, common to most of eastern Tennessee. These trees stood inside the Cordell Hull Birthplace State Historic Park, named for the native son who served as FDR's secretary of state. Hull, who authored both the income and the inheritance tax laws, wasn't all that popular with the locals. His daddy, though, enjoyed a solid reputation as the owner of a thriving moonshine enterprise. The park even featured a visit to Bunkum Cave, site of Hull Senior's former distillery.

I could use a drink right about now, Sam thought.

"Morning, Sheriff Tate." Detective Abdi Issen's slow drawl rolled across the clearing. He rose from his crouch, put a reassuring hand on the runner's shoulder, and walked over. Though he'd likely been a half hour at the scene, he looked as crisp and pressed as she did. He favored his boss with a wide smile that lightened her mood.

Sam routinely thanked the fates that Abdi had agreed to move up to Pickett County from Nashville to help her out. In the process, he'd left a promising career and his close-knit family. It couldn't have been easy being a dark face in a light community. Yet Abdi made it work.

"Morning, Abdi. What do we have so far?"

"Our Good Samaritan over there is Rich Deckler." Abdi indicated the young man on the rock dressed in shorts and a sweat-stained T-shirt. "He ran by the body, stopped, called us, and upchucked, in that order."

"Understandable. Might as well send him home. Any idea who she is?"

"Not yet. I took a digital scan of her fingerprints, but DOJ is slow to respond and not everyone is in the system.

Seemed like a visual ID might be faster. Sent an image out to see if it connects to a recent missing persons report."

His phone pinged. "Well, what do you know? Hold on here. Missing persons report was filed at the Madison precinct an hour ago. The woman is tentatively identified as Elizabeth Newsome, aka Bitsy, a Nashville real estate agent specializing in commercial properties."

"Huh. Nashville is more'n two hours away. How'd she end up here?"

"No idea." Abdi swiped at the screen. "The report was filed by a Mark Talcott, a lawyer who says he's her fiancé. Their wedding was scheduled for mid-May. Ah, damn."

They both took a couple seconds of silence.

"Abdi, I want you to call over there and let the officer who took the report know what we've found. They'll assign a homicide detective. You know the drill. Make that person your best buddy. We need information on Ms. Newsome's movements over the past few days. Everything from GPS and cell phone data to street cameras, if possible. Be cooperative, but make sure the detective on the case knows we own it."

"You got it. What about TBI?"

Rural counties partnered with the Tennessee Bureau of Investigation for help with serious crimes such as drug or sex trafficking, kidnapping, and homicide. Sometimes the request ran through the district attorney general's office. Other times a local officer would call directly to an agent they knew within the Criminal Investigative Division. Sam's contact was Nate Fillmore.

"We will need their expertise," she said. "I'll call Nate as soon as I speak with Doc Holloway. Meanwhile, keep an eye on Ken." She tilted her head in the direction of the focused young deputy. “I’m sure he’s being thorough. Still, you’re going to do some mentoring on this one, Abdi. We both are.”

Abdi nodded. He’d come up five years behind Sam at Metropolitan Nashville Police Department (MNPD), the last three as a homicide detective. Pickett County deputies, on the other hand, had little need to know much about murder investigations. Until recently.

Dr. Jedediah Holloway rose stiffly at Sam’s approach. Tall and silver-haired with a slight stoop, he appeared every inch a courtly country doctor, albeit one with emergency room experience and a stint as an army medic. The man had seen all manner of mayhem.

“Good morning, Samantha.” Doc Holloway was the only one who didn’t call her Sam or Sheriff. She found it rather sweet. “Although not good for this young woman,” he continued. “If you're expecting me to provide details at this juncture, expect to be disappointed. I won’t speculate.”

“I understand. We believe her name is Elizabeth Newsome.”

“Good to know. Ms. Newsome wore nail extensions and false lashes, both removed. Her face is makeup-free, her hair freshly washed, all things being relative. Based on lividity and temperature, she’s been dead more than a day but less than three. That’s all I know. Well, except what might appear obvious, which is that this is a homicide.”

Sam waited. She knew Holloway’s routine.

“Preliminary evidence indicates she died from a cut on each side of her neck. We’d call that sharp force trauma. The killer knew quite a bit about human anatomy.”

"How's that?"

"The cuts are neat and deep, one across each carotid artery. The killer didn't bother to slice across the throat. That way is messy but not always fatal. Hit the carotid arteries, you can count on exsanguination in less than a minute."

"Wouldn't a person have to saw through the upper layers to cut the deeper arteries?"

"Depends on the instrument used and the user's skill. This killer earns high marks for expertise. An optimal stroke would require the victim's head be pushed forward. The muscles become looser, which make them easier to slice. None of this head-thrown-back business like you see in the movies. Dramatic but unproductive."

Holloway rubbed his neck. "Still, a set of cuts like this should generate a lot of blood. We have nothing. Wherever this happened, the perpetrator cleaned up thoroughly. Which suggests a working knowledge of forensic investigation or a neatness pathology."

"Or both." Sam bent down to look more closely at the victim's throat. "Weapon?"

"Something sharp."

"Doc."

"Perhaps a knife. The Internet is filled with ads for military-style weapons. The forensic pathologist can tell us more, no doubt."

"What about the ring finger?"

"If I had to guess, I'd say a cleaver. As you may have surmised, Samantha"—Holloway leaned over with a grunt and lifted the dress—"Elizabeth Newsome is wearing stockings with blue garters." He dropped the hem.

"Just like the other four."

"Including our own Claire Hooper, I'm afraid."

Sam recalled an April day much like this one, the seasons suspended between spring's promise and summer's heat. A body under an oak tree in the corner of a park just inside Pickett County. Brown hair, mid-twenties, pretty, dressed like a bride. A local girl named Claire Hooper who looked forward to a June wedding.

Hooper followed three other victims, two in Florida and one in Georgia. All were twenty-something brunettes with only their premarital status and the details of their murders in common. The FBI came on board after victim three. The lead case agent, Terry Sloan, remained in pursuit of a serial killer his agency dubbed the Wedding Crasher.

Despite the involvement of multiple agencies, the investigation stalled. Four years, four ritualistic murders, no leads. No who or why, only when: at the top of the fourth month of the year.

Then last April passed without incident.

"Maybe the killer quit," Abdi observed back then.

"Or he paused for personal reasons," Sam suggested. "He might be staking out new territory. Either way, it's not our problem. I'm not about to quarrel with fortune."

Fortune was apparently not done with Pickett County. How else to explain another dead young woman dressed like a bride and laid out like a damned sacrifice?

"I'm guessing our victim was knocked out before her throat was slit." Sam made a statement, not an inquiry.

"An autopsy will confirm," Holloway replied.

"Coincidence? Copycat?"

"That's your call, Samantha."

"Goddamn it all to hell."

Holloway looked at her, his eyes narrowed. "Has the Wedding Crasher returned to Pickett County?"

"You know me, Doc. I hate to speculate." She intended it as a joke, but neither of them so much as cracked a smile. "Excuse me. I need to make a call."

Sam had Nate Fillmore on speed dial. She'd met the agent when they worked the Hooper murder. A droll man with a supremely dry wit, he was married with two kids and a mortgage. He reported to the TBI offices in Nashville but lived in Algood, which put him closer to the region he served. Sam remembered he worked from home on certain days. She hoped today was one of them.

A child answered his phone. A little boy or girl. Sam couldn't tell.

"Hey, there." She spoke with the forced cheeriness of someone inexperienced at dealing with children. "Can I talk to your dad?"

"Can you?"

Sam briefly closed her eyes. "I should have asked if you'd let me talk with him. Will you?"

"Why?"

Sam didn't have the time or the inclination to deal with a deliberately oppositional young human. She debated whether to get into a lengthy discussion with this small creature about the responsibilities and obligations of a citizen of any age to help serve justice and the greater good. Then she heard Nate's voice in the background.

"JoEllen, what did I tell you about answering Daddy's cell phone?"

"This lady wants to talk with you."

"Thank you, sweetie. I'll talk and you get ready for school. Don't forget your pink sweater." The phone transferred hands. "Sam Tate, didn't expect your name to pop up on my cell phone this morning. What's going on?"

"I'm afraid I may be needing your services, Nate. We've got a body in the woods. Female. Mid-twenties. Throat slit. Laid out under the trees and dressed—"

"Like a bride. Ah, shit."

"And then some."

"You gonna make some other calls?"

"I'll probably reach out to Cookeville." The nearest FBI field office was a satellite of the larger one in Memphis.

"And our mutual friend in Tampa."

Sam almost faltered. "Of course."

"Because this may be a repeat performance."

"Or a copycat."

"Come on, Sam. What's your gut telling you?"

How she hated that question. "I can't afford to guess, Nate. The evidence as of this moment, evidence I need your people to review, suggests an MO identical to that used by Claire Hooper's killer. It likely matches the three other open homicides as well."

"So, the Wedding Crasher has returned to our fair county. Or never left."

Sam didn't answer. She swallowed the bile that rose in her throat and looked up again, hoping the old trees would deny the obvious. Instead, they stood as silent witnesses to an incontrovertible truth.

Chapter 2

Two hours later, Sam sat cross-legged on the floor of her locked office, hands at heart center, trying to slow her breathing and corral her racing thoughts. She wanted five minutes to steady herself before she went out to face the staff and let them know that the serial killer known as the Wedding Crasher might have made a reappearance in their sleepy burg.

What was she doing, anyway? She never intended to be sheriff. Her plan had been to scale back. Her decision to leave MNPD for a rural department took many of her colleagues by surprise. Abdi Issen. Her captain. And, of course, Larry Zielinski, her partner.

"I don't know why you wanna leave now, when everything's going your way," he told her. "Your close rate is through the roof. You're one of the youngest detectives we have. The squad respects you. The captain adores you. You're a hero and I ought to know, since you were the one who saved my ass during the warehouse shooting. Why would you move to Birdshit—?"

"Byrdstown, Larry. Pickett County, actually. I'm going to be their first-ever investigative detective."

"Whatever. Why move to the sticks when you've got it all going on here?" Concern swept across his weathered face. "Maybe you just need time off. Hell, between the shootout and Jay's death, not to mention your deployment, it's a lot to deal with for . . ."

"For a woman?" she retorted. She'd felt the misogyny, along with racism and homophobia, that percolated beneath the surface of the proudly reimagined police department. The new Nashville, with its international

Music scene and its rising reputation as a hot destination, continued to trip over its Southern roots from time to time.

"For anyone." Larry retorted.

"Sorry."

"All I'm trying to tell you, Tate, is you can fix whatever ails you without throwing away your career. Maybe you're suffering from PTSD. What does Doc Sommers have to say?"

"Zielinski." She invested the word with warning.

"I know, I'm out of bounds. I just don't want to lose my partner."

She tried to match his conciliatory tone. "Look, it's not any one thing." *More like three things.* "I just need a change of pace. Something less, I don't know, high-pressure."

Someplace where my nightmares won't find me, she could have added but didn't. Sam liked Larry and she trusted him with her life. Just not with her secrets.

Now, a little more than two years later, she found herself in charge of policing the sparsely populated county she'd fled to for solace. Hard enough to be a woman, a newcomer, and an outsider who rented a room from a gossipy widow and kept all her business in Nashville. Worse, she'd apparently been followed by a serial killer enamored of all things bridal. The irony was not lost on her.

Bitsy Newsome's body was on its way to a morgue in Nashville, with Holloway close behind. Abdi had reached out to Eddie Gould, a homicide detective from the Madison precinct, who was on his way to Newsome's condo. Warrants had already been requested for her phone records, her car's GPS, and her social media accounts. Nate and a forensic technician were on-site.

Sam had made a series of phone calls on the way back to the office to assure the higher-ups from the mayor to the county executive to the district attorney general that yes, she was on top of developments and no, she didn't intend to leave anyone out of the loop.

She still had to call FBI Special Agent Terry Sloan. He of the broad shoulders, crinkly smile, and amber eyes like gemstones.

"Jesus, Tate, give it a rest!" She clamped her hand over her mouth, too late to avoid the discrete knock.

"Sheriff?"

At the sound of Abdi's voice, Sam popped up off the floor and turned the lock.

"Come in. I thought it might be Kaylee. She tends to hover by the door."

"I've noticed. You okay, boss?"

"Not even close."

"I can't believe he's back after two years."

"Not necessarily," Sam replied. Unconvincing. Unconvinced.

"Sorry, Sheriff, but if it walks like a duck and talks likes a duck . . ." He noticed Sam rubbing her forehead. "You need coffee?"

"God, that's the last thing—"

As if on cue, Kaylee Simpson walked through the door carrying a fresh pot. As usual, she'd dressed more like a high school girl than a married forty-something mother of three sons. Multiple ear piercings lined one lobe, bangles filled one arm, and a small tattoo graced the inside of a wrist. She wore a neon-green crop top that barely reached to the waistband of her fitted black jeans.

"The poor woman may not know she comes across like a streetwalker, bless her heart," Sam's landlady once commented. Cora Granville was nothing if not blunt. Sam decided to ignore the old woman. No one else—including the mayor and the county commissioners—ever once complained about what Mrs. Simpson wore in or out of the office. They paid her salary. And Sam's.

Besides, Kaylee was an engaging and efficient assistant who'd been with Sam since Tom Jackson's fatal heart attack had elevated Sam to sheriff. She made god-awful coffee, though. She also had a habit of walking into Sam's office unannounced. The sheriff had tried and failed to broach the subject, but Kaylee's injured pout effectively derailed the conversation.

Sam suppressed a grimace, then pasted on a smile. "Coffee. Perfect."

"I know y'all don't like my coffee, Sheriff," Kaylee pouted. "Even though I went and mail-ordered those Arabica beans special for this office."

"We love your coffee, Kaylee," Abdi insisted. "Maybe you could use a little more water is all."

Kaylee put a fist to her waist in mock protest. "Abdi Issen, you don't understand anything about proper brewing!"

Most days, Sam found their banter mildly amusing. Not today.

"Enough, you two. Kaylee, let me know when everyone is gathered out front. Then I want to start the meeting."

The assistant grabbed the mug and flicked a triumphant look in Abdi's direction. She exited, hips swinging, long blond waves bouncing. Sam heard the sound of running water, then the less-than-reassuring gurgle of the coffeemaker.

Abdi stood in front of her, waiting.

"What?"

"Have you called the FBI?"

"In a minute."

As soon as he left, Sam took out her cell phone. Almost immediately, Kaylee reappeared at the door. "We're ready."

"Let's do this."

Sam read the concern on the faces of the people who reported to her. No one liked the idea of a homicide in the quiet community, much less one tied to a serial killer. Moreover, everyone knew a brunette in her twenties.

"I want to talk with you about the victim we found over at Cornell Hull today," she began. "Preliminary evidence indicates a homicide."

"A woman dressed like a bride, right?" someone called out. The statement prompted a wave of incoherent babbling.

"One at a time," Sam ordered. Hands shot up like weeds. "Ralph."

Ralph Cook, former quarterback at Pickett County High School. An all-around stand-up guy. "Is it the Wedding Crasher, Sheriff?"

"The crime scene suggests it could be." More mumbling. "*Could* be, people. Maybe it's staged. We're working with MNPD and TBI. I've also asked FBI Special Agent Terry Sloan to come up. He'll be here late tomorrow."

"We're turning this over to the Feebs?" asked a veteran named Cornelius "Cob" Atkins. Cob had three years with the state police and twenty-one with Pickett

County Sheriff's Office. In all that time, he had only worked one other homicide. He briefly considered a run for the top spot after Jackson's death, then changed his mind. Claimed he didn't need the pressure.

"We're not turning anything over to anyone, Cob. It's our case. We simply can't do the work on our own. FBI involvement will be limited for now to Special Agent Sloan with an assist from his local liaison until we decide what we're dealing with. As you all know, he's been leading the investigation into these serial killings for several years."

"What's he got to show for it?" asked Felix Booth, another old-timer.

Sam plowed ahead. "Look, we need their help, but they also need ours. Whatever kind of task force we assemble, this office will lead. Most of you will have some connection to this investigation. This case is a priority. We all want to catch the bastard who did it, don't we?"

Firm headshakes and set jaws told her she'd made her point.

"One more thing, people. I expect you to be smart about this situation. We're a tiny community and a dead body is gonna shake everyone up. Reassure your friends and family, but do not encourage speculation and don't indulge in it yourself. Thank you. Okay, back to work."

Her cell phone vibrated as she entered her office.

"Hey, Tate, long time."

Her stomach fluttered. *Stop.* "I was about to call you, Terry," she said.

"Yeah? What's going on?" She felt him shift to high alert.

"What's going on is I have a dead brown-haired woman in her mid-twenties, dressed like a bride, throat slit, fourth finger missing, lying in a state park in my goddamn county."

"Fill me in."

She gave him the details she knew matched those he'd committed to memory.

"I expect you'll want to take the lead on this, Terry."

"We'll work it together, Sam. I know the background, you know the area. I know you've considered other possibilities: imitator, admirer, misdirect."

"I'm not taking anything off the table. It's just . . ."

"Your gut tells you it's the Crasher."

She didn't answer.

"Sam, how are you with all this?"

She felt her face tighten. "Which part, the two dead brides since I arrived in Pickett County or the whole wedding-gone-wrong thing?" She took a breath. "Damn, I'm sorry, Terry. That was unnecessarily bitchy."

"Yeah, well, given the circumstances, you're forgiven."

"I feel like he's following me."

"Are you having those dreams again?"

The conversation seemed odd, at once distant and familiar, as if they were in the same room instead of separated by geography and circumstance.

"Not really," she lied.

"Because if you are, you could see the doctor—"

She cut him off. "When will you be up?"

"End of day tomorrow. I can't get there any sooner."

"It's fine, Terry. Good news, in fact. I can't tell you how much I appreciate this."

"Wild horses couldn't keep me away, Tate. Bye."

She disconnected. Her hand strayed not to her head but to her heart. Her efforts to keep feelings locked up and memories shelved felt at risk. Yet in that moment, she didn't care.

Chapter 3

Sam saw the foot in silhouette at the bottom of her office door.

"Kaylee, damn it, what have I told you about lurking outside?" She yanked at the knob. The door swung open onto a lush backdrop that could have been anywhere in the state. Not a park, though; the area appeared poorly tended. Vines wound themselves around old trees, primarily oaks. Tall grasses and thorny bushes created a formidable wall and blocked the sky. She saw nothing; no people, no animals, no birdsong. Even the insects had gone quiet. Day or night, she couldn't tell.

Sam fought her way through the dense undergrowth, drawn by a patch of light. A break in the trees, perhaps a glade. The closer she drew to the spot, the more she began to notice signs of life. A bird screeched nearby. A rodent scurried underfoot.

The landscape changed. More arid, less verdant. Green gave way to beige. Acoustic music played, some kind of stringed instrument. Singsong voices reached her, punctuated by laughter. She picked out words in Pashto.

The soundtrack continued, but no one appeared. She came upon a small white tent, the interior tossed or perhaps abandoned. Strings of tiny white lights dangled haphazardly from the support beams. The sand half-buried overturned baskets of food on brightly covered woven mats. Flies swarmed around a discarded goat carcass. A crimson mist lay across every surface. What happened? she wondered. Where were the occupants?

At the far end, a slight figure in creamy white lay prone on an elevated platform. A woman dressed like a princess or a bride. She might have been sleeping—or dead.

Sam approached the makeshift stage and gingerly rested her hand on the body. Except there was no body; Sam clutched an empty dress, a piece of satin fabric.

"Ah, there's the intended." The words came out on a sigh, as if the wind were speaking.

"Not me," Sam said. "I think there's been a mistake."

"No mistake," the voice replied affably. Sam felt a pinprick at the back of her neck. She sank to the ground. Someone lifted her to the platform. An apparition dressed in a heavy veil appeared above her. The left hand, minus a fourth finger, held a hunting knife.

"Congratulations, Sam Tate."

"No," Sam whispered. "No," she repeated, louder this time. The hand with the blade hesitated.

"Damn it, no!" Sam thundered. She bolted upright, clawing at shadows. Her three-season quilt lay in a heap on the floor of her room. She noticed the ever-present chorus of night creatures that croaked and hummed outside her window: Katydids, tree frogs, even a whip-poor-will added a forlorn note. Nothing human moved.

At least I didn't wake Cora with my hollering.

She fumbled for her digital clock, which she'd turned away so she could sleep without watching the hours drag by. Four o'clock. Her sour stomach protested. When or what had she last eaten? In the faded moonlight, she could see a glass on the bureau nestled next to a half-empty bottle. Liquid dinner.

Way to go, Tate.

She kept a pad and pen on the nightstand. Should she write down her dream, with this latest incubus, as she'd been instructed to do? Why bother? She rarely forgot them, not when they were simply variations on a theme.

Screw this.

She jumped out of bed, pulled on her running gear and tiptoed out the door. Cora's tabby mewed once, a note between inquiry and irritation, then fell back to sleep.

The road between Lovelady and Byrdstown was predictably deserted. Sam leaned into the wall of humidity and drove from her mind all thoughts of ivory dresses, silver knives, or copper droplets of blood. She ran until her lungs burned, her hamstrings ached, and the compartments of her mind resealed themselves. After a quick shower, she headed into the office. Time to work.

She plopped herself in front of her laptop and popped on a pair of glasses. Thirty-four and her eyes were going. *What's next?* she asked herself. *The hearing? The lower back? The memory?* Although that might not be so bad.

She clicked a file folder marked "TWC" and five subfolders opened in front of her. One for each victim.

Janet Barnes was a student at Florida State University in Tallahassee when she died. Twenty-two, a month away from graduating, and recently engaged. The date had been set for the following spring, fourteen months in the future, which would have allowed time for planning. If she'd had a future.

Sam and Jay had discussed eloping. Rather, she had. "I don't do weddings," she reminded him.

"It won't be a wedding, Sam. Couple of friends, a mutually agreed-upon dive bar, preferably with a great band and an easygoing justice of the peace. We'll call it a tie-the-knot party. What could go wrong?"

She closed her eyes against a wave of pain and opened them again.

The second victim, Barbara Kopeck, co-owned a flower shop in Lake City, Florida. Natalie Garcia, the Georgia "bride," had a position as a nurse's aide. Claire Hooper worked as a mortgage banker in Cookeville. She'd had a stalker in her past. Unfortunately, he provided an unassailable alibi: At the time of the murder, he was in the hospital recovering from a beating by another woman's boyfriend.

Bitsy Newsome, real estate broker and Nashville resident, was the fifth victim. Why here? Why now? Why did the Wedding Crasher miss a year? Was he indisposed? Working? Wandering? Had he settled down in her region? In her community?

Abdi found her at her desk two and a half hours later, staring at her screen. She lifted her head and sniffed the air like a hound on a scent.

"Lynne's Bakery," he announced, brandishing a rumpled bag and a pair of steaming paper cups. "Fresh muffins and drinkable coffee. Which, no offense, you look like you could use."

"Is it that obvious?"

"I couldn't sleep, either. Good news is I got the go-ahead late yesterday to search Bitsy Newsome's social media accounts."

"Anything interesting?" she asked.

Abdi rolled his eyes. "She was running a pictorial diary of her wedding plans on Instagram, which she shared on Facebook with an occasional aside on Twitter. She even put a couple of her videos on YouTube. Actually, it's part diary, part advice post about how to plan a Nashville wedding. Who to hire, who not to hire. That sort of thing."

"Really? Sounds provocative."

"Bitchy, if you ask me. She knew who she wanted to use from the get-go. Cream of the crop. Best of the best. She just went around to the other places so she could take selfies in front of the stores or tape encounters with florists or cake bakers she argued with and then post reviews. Almost all of them negative, by the way."

"Reality TV stuff."

"Oh yeah. Hissy fits, name calling, and phony as a three-dollar bill."

"Do you think someone paid for her endorsements or her pans?"

"Maybe. Or maybe she was setting herself up to be an Internet star, although she was a little old for that. Those girls start when they're twelve and that's all they do." He caught Sam's smile. "Come on. You know I have five sisters."

"Where were Bitsy and Mark getting married?"

"Where else? Cheekwood. 'The people's choice,'"— Abdi used air quotes— "if by that we mean Nashville's one percent."

Cheekwood was a fifty-five-acre botanical garden and art museum just eight miles south and west of the city. Old money and new climbers who wanted to get next to old money joined as members and became at least nominally involved in one or more committees open to generous donors. In return, they had access to the astounding array of facilities they could use to host fund-raisers, charity events, and weddings. Membership at Cheekwood would make sense for an ambitious real estate broker and her undoubtedly ambitious lawyer fiancé.

"Anyway," Abdi continued. "I went through everything—she posted a hell of a lot—and compiled the digital highlights. Get ready for 'Bridezilla, the Southern edition.'" He sent a video to Sam's computer from his phone and came around to her side of the desk.

They watched as Bitsy verbally pummeled the owner of a flower shop, her stinging remarks dripping with honeyed condescension. She then addressed the viewers with, "Well, my goodness, *that's* not going to work, is it? Maybe the owner needs to branch out, sell fruits and vegetables. He could knock down a wall, bring in a little straw, and bill the store as a farmer's market. As long as he stops using the word 'florist,' wouldn't you agree, fellow brides?" Bitsy winked and zoomed the camera away from her smiling face to the flower shop entrance.

"Well, ouch," Sam remarked. "When did this go up?"

"About six weeks ago."

"And how many followers does she have?"

"Couple thousand."

Sam clicked her tongue. "That could put a damper on business. Let's see more."

The second video featured Bitsy, in a smart navy suit, standing at a department store perfume counter bemoaning the selection in front of her. Someone hovered just outside the shot.

"If I smell one more citrus/jasmine combination," Bitsy was saying, "I will lose my mind. And trust me when I tell you, friends, do NOT pick anything that reminds you of lilies. You will smell like death, I promise you."

Prophetic.

Sam leaned in. "That's a department store. Upscale, by the looks of it. Could that be Nordstrom over in Green Hills?"

"Might be."

"Who's the other person? Can you zoom in?" The grainy picture didn't tell them much. A light-skinned male of indeterminate age.

"Maybe he wanted his minute of fame," Abdi suggested.

There followed a few mouthwatering shots of Cheekwood (perfect for any sized, absurdly expensive nuptials) and another video in which Bitsy, along with fiancé Mark, stood in a baker's shop, making faces and expressing extreme disappointment with the quality of the sugary samples. The commentary was occasionally humorous but more often cruel. Mark participated with good cheer and tacit approval of Bitsy's withering remarks.

"Groomzilla?" Abdi asked.

"Maybe he's playing the role of loyal partner. She doesn't like it, so neither does he." Sam paused the video and studied Talcott more closely. Thirty-something, moderately tall, quite fit in his polo shirt and blazer. Light brown hair worn short, angled jaw, pleasant features except for the dark, flat eyes that somehow reminded her of a shark. Attorney as predator. He might even have a future in politics.

"What kind of law does Mr. Talcott practice?"

"Mostly corporate, although he spent a year as a prosecutor."

A thought streaked like a comet across Sam's consciousness, then disappeared. "Is Detective Gould planning to interview him?" she asked.

"Not sure. He contacted Talcott yesterday after he spoke with the victim's parents. Dad Conrad lives with his second wife in Houston. Mom Alice is in Nashville. There's also a married sister in San Francisco. Talcott was apparently put out because he wasn't notified first. Got huffy when reminded he wasn't yet next of kin. Got even more irritated when Gould politely asked him where he'd been the weekend of his fiancée's murder."

"Did he have an answer?"

"An answer, an alibi, names, telephone numbers, receipts," Abdi replied. "I should say, he offered all of those things. Gould told him it could wait until after the funeral. Which they were going to schedule once everyone convened today."

"Mark Talcott sounds very prepared."

"Those are the ones who end up being least cooperative."

"You have a point, Abdi. Talk to Eddie. Ask him if he minds if we tag team on any discussion with Mark Talcott. Something is bugging me about the guy, but I can't put my finger on it." She sat back, hands behind her head. "Our Ms. Newsome seemed to have high standards and higher expectations."

"Maybe she stepped over the line with one of the vendors."

"Or the Wedding Crasher," Sam replied.

They let that possibility sink in.

"Not sure you noticed the last picture, Sheriff." Abdi pointed to an image of Bitsy standing in front of a quaint-looking sign that read HATTIE'S VINTAGE WEDDING SHOPPE.

"That's right down the road in Livingston. I know that shop."

"Doesn't seem your style." Abdi's voice was noncommittal.

She cut her eyes to him. She'd never really talked with him about her visceral distaste for all things wedding-related. Abdi was good at reading people, though. It was part of what made him such a superior investigator. He'd picked up on it. Maybe he assumed her own thwarted nuptials were a factor. Maybe he knew more than he let on.

"Sheriff?"

"Sorry, went off on a tangent." Sam looked at her screen. "We tried to visit that shop during the Hooper investigation. The place was locked up. We never got to interview the owner."

"Might be worth a visit. Let me see if I can expedite the forensic report on the dress, so we can confirm if it's vintage or not."

She felt like someone had stepped on her chest. "That's a good idea."

"'The past is never where you think you left it.'" Abdi said.

"Excuse me?"

"It's a line from *Ship of Fools*. The book. This case brings that quote to mind."

She knew the quote; she saw it as a rebuke to people like her, who thought they could control their own narratives. She'd tried to leave her own past safely boxed up and away from her present-day life. Unfortunately, it refused to stay hidden.

Chapter 4

Special Agent Terry Sloan poured himself a cup of coffee and inhaled, willing the hot beverage to wash away his exhaustion. He pushed back the sliding door and walked onto the small balcony. In the predawn dark, twinkling lights illuminated the Sunshine Skyway Bridge. Twin sail-like structures at the bridge's center gave the illusion of motion across the Gulf's inky waters. Brilliant design. Gorgeous views. Literally a jumping-off point for the desperate people who decided to end their lives.

He looked at his watch. Four o'clock.

"Mercy, you didn't have to get up just for me," he told the woman who followed him outside to lean against his back and wrap her arms around his waist.

"I don't mind. I wanted to see you off. Besides, it's only an hour and a half before I usually get up. Think of how much more I can get done today."

Terry had no doubt she'd cram in a lot before she headed into her office at WFLA, Tampa Bay's leading local news station. He considered the long ride he had ahead of him. Ten and a half hours, not including the stop he intended to make in Atlanta. That would eat up the day. Still, he looked forward to it. Driving relaxed him. I-75 offered nothing in the way of remarkable scenery, but the route was efficient. And away from here.

Mercy squeezed as if she'd never let go. "How long did you say you'd be gone?"

He looked down again, noting she was dressed. A second glance told him she wore one of his shirts. He fought off claustrophobia.

"Three days or three weeks; I can't be sure. It depends on what Sheriff Tate and I determine is the best course of action after going over the evidence. You know the drill."

"You trust this small-town sheriff?" She tried for lighthearted, but he couldn't miss the apprehension in her voice.

"I trust Sam Tate with my life," he said.

The strain left her small body. She smiled up at him. "I'm glad you said that. I feel better." She hugged him once more and released him. Terry realized he'd been holding his breath.

He turned to face her, holding her arms lightly, holding her away. He had to look down. Mercedes Rodriguez, at just over five feet, didn't even reach his shoulder. He could see how rivals, colleagues, even her employers might once have underestimated her. That is, until her grit and determination vaulted the affiliate to first place and earned it a Peabody nomination. Now both the New York and Washington NBC news bureaus had their eyes on her. She hadn't yet turned thirty.

Though a powerhouse on-air and in her dogged pursuit of a story, she remained insecure about her personal relationships. Terry understood: a volatile father, an early failed marriage, a succession of disappointing men. No wonder she found his apparent steadiness a comfort.

Terry didn't expect to end up in Tampa. You went where you were sent, particularly when you've been allowed to stay on while you "work through" your issues. It wasn't so bad. He lived in a condo with a terrific view of the Bay. His commute was far shorter than when he lived in D.C. Traffic was light, except in February. He enjoyed far better weather. As a bonus, he met Mercy Rodriguez.

Her piece on his role in the takedown of a violent criminal made him out to be some kind of hometown hero. He heard from old friends, even made some new ones. HQ seemed pleased. Terry almost believed he might turn his life around.

Almost. Mercy was strong and sexy, with plenty of experience in and out of bed. She knew the best places to eat, the most fun people to hang with, the movers and the money people in and around Tampa. He loved her energy and the attention she heaped on him. He enjoyed being part of a couple. She eased his grief. Her attention made him feel complete, at least on the surface.

Mercy didn't want surface, though. She wanted attachment, roots. He should have seen it, but he wasn't paying attention. At some point, she decided she'd found her man. Someone she respected, trusted, and loved. Someone who would be her rock, her harbor, her safe spot forever. Terry Sloan.

Terry couldn't pretend to be any of those things. Not for her. Maybe not ever again for anyone. He just didn't know how to tell her. Terry Sloan, who had faced psychopaths and predators, who had hunted down drug lords and depraved killers, couldn't handle the expectations of one small woman.

"I gotta get going," he said. "I'll call you from the road."

"Promise?" She lifted her face up for a kiss.

"Absolutely," Terry replied. He brushed her lips with his, picked up his bag, and walked out. He heard her call out "text me" and delivered an over-the-shoulder wave without looking.

The guilt hit like a sledgehammer. He hadn't hurt Mercy yet, but he would.

The oppressive heat followed him north and into Georgia. Barely April and the temperatures were into the eighties. He turned the air-conditioning in the Prius to high. It didn't help. Terry had never grown used to hot and steamy weather. He'd been raised in Colorado, where spring arrived on dry air and blue skies that served as a backdrop to jagged, snow-capped mountains.

At least the drive was quiet. Terry kept the radio off when he drove. The silence and the blur of scenery out his windows soothed him. The Zen of the *whoosh,* a friend called it.

As he pulled at his iced coffee, his mind zeroed in on the latest iteration of the case that had attracted and plagued him over the course of four years. How did the Wedding Crasher choose Bitsy Newsome from Nashville? What was she doing in remote Pickett County, anyway? Working? Playing? At least he could find out that much. Meanwhile, he'd get to partner with Pickett County Sheriff Sam Tate.

Sam Tate. The star of the Tennessee Law Enforcement Academy the year he visited to talk to the students about investigative work. Her classmates couldn't get over the striking-looking woman with the criminal justice degree and the glamorous past as a singer and then a lieutenant with an elite all-women's unit stationed in Afghanistan. They fell all over themselves to impress her, as did most of the instructors.

Terry, who'd once considered joining the Behavioral Analysis Unit, couldn't resist profiling the capable young woman. Friendly but closed off. Flashes of humor along with a deep-seated anger. Pain tucked away beneath the reserved exterior. He wondered if the sorrow that trailed her like a veil made her professional and personal lives more difficult.

By the time they met again, she'd left her job with MNPD. Something about stress. He could relate. The aneurysm that felled his pregnant young wife nearly ended him. His deep dive into pills and booze earned him an involuntary transfer to a field office in Tampa. Just another widower in Florida, albeit younger and still working.

At least the Wedding Crasher filled his mind and ate up his time. Yes, other cases intervened, other pleasures and irritations made themselves known. But something happened to him each March. Anticipation. Excitement. The smell of blood or the thrill of the chase; he couldn't say.

He made good time and reached the Atlanta office before lunch to touch base with the lead agent on the Natalie Garcia murder. Terry preferred personal interaction to texts, emails, or phone calls. He planned to meet later with Darryl Cutler up in Cookeville, the FBI's satellite office nearest to Byrdstown. Cutler would be the local lead, as he had been on the Hooper investigation, though Terry remained the overall special case agent. A mixed blessing, to be the face of an unsolved string of homicides.

He heard Lena Small's smooth contralto as soon as he stepped off the elevator inside the FBI's Atlanta headquarters.

"Terry Sloan. As I live and breathe. Come on in."

Lena wore a well-cut gray suit with rust-colored pumps and a striking copper necklace. Her spikey silver-streaked hair perfectly complimented her oval face and café au lait complexion. As usual, she projected an assured confidence. A talented field agent and an admired administrator, she was married to a rising local politician. Each of them harbored aspirations that went beyond Atlanta.

Terry entered her air-conditioned office and took a moment to admire the mix of artwork, laudatory letters, and photographs with local and national celebrities. Without a doubt, the woman was going places.

"Sit down, Terry." She gestured to a comfortable chair. "How's Florida?"

He grinned. "Hot and muggy. Just like here. So, when are you running for office?"

"Slow down, hombre. Let's not get ahead of ourselves." Her smile and the twinkle in her eye told him the idea had crossed her mind. "First, I have a case to close. It would appear we're chasing the Wedding Crasher again." She leaned back in her chair and cocked her head. "And what do you know, he's reappeared right back in Sam Tate's county. That should be interesting for you."

"Lena, I don't know what you heard . . ."

"Doesn't matter what I heard, Terry. Two colleagues working an ugly case, both of them single, each of them recovering from a devastating loss." She shrugged.

"Ancient history—"

"Is it?"

He put up a hand. "The only thing I can think about right now is the return of our perp after a two-year hiatus. I've got to take a look at every piece of the puzzle. I've got questions without answers."

"Then let's talk it through. I ordered in from the Cuban sandwich place. Hope you're hungry."

"For Cuban? Always."

They discussed the specifics of Natalie Garcia's murder over lunch at Lena's desk. Terry had already consulted with two agents from the Florida Bureau of State Investigations who'd worked the Barnes and Kopeck homicides, he told her.

"No changes in methodology?" Lena asked.

"The only difference is the missed year. And the repeat location."

"The killer is in Pickett County."

"Or traveled north and circled back."

"Uh-uh." Lena put down her sandwich. "You don't believe that and neither do I. Something has tied the Wedding Crasher to Pickett County. Maybe the same thing that resulted in the year off."

"Real life."

They turned to other topics. Terry promised to keep his colleague in the loop. Then he pushed on, his belly full and his mind in overdrive.

The killer would be caught. Terry believed that without hesitation. He considered what the end would mean for him. What would consume him? More significantly, what would keep him sane? He didn't yet trust himself and didn't want to rely on any of his acquaintances. Self-medication hadn't eased his insistent grief.

Mercy did her best to fill the hole. For all the love she offered—love he didn't deserve—she couldn't release him from the prison of his own pain. Only the Wedding Crasher seemed capable of doing that. Yes, the murders angered him. Of course, he ached for the families of the victims. Yet he couldn't deny that the killer's reappearance ignited a flame deep within him. He felt focused, alive. Repurposed. Renewed.

Was that sick? Part of what made him a damned good investigator? Or both?

And what about Sam Tate? How did the latest murder affect her? She relished a challenge, that much he knew. Still, she faced a lot of pressure over this case. From a public worried that a killer lived among them. From the burden of her own painful past.

The stress could knock her off her game.

Not gonna happen, he reminded himself. The Sam he remembered—the whip-smart trainee, the no-bullshit detective, the passionate woman—wasn't some tightly wrapped bundle of neuroses. She was a fearless and resolute officer of the law. The Wedding Crasher's return might stir up old memories. It would also imbue her with a sense of purpose. No ritual-worshipping, bride-loving fetishist was going to terrorize her county, not while Sam Tate was sheriff. She would kick his ass. And Terry would be by her side when they took the serial killer down once and for all.

Chapter 5

About when Terry left the Atlanta field office, Sam and Abdi pushed open the door to Hattie's Vintage Wedding Shoppe in Livingston. Tinny mechanical trumpets played the first four notes of "The Wedding March." It was an odd little announcement, yet in keeping with the kitschy appearance of the place.

Sam broke into a cold sweat that had nothing to do with their passage out of the humid day into the chilled store. She didn't want anything to do with weddings. Ceremonies these days were nothing more than part performance art, part competition, and part fairy tale. An entire industry had grown around thoroughly unrealistic expectations about love, fealty, happiness, and even memory. Perception mattered. Whoever has the biggest, most elaborate celebration wins. Bitsy and others like her had willingly, sometimes urgently, participated in the sham.

That wasn't the only reason Sam detested the entire process of planning and implementing the ritual. In her experience, weddings weren't cause for celebration.

Although small, the store was crammed. Dresses—there must have been a hundred or more—hung from racks or draped across chairs. Tulle, chiffon, silk, and lace gowns in every imaginable style seemed to dance around them. She'd never seen so many variations on white: shades like ivory, pearl, crème, and snowdrop.

"These are all vintage?" Sam asked in a low voice. "What does that even mean anymore?"

"Anything not made in the last, oh, twenty years, I'd guess," Abdi replied. "Newer than that, it's used. Pre-twentieth century, you'd be dealing in antique couture."

Sam gave her detective the side-eye. "You seem to know a lot about it."

"I have a lot of women in my life." He laughed. "I've been in these stores."

A stout woman pushed through a set of curtains in the back and hurried to them. She had piled her flame-colored hair carelessly on top of her head. Her low-cut lavender dress emphasized her ample cleavage. With the addition of a bright yellow scarf, she stood out among the pale couture like an early spring crocus. Sam pegged her as perhaps late fifties.

"Welcome, welcome. Thank you for coming." The voice was high and youthful; the accent suggested upper-class Southern breeding. Above her wide smile, her small blue eyes moved back and forth between Abdi and Sam. The two of them had decided against wearing uniforms. Sam's badge, clipped at the waist of her jeans, was hidden by her blazer.

Without so much as a twitch, the cheerful shopkeeper said, "The happy couple, I presume."

Maybe times really were changing, Sam thought. Maybe the woman had a diverse clientele with a shared love of old dresses. Or maybe she believed in covering her bases.

"Actually, I'm Pickett County Sheriff Samantha Tate, ma'am." She pointed at her badge and produced her identification. "And this is Detective Abdi Issen. Are you the proprietor?"

"I am indeed. Thirty-five years now." She cocked her head, an inquisitive bird with bright plumage and a sharp eye. "What brings a neighboring county sheriff and her detective to my shop? This wouldn't have to do with a body someone discovered in a park yesterday, would it?"

"Why would you say that?" Abdi asked.

"Now, Detective. It's pretty hard to keep such a thing quiet. It's not as if this area has a lot of bodies lying around, although I suppose the drugs are killing off more than a few these days. I stay informed, thanks to a well-placed network of fellow busybodies. I'm in the business of dressing brides, for heaven's sake. So, is it him? The Wedding Crasher? Should I warn my customers? Are you bringing in that handsome FBI agent who worked the other case?"

Sam fought the urge to pivot and flee. "Ms., uh—"

"McCoy. Henrietta Courtney McCoy. You may call me Hattie. I know; Hattie McCoy. It seemed funny at the time. Of course, now that my husband is gone—"

"I'm sorry," Sam said instinctively.

"My dear sheriff, don't be. He left me for his young secretary years ago. She in turn left him for another woman after bankrupting the fool. He's living on scraps, last I heard, while I am making quite a nice living selling to clients all over the world. I hope his ex comes to me. I'd love to outfit two women. As you may have gathered, I'm a great fan of karma." She chuckled amiably.

"Ms. McCoy, we're very early into our investigation. We hope to know more in the next few days."

"I shall follow the news, then."

"Is all your merchandise from past eras?" Abdi asked.

"It is. We have nothing made after the 1980s. I stop just before the onset of grunge, which had a deleterious effect on bridal fashion, let me tell you. Some of the dresses in the nineties even featured rips! Can you imagine? I realize it's in style with two-hundred-dollar jeans, but a dress you wear in a commitment ceremony?" She made a dismissive gesture, as if she were shooing away an irritating insect.

"The 1980s was the height of repurposed romanticism," she continued. "That look is becoming popular again, by the way, without all the excessive head pieces, thank goodness. The other popular looks are from the late 1950s. One style features the sweetheart neckline and small waist and full skirt. I like to call it the Doris Day virgin look. Don't be shocked, Detective. We trade in fantasies." She ran her hand lightly over the gowns nearest her.

"The Hollywood glamour designs from the late fifties are my favorite," she continued. "The full or A-line skirt remained, you see, but the necklines became more daring, though not by today's standards. A bateau neck or cowl, cap sleeves, even strapless gowns. Nothing anyone would find at a local garage sale, but I shop all over the world. Silk or taffeta, some chiffon, tulle and lace. Such fun."

"I can see why you'd love the film-inspired designs," Abdi said. "They really do flatter a woman's figure. Not everyone wants to be a princess, I'd imagine. Besides, taffeta and silk drape nicely, and silk has the advantage of working well in sticky weather."

"Why, Detective, you do know something about dressing a woman," Hattie replied coyly. "Is it an interest of yours, something you do in your spare time?"

"I have five sisters, ma'am, two of whom were recently married. And a girlfriend who would probably like to be. They've supplied me with my education."

Hattie's laugh rang out like church bells.

"What about alterations?" Sam asked. "Do you provide that service?"

"We may. Often as not, whoever buys the dress does her own needlework or has her personal seamstress or tailor do it. There are several men and women who specialize in working with older and presumably more fragile material. Fine by me. The money is in the sales."

"Do you sell other accessories? Veils, shoes, garters?"

"Headbands, veils, and some handbags, yes. Used shoes? Never." She gave a shudder. "The brides go on eBay or Etsy. Sometimes they may try a thrift shop. Or they buy a perfectly plain shoe that could come from any era after 1940. You'd be surprised how many modern brides wear low-heeled pumps, Mary Janes, or even flats. Comfort is in."

Sam's attention was caught by a dress with a capped-sleeve brocade top, fitted with darts. The skirt, chiffon over lightweight taffeta, flared out from a nipped-in waist. She fingered the material.

"I see you in something a little sleeker, Sheriff," Hattie said. "A long sheath with a subtle slit up one side. Do you remember what that actress wore when she married England's Prince Harry? Very Audrey Hepburn. Something along those lines."

Sam blushed. "Me? Oh, no, I'm not in the market. I was wondering what something like this would cost?"

"That's a designer dress," Hattie said. "Worn once. It sells for twelve hundred dollars. The dresses start at four fifty and go up to thirty-five hundred or four thousand, mainly because the clothes are in impeccable condition. I have one gown here I won't sell for less than ten thousand."

Even at the low end, that represented a sizable investment for a serial killer, Sam thought. Unless he was a spare-no-expense kind of guy. She looked over at Abdi and knew he was calculating the cost as well.

He'd moved down the rows of dresses and was studying a high-necked chiffon number. "Where do you get your dresses?"

"As I said, all over. Estate sales, auctions, and the like. I've got people looking for me in North Carolina, Texas, Louisiana, Kentucky. Sometimes New York City and Los Angeles, though the prices tend to be too high. I even have a scout outside London and another in the suburbs of Paris."

"That's impressive," Abdi said. "And how much of your business is mail order?"

"More than half, if you can believe it. I still get walk-ins, mostly local, but the number of people willing to buy dresses without trying them on has grown."

The proprietor crossed her arms over her generous bosom. "I don't feel as if I'm being all that helpful, officers. Especially if you want to know if a killer walked into my shop and bought a dress. We don't see too many men, but there are enough of them. As for orders through the mail, I don't really know who's on the other end, do I?"

"Can you tell whether this is one of your dresses?" Sam handed her phone to the woman. On it was a shot of the dress Bitsy Newsome had been wearing when her body was discovered.

Hattie pulled up a pair of reading glasses tethered to an ornate chain around her neck and peered through them. She shook her head.

"I can't say for certain. It would help to see the dress itself and not a picture of it. I suspect it started as a strapless gown, though. Were the sleeves added later, do you know?"

"Forensics says the fabric that makes up the, uh, body of the dress dates back sixty or seventy years ago and the rest is new."

"I can believe that. The sleeves are at odds with the rest of the dress. This piece of added fabric"—Hattie touched the screen with a red-tipped nail— "creates a completely different neckline. Perhaps this is someone's idea of modesty but frankly, it ruins the look. I don't know why anyone would buy a vampy gown and then cannibalize it. Except, oh dear—" She handed Sam the phone as if it were a hot potato. "Was this worn by the latest victim?"

"I'm afraid it was. Perhaps you have receipts from, say, January to March of this year?" Sam had no way of knowing whether the Crasher shopped here, but she couldn't leave anything to chance.

"I'll get those for you." Hattie went back through the curtains and returned a moment later with a small metal file box. "My niece is on me to digitize," she said with a sigh.

"Looks to be about fifty here, Sheriff," Abdi said, glancing at the box.

"I can pull out the period strapless gowns we sold. Shouldn't be more than three or four. Although I honestly can't tell. As I said, I hate what has been done to this piece, but I have to admire the handiwork, what I can see of it."

"Do you take returns?" Abdi asked, still looking through the dresses.

"Never. You buy it, you keep it. Unless something prevents the marriage from taking place."

Abdi and Sam both jerked their heads up. "Did something like that happen, say, two years ago?" Sam asked.

"The shop was closed two years ago," Hattie replied. "I took time off between March and November." She didn't elaborate. "I did let my clients know I planned an extended vacation and word got around. I sold a record number of dresses over the holiday weeks that preceded my absence."

"And you have receipts for that period of time?" Sam tried to keep the eagerness out of her voice.

"Of course. Same box, just a little farther back. Let's see. December two and a half years ago. What name are you looking for?"

"Claire Hooper." Sam and Abdi spoke at the same time.

"I remember that name from the news. She was the previous victim. Oh, no!" Hattie looked stricken.

"May I?" Abdi rifled through the cards and pulled one out. "Hooper," he said, holding it aloft.

Sam brought up another photo on her phone. "I'm sorry to do this to you again, Hattie, but can you look at this dress and tell me if it's something you might have sold? I realize some time has passed."

"I don't forget dresses, Sheriff." Hattie put her glasses back on and studied the picture. "That was our Grace Kelly model. Modest, regal, quite popular in its day. Only a very few brides order that sort of style anymore. Now that I recall, Miss Hooper was planning a traditional church wedding." She sniffed. "And this is the dress she was killed in?"

And buried in, Sam might have added. She never questioned the parents' decision in the matter. Grief worked its own black magic on the psyche.

"I'm afraid so."

Chapter 6

According to the clock Sam was trying not to watch, Terry walked into the two-story brick building on Main Street at exactly 5:23 P.M. He ran a hand through his hair, tugged on his damp collar, tried to smooth his rumpled slacks, and took a minute to look around. Sam peeked at him from behind her door like a shy schoolgirl.

When she stepped out of her office, she saw his hands go to his stomach. The gesture was both unconscious and self-conscious. He needn't have worried. He was still lean, if somehow more substantial. A bit craggier, which gave his face character. Despite the long drive, he seemed more relaxed. Maybe the "steady friend" to whom he'd alluded had something to do with that.

And what did he see? A well-run office? A staff hard at work? A sheriff who'd changed in the last two years? Thinner, if her prominent cheekbones and loose slacks were any indication. Less rested, without a doubt. The occasional silver strand that mixed with the rich mahogany of the hair she'd pulled back in a ponytail. A faint web of fine lines at the corners of her pale jade eyes. The ever-present forehead crease.

"Sheriff Tate," he called out. "You're looking well."

"Hope the long drive didn't present too many difficulties, Special Agent Sloan." She felt like a character in a play. "Do you need something cold to drink? Or hot?" She lowered her voice. "You don't know how glad I am to see you."

"The feeling's mutual." Were they talking about the case? She couldn't be sure.

He headed to the coffee station and helped himself to a large mug.

"Let me just refuel."

"Don't drink it black," she said quietly. "Kaylee's coffee is kind of stro—"

Terry took a sip and nearly gagged. He managed to lift his cup and smile at Kaylee, who tracked his movements like a hawk.

In the privacy of Sam's locked office, he held the steaming mug away from him as if it were poison. "Holy crap, that's hard core!"

"Tried to tell you. Dump it out the window. That's what everyone else does. Most of us in the department steer clear. All we need is something else to contribute to our acid stomachs and sleepless nights."

Terry placed his briefcase on her desk, pried open the nearest window, and poured the coffee on an unsuspecting bed of pansies. He looked out after them. "That poor flower bed," he remarked. "You must do a lot of replanting."

"A fair amount." Sam pulled a Coca-Cola Classic out of a cooler she kept near her desk for visitors who fell victim to her assistant's coffee. "Here you go."

He drank half the bottle in one gulp.

"Better?"

"Absolutely."

He looked drained. Should she suggest dinner first, give him time to recharge? Not that she wanted to spend an hour on small talk. "Here's the thing—" she began.

"Tell me about—"

Their words collided.

"Great minds and all that," Terry said with a laugh. "You go first."

"Did Darryl catch you up?"

"You mean on what TBI didn't discover at the scene? I'm afraid so."

"Nothing, Terry. No fingerprints, no footprints, no DNA, no blood or skin trace belonging to anyone but the victim. Nate's people were thorough. As for the body, it's practically been sterilized."

"Just like the other crime scenes."

"It's all the same. Small white satin pillow, like the kind you see in a casket or at a communion. Cheap candles, maybe purchased at a five-and-dime. Flowers could come from anywhere: a garden, a field, a florist shop. Shoes appear lightly used. Thrift shop or garage sale. Stockings and garter are new, though. Who knew those were still around?"

"Obviously not you," Terry said. He ventured a smile she didn't share.

"Not my thing, Terry. I can tell you about the dress, though. It's been altered. Part old and part new. The new part adds more modesty, believe it or not. Made me think of *Bride of Frankenstein,* but the stitching is much neater."

"Hmm. Janet's dress was homemade, maybe by her killer. Modern fabric, old-fashioned design. Barbara Kopeck's outfit had a vintage jacket added. No additional alterations needed. Natalie was found in her mother's gown, the one she planned to marry in. No modifications necessary. We never traced the source of Claire Hooper's dress."

"Actually, we did." She told him about the visit to Hattie's store. "She sold three gowns that might have been used to dress Newsome, but we won't know until the clothes are released from evidence."

"Buyers?"

"All three were mail-order."

Terry's shoulders slumped. "Not helpful. What about the murder weapon?"

"The official autopsy is tomorrow. Probably a knife plus a small cleaver."

"Sounds like our guy."

"Welcome to my world. I've pulled together a task force. We're going to meet in the morning. Take a look, see if there's anyone I need to add."

Terry scanned the list she handed him. "Looks like you have who you need. We'd better start the meeting early. We need to hold a joint press conference tomorrow afternoon."

"So soon?" Sam couldn't keep the dismay out of her voice. "Can't we at least wait until we have all the forensic reports?"

"The situation isn't ideal, Sam. Calvin Jakes, the FBI's regional PR guy, will run it. We'll keep it short. You know as well as I do how these things work. We have a second dead woman in two years dressed like a bride. The victim is a high-powered broker from Nashville. The serial killer who's been murdering brunettes across three states is still at large. Possibly still here. When word gets out . . ."

Sam thought of the earlier visit with Hattie McCoy. "I think it already has."

They didn't know the half of it.

Overnight, the online version of *Pickett County Press* quoted a "reliable source" within the sheriff's office as having "credible knowledge" the homicide was a victim of the Wedding Crasher, a "notorious serial killer who last struck the area when Sheriff Tate was new on the scene." The report also confirmed the presence of Special Agent

Terry Sloan, the FBI officer who'd been pursuing the killer for years.

By the time Sam got in the next morning, a reporter from Nashville's main daily, *The Tennessean,* had already called the office and had also reached out to the Madison precinct captain, according to Eddie Gould. Meanwhile, Kaylee discovered the hashtag #ReturnoftheWeddingCrasher gaining ground on social media.

"It's hitting the newswires," she announced. "We're gonna be swamped."

"You'll need to handle all the case-related inquiries until we coordinate with the FBI's press machine."

"I already heard from Agent Sloan's man in Memphis this morning. Mr. Jakes. I guess you and Agent Sloan must have sent him a statement last night. The press conference is this afternoon." She smiled, energized. "Don't worry, Sheriff. I know exactly how to handle callers. I'm good at stonewalling. Oh, and I've got coffee set up for your meeting."

The task force assembled at eight thirty. Abdi, Darryl Cutler, Nate Fillmore, Doc Holloway, and Eddie Gould represented their various employers. The state police sent Captain Gerald McHenry, a practiced investigator. The Tennessee District Attorney General's office assigned a lawyer named Karen Polk to observe. The woman, a petite blonde, sat with her head down, eyes glued to her cell phone. Even a state park ranger by the name of Watson showed up in full uniform, right down to the hat.

"Guy looks like Smokey Bear," Sam grumbled as they entered the conference room. She made introductions, then turned to Terry.

"The most obvious question will be whether this is the Wedding Crasher," he said. "Everything seems to point in that direction. Same details, from the method of the murder to the victim type to the way the killer dressed her. The location—a glade within a park—matched the other homicides as well."

"Is that the official story?" Eddie asked.

"It explains Agent Sloan's presence," Sam replied. "It's not the only story, not yet. I want you and Detective Issen to look at the murder from a more conventional angle. Did the victim have any enemies? Angry clients? Disappointed exes? What does her cell phone tell you about her movements?"

Eddie cleared his throat. "We don't have her physical phone. Or her purse. Oh, and she was apparently having a problem with her phone battery. At least that's what her fiancé told us. Who knows if or when it stopped working?"

"What about her car GPS? How did she get up here from Madison?"

"It's not clear, Sheriff. Her car is still at her office." Eddie caught Sam's frown and added, "Early days yet."

"What do we know about the Wedding Crasher, Agent Sloan?" McHenry, the state police investigator, asked.

"Thirty to sixty years of age. Trained in how to use a knife or similar instrument. A chef, ex-military, even a butcher, although the cuts suggest someone with some medical knowledge. Possibly a doctor."

"Dr. Death," Ranger Watson muttered.

"The year off is a deviation," Terry continued. "Otherwise, the profile remains the same. He—I'll use one gender designation for now—is detail-oriented.

Meticulous, which might indicate an obsessive-compulsive disorder, likely well hidden. That is, he doesn't come across as peculiar to the people who encounter him. He might travel for work. Probably lives an ordinary life. Very possibly married. Possibly even a parent. Nevertheless, emotionally immature. He operates either from a sense of entitlement or aggrievement. Likely both."

"Well, that narrows it down," Eddie groused.

"Those details help, trust me. They lead us into the motives behind the killings."

"I assume you checked to see if the very first victim back in Florida had an ex-fiancé in her past." Captain McHenry again.

"We did and she didn't."

"So, this isn't about jealousy?" Ned asked.

"We don't think so," Terry replied. "The victims aren't viciously attacked. They're knocked out before they're cut. They're not stabbed or beaten. The finger is removed post-mortem. Our killer may see himself as behaving respectfully. The ritual may channel his wrath. He may even believe he's doing his victims a favor."

"Please tell me you're joking," murmured Karen Polk without lifting her head from her phone. No one paid her any attention.

"I don't understand how a profile is going to help us," Ranger Watson complained. "We already know the killer has it in for young brunettes. We know he kills once a year. Does it really matter why? We need something more concrete. A physical description. Some kind of evidence. The perp is young. He's old. He's strong. He walks with a limp. He's bald. He's blind. He's a she."

"Except we're dealing with someone who leaves no evidence, at least none we can find," Sam responded. "I realize this is frustrating, but we have to consider the killer's motives if we're going to move ahead. The media will want an updated assessment."

"The media," Eddie scoffed. "I wouldn't wish that shit show on my worst enemy. No offense, Sheriff."

"None taken, Eddie. If I could trade places with you, I would."

Chapter 7

At noon, Main Street began to fill with journalists, reporters, stringers, bloggers, videographers, and their support staff. Combined with the curious and the obsessed, their numbers threatened to double Byrdstown's tiny population in half a day. Clay and Fentress County sheriff's offices sent over deputies to help manage the traffic. The town's three eateries overflowed with spectators.

A couple of enterprising media outlets set up their trailers at the edge of town. Others checked their people into the Sportsman Lodge Motel in Dale Hollow Lake. One of the deputies reported seeing a NO VACANCY sign hanging above one that read, NOW HIRING.

"I'm sorry I can't offer you a place to stay, Terry," Sam had told him the night before. "I mean, an extra bed." She smiled to cover her discomfort. She couldn't decide what bothered her more, that she lived like a graduate student in a rented room, or that she didn't know where Terry would choose to sleep if she had her own space. Or where she'd want him to sleep.

"No problem. I'll fend off nosy reporters with my famous glower."

An hour before the 2:00 P.M. press conference, Sam, Abdi, and Terry stood in Sam's office and munched on sandwiches brought in by one of the deputies.

"Seems murder is good for business," Abdi noted.

Terry shrugged. "Retailers might as well cash in. Maybe people have persuaded themselves the Wedding Crasher is shopping for victims in Nashville instead of up the street."

"And leaving them here?" Sam asked. No one responded.

Kaylee stuck her head in the door. "Mr. Jakes has arrived." She stood aside for a short, neatly dressed man with curly black hair and round brown eyes behind rimless glasses.

"It's getting crowded out there," he observed with a jovial smile.

"Are you going to be able to keep this contained, Calvin?" Terry asked.

"That's my job, Agent Sloan. You and Sheriff Tate will be there to answer a few questions. Keep your responses short, emphasize that information is still coming in and assure your audience that as you have said information, you will share it. I haven't asked anyone else to the platform. I know how some local officials like to talk, but I don't think that needs to happen here. Am I correct, Sheriff?"

"I work for them, Mr. Jakes, not the other way around. They've agreed not to say anything at this press conference, but I can't guarantee what happens afterwards."

"One step at a time, then. Shall we go?"

Jakes stood on the makeshift platform in front of the municipal building with Sam and Terry on either side. Terry looked relaxed, his pants pressed, his blue shirt crisp under his blazer. Sam felt exhausted. The dark circles of sweat under her arms mirrored those under her eyes. She'd left her sunglasses off; she didn't want to come across as a caricature of a county sheriff. She felt vulnerable, exposed in the bright April sun.

Don't squint, she reminded herself. Make your face blank. Behind the mask she adopted, she scanned the audience. *Is the killer here?* she wondered. Standing among the reporters and bystanders. Pretending to be interested. Secretly amused? Or thrilled?

Jakes read the prepared statement, outlined what he called the rules of engagement (five minutes for questions, tops), and pointed at the sea of waving hands.

"Agent Sloan, can you say definitively this is the Wedding Crasher?" Sam recognized the reporter from *The Tennessean.*

Terry stepped to the mike. "Not yet. The evidence indicates that it may be. That's why I'm here."

"Do you know why he skipped a year?" an *Associated Press* correspondent asked.

"We're working on theories about that."

"Isn't six years a long time for a case to be open, Agent Sloan?" The question came from a cable news reporter. Sam couldn't see which outlet.

"The case didn't move to the FBI until the third victim. Still, an open-ended case like this is troubling. The infrequency of the murders and the change in locations are inhibiting factors in catching this particular perpetrator. But we will catch whoever did this."

Jakes moved in. "Thank you, Agent Sloan. Now if there are no more—"

"Sheriff Tate, how do you feel about having a serial killer back in your county?" Sarah Moss from Channel Five. Directly to Sam. No way of deflecting.

"I don't know that I have a serial killer in my county, Sarah," Sam answered carefully. "The victim was from Nashville, two hours away. The killer might be passing through. This may not be"—she almost said "not a serial murder at all" but caught herself just in time; no point in muddying the waters—"anything we can solve overnight.

But we will solve this case. Because what I do have is a dead woman in Pickett County. And I take that very seriously." She stepped back, relieved to be out of the spotlight.

Her respite turned out to be short-lived. Over the next few days, she discovered the press had become enamored of Sheriff Sam Tate. Some seemed to romanticize her past: the unsuccessful attempt at a singing career, the praiseworthy tour in Afghanistan, the commendations she received as detective, the tragic loss of her fiancé. Others saw in her unexpected promotion to sheriff a story of female empowerment.

At the same time, the current situation encouraged darker speculation. How did the Wedding Crasher happen to appear in Pickett County just after then-Detective Sam Tate arrived? Did the killer follow her? Had he settled in the area? Was he taunting her? Might she become the next victim?

And by the way, how did she feel about once again pairing with the handsome FBI agent, who also happened to be single?

Sam stormed into the conference room three days after the press conference and threw down a print copy of a national paper. "Did you see this garbage?" she asked Terry. "They make it sound like we're starring in a TV movie. What the hell am I supposed to tell the mayor or the commissioners?"

"Tell them you're trying to do your job. Or tell them to let the press know. They seem to be pretty cozy with the fourth estate."

Byrdstown's Mayor Jerry O'Neil and Pickett County Executive Billy Owens kept mum the first day. After that, they engaged the reporters one on one, a strategic deployment that combined Southern charm and aggressive promotion of Pickett County as a lovely place to visit and live. Sam wasn't sure if their maneuvers helped or hurt.

Calls and visitors threatened to overrun the sheriff's office. Sam finally hired a woman named Becky Rattle to physically keep out anyone who did not have legitimate police business. Becky, a fifty-year-old woman with short salt-and-pepper hair and a voice roughened by years of cigarettes and whiskey, worked as a bouncer at a dive bar out on Route 111. She proved impervious to threats, bribes, promises, or lectures about the First Amendment.

Sam also assigned a young deputy named Seth Yardley to work with the FBI's cyber division. Years earlier, the FBI set up a website dedicated to information about the Wedding Crasher case. The purpose was twofold: to educate the public and to provide a counterpoint to the sensationalist and often erroneous media reports.

After a period of relative quiet, the site was now in danger of crashing. While some people logged on to get new information, others posted lengthy commentary or claims about new information. Each and every lead had to be tracked down, no matter how far-fetched. Seth, a local boy, proved more than equal to the task of ferreting out the conspiracy theorists.

Bitsy Newsome's funeral was held in Nashville just over a week after the discovery of the body. Most of the press moved to cover the services, which gave Byrdstown a much-needed respite. Nashville's mayor, the police commissioner, and a number of corporate and political types figured among the several hundred mourners, along with family and friends. Neither Sam nor Terry attended, though at least one Pickett County commissioner did. Among the marquee names were those of representatives Dora Briscoe and Lincoln Charles.

Sam found their presence interesting enough to merit further research. Briscoe represented Nashville. The high-profile case warranted an appearance. The congressional district covered by Lincoln Charles included seventeen counties far east of the city. Why did the representative from the neighboring district show up at the funeral of a local real estate broker?

At her desk the following day, she typed in Lincoln Charles and Bitsy Newsome. No shortage of stories about Charles, who held several key House committee appointments. The man seemed more than capable of getting the press to cover him. His sparsely populated district loved him, returning him time and time again to D.C.

Predictably, Newsome's public profile was thinner and limited to articles on her engagement, an appointment to a position at Cheekwood, and an industry award she won. Most of the press coverage came after her death.

On a hunch, Sam paired Charles with Mark Talcott. More interesting. Several stories with images attached showed the two shaking hands over the course of fifteen or twenty years. Further reading revealed that Talcott, who grew up in the small town of Celina, Tennessee, met the congressman during a high school field trip and ended up as a summer intern the next year. He went back to work in the congressman's office between college and law school.

According to *The Tennessean*, Talcott and Newsome planned to move to D.C. after their spring marriage. No mention as to whether Lincoln Charles helped make that happen. However, the congressman attended the couple's lavish engagement party—and Newsome's funeral.

Celina, whose population remained steady at just under fifteen hundred people, was a very small town. Claire Hooper was from Celina, Sam recalled, and a few years behind Talcott. She'd moved a little closer to Nashville, but her family remained in place. Talcott had attended college in state and went east for law school. Then he came back and spent a few years with the Office of the District Attorney General, which prosecuted all crimes committed within a seven-county district. Just two years ago, he joined a private law firm in Nashville.

"Two years," Sam said aloud, and the fog lifted.

Chapter 8

"We appreciate your time, Mr. Talcott," Eddie Gould began. He glanced down at a blank pad of paper, then looked back up. His dark eyes radiated sincerity. "Mark—may I call you Mark?"

"Mr. Talcott is fine. I trust we can make this brief. I've only got a few minutes before a client meeting. Unless . . . do I need my lawyer present?"

Eddie chuckled and raised an eyebrow. *Come on,* the gestures seem to say. *It's just us boys*. Which made sense, given that the lawyer hadn't even glanced in Sam's direction since the interview began. Nor did he look at the one-way mirror behind which Abdi and Terry stood.

"I wouldn't think so, Mr. Talcott," Eddie said. "You're doing us quite a favor, coming in on such short notice."

The lawyer smoothed his blue silk tie and made a show of looking at his stainless steel watch. A Piaget, worth nine or ten thousand dollars. Jay had coveted one just like that, to Sam's everlasting amusement. She imagined many otherwise normal people aspired to own such a watch, just as some drooled over a car.

For the attorney, the timepiece seemed more like a reminder to others that he occupied a rarified world. Maybe he chose his preferred status level early on, which in turn influenced his choice of career, neighborhood, social club, friends, and fiancée. Everything about Mark Talcott suggested class and taste. If not old money, then new money well spent. Shiny brown hair, skillfully barbered to minimize a high forehead. An immaculate shirt under a tailored linen jacket. Buffed nails. An even tan that didn't quite disguise an unhealthy pallor. A dazzling smile that had clearly benefitted from a cosmetic approach to dentistry.

"I assume you received the packet my assistant sent over," he said. "The itinerary and copies of bills and receipts for my business trip to Washington, D.C., two weekends ago. When Bitsy was killed." He looked down and away, the epitome of controlled grief.

"We did receive the materials and we appreciate your cooperation—" Eddie began.

Talcott kept going. "As for what I can tell you about Bitsy, I'll repeat what probably everyone—friends, family, coworkers—said about her. She was an amazing woman. The whole package. Fun, popular, beautiful, and brilliant. Social skills like you wouldn't believe. A head for business, I can tell you that. Nashville is a hot market right now and she was at the top of her game."

He sounded as if he were ticking items off a résumé.

"How did she feel about leaving all that behind?" Sam asked.

Talcott startled. "You're the Pickett County sheriff, aren't you? Tate? Where's your partner, the FBI agent?" He looked faintly disapproving, as if he deserved to be questioned by federal, not local authorities. Or men, not women.

"He's elsewhere at the moment. Let's get back to my question. Was Bitsy looking forward to leaving Nashville?"

"What do you mean?"

"Someone who's popular and well established in her field might want to stay where she had some leverage."

"Bitsy is—was my fiancée, Sheriff. She was also an ambitious woman, as I am an ambitious man. Fortunately, our goals aligned. Washington would have been the best possible move for both of us. She'd even lined up a job with a respected high-end real estate firm."

I wonder how much Lincoln Charles had to do with that. "Are you still planning to move?" Sam asked.

His sorrow appeared practiced. "There's nothing holding me here."

Sam looked down at her own notepad, which she kept in her lap. It was blank, but Talcott didn't know that. "So, you both had offers. Very helpful for a bright young couple. What kind of corporate law do you practice, Mr. Talcott?"

"I don't see what any of this has to do with Bitsy's murder." He looked at Eddie, who shrugged as if to say, "I have no idea where this is going."

"Ms. Newsome dealt primarily with commercial properties and development, I believe. You practice corporate law. I'm looking to see whether your professional interests may have overlapped."

"Corporate law typically encompasses a range of legal activities on behalf of business clients, Sheriff. Our role is to counsel those clients, to negotiate, draft, or review contracts or other agreements, and to advise on governance and operations."

Sam smiled. "I'm familiar with the outlines of your profession. Perhaps I should have been more direct. Did you counsel or advise any clients who might also have been working with Ms. Newsome?"

Talcott stared at her. She looked into eyes so dark they could have been all pupil. Once again, she was reminded of a predator fish or a bird of prey, like a peregrine. She saw no life, just a flick, as if someone lit a match and quickly extinguished it.

Then his face rearranged itself into a sneering sort of smile, as if he found her question adorable and foolish, something a child would ask.

"What an interesting train of thought. You're wondering if either of us made work-related enemies. Which suggests you aren't absolutely certain she was murdered by the serial killer."

"Doesn't have to be either or, Mr. Talcott," Eddie said. "The Wedding Crasher may have settled down in the region a couple of years back, taken a job, made friends, become an upstanding citizen, maybe even married."

"I hope you're not implying that one of our friends is a serial killer, Detective. I find the idea both ludicrous and offensive. I don't know everything about Bitsy's clients. The notion that one of them was moonlighting as a murderer seems far-fetched. You'd have to talk with her superior or her colleagues. And no, Bitsy and I did not share clients."

"Did she know Lincoln Charles?"

"Obviously she did, Sheriff. He was at her memorial service. I knew him first, as I'm sure you learned." Talcott shifted his attention to Eddie. "Is this going to take much longer? I really need to leave."

"You'll have to ask Sheriff Tate. She's the lead investigator on your fiancée's case. I'm working as a liaison."

"Oh, well," Talcott said with a wave of his hand. "Investigate away."

"Thank you, Mr. Talcott," Sam said. "I'll move things along. Would you consider Congressman Charles a friend of yours?"

"More a mentor. He gave me an internship, then a job. I loved Washington, I don't mind admitting. I wanted to stay. Unfortunately, I had family obligations that brought me back to the area."

"And when did you meet Ms. Newsome?"

"About two, no, three years ago."

"In Nashville. But you were born in Celina." Sam looked down at the gibberish she'd scribbled in her notebook.

"It's not a secret, Sheriff, and I'm not ashamed of my roots."

"I'm not suggesting you are. You were able to work in Nashville while you fulfilled your family obligations?"

"No, I got a job locally in the DAG's office so I could be closer to home. My mother took a long time to die."

Sam ignored the trace of bitterness. "While you were with the DAG, you prosecuted, among other suspects, a man accused of stalking a local woman named Claire Hooper."

"Common knowledge, Sheriff. Surely you figured that out back when you and the old sheriff were trying to solve the poor woman's murder."

"We looked at the stalker, naturally. Your name didn't come up. Now it has. Over and over again. It's awfully coincidental that the same man who helped protect one victim was another victim's fiancé."

"One thing is not remotely like the other, Sheriff."

"Except you didn't just work to find justice for Claire Hooper. You also dated her."

At the edge of her sightline, Sam saw Eddie's eyes widen. She kept her focus on Talcott.

"We bonded during the trial. We went out for a few months once the verdict came in, you may note. What's wrong with that? Since we were adults, both single at the time, I'd say no harm, no foul."

"Who broke it off?"

Another hot flash in those opaque eyes. Another smile.

"I don't know when you last dated, Sheriff Tate, but it doesn't work that way nowadays. One of us got busy or occupied elsewhere. Interest faded. Those things happen."

"Very modern of you. You seemed to have an issue with rejection in high school, though. Bit of a stalker yourself, weren't you?"

The veneer cracked, just a little. "If you're referring to an isolated incident from fifteen years ago, based on a juvenile miscommunication and long since resolved, you are clearly off the mark, Sheriff. I can only hope the special agent has a better track record when it comes to homicide investigations. Although," Talcott looked directly into the one-way mirror, "Agent Sloan seems to have come up short on the Wedding Crasher cases."

He put his arms on the table and leaned over far enough that Eddie rose an inch out of his chair.

"Let me give you a piece of legal advice, Sheriff Tate. Stay away from me and my family and my friends. Your inquiries and insinuations verge on harassment. I have some experience with shoddy treatment by overeager law officers with aspirations beyond their abilities. I'd be more than happy to slap your sorry"—he hesitated—"excuse for a police department with a lawsuit that could bankrupt the county."

"Is that a threat, Mr. Talcott?"

"It's counsel, absent my usual fee. You're welcome. Now, if you'll excuse me."

He rose, brushed off an invisible piece of lint, and picked up a soft leather briefcase worth about a month of Sam's salary. She kept her eyes on him as he exited.

"I think you ticked him off, Sheriff," Eddie observed.

"No, he came in hot, Detective. Not grief, though. Something else. I wonder what."

Chapter 9

Sam leaned into the warmth of the spotlight. She reminded herself to concentrate not on the frigid air-conditioning but on the audience, even though she couldn't distinguish one face from another. Her on-again, off-again agent had recommended she wear the slithery 1940s-era dress he'd picked up from God knows where. Long sleeves, plunging neckline, a twilight-blue number that would look good at a theme party.

She hated the outfit. The dress marked her as out of step with the times and overdressed for the club, which deliberately cultivated a laid-back, low-rent vibe. Like she was trying too hard. She lobbied to wear jeans.

"Everybody does that," the agent countered. "If you played guitar or fronted your own rock band, maybe. This look works for you, trust me. It's classy. A cut above. Vegas-ready. You want that. Vegas is where the money is."

She acquiesced, though she pushed back on his song selection. He favored "Daddy's Hands," a popular tune about a girl's beloved but strict father with hands that could be loving or punishing. Sam couldn't listen to the lyrics without wanting to scrub herself clean.

In the end, she settled for "Crazy." Done almost to death by almost every would-be female songstress. She sang it better than most, though, and she knew it.

Sam asked the house band to pitch the song in A, which gave her a rich low note at the beginning and room to riff at the end. The enthusiastic applause told her she'd made the right choice. She bowed. The crowd continued to show its approval. The affable if slightly sleazy host materialized at her side.

"What do you think, ladies and gentlemen?" he asked. "Isn't she something?" He held onto her arm as she tried to exit. "Hang on, honey, no need to run off just yet. We're going to take questions from the audience."

"We are?" Sam asked. She waited for the houselights to go up. Instead, the place got darker. She stood alone inside a small ring of light, like a circus animal. Or a suspect.

"Why haven't you made any progress?" someone called out. "What's holding you back?" another asked. She assumed they were referencing her slow-to-start singing career. Rude, but she could come up with some sort of answer, couldn't she?

Then the questions came faster and faster, like balls from an out-of-control pitching machine.

"Do you think you're doing a good job?" "How would you rate your performance?" "Come on, Sheriff, tell us who you really suspect. Who is the Wedding Crasher? We think you know."

"I don't know," Sam replied.

The lights came up briefly. Terry, Abdi, and Ralph sat in the front row, grinning like they'd been let out of school.

"Terry? What are you—?"

"The performance was perfect, kiddo," he called out. "Now tell these people what you know."

"I—I honestly don't know anything," she protested. She sounded childish.

"She may be suppressing," Abdi told Terry in a stage whisper.

"She knows!" A figure rose in the back, tall and imposing. Her father. Blood trickled from a round hole in his forehead. He looked disappointed in her. "You need to tell them what you know," he commanded. "I raised you better than this."

"Daddy, I don't know—shit!" she yelled because she'd smacked her head on the desk and it hurt. She blinked, took in the familiar surroundings of her office. How long had she been out? Long enough to have another dream in which she was again a victim. Of what, exactly? A failed career move? The Wedding Crasher? The past? A nagging memory? Her own incompetence?

Sam pushed upright and glanced at her watch. Midnight on a muggy evening in early June. Technically spring, but tell that to the humidity. She rubbed her head where she hit it. *That'll leave a mark,* she thought. Just one more thing for the reporters to ask about.

Just before Memorial Day, the FBI had announced it was diverting resources. Bureaucrat speak for, "We need to return our people to their field offices. We'll work on the case in between our other cases. Meanwhile, your friendly cops will work the local leads."

The press conferences became less frequent, the media representation smaller. The news cycle moved on and so did the attention span of most citizens. One way or another, they decided, whoever killed Bitsy Newsome was done for the season. Maybe gone for good. Meanwhile, they were going to enjoy the summer.

Terry left with assurances he would keep in touch. She sensed he wanted to stay and not just because work required it. She slapped aside those notions, told herself too much distance—physical and emotional—existed between them to try to light that spark again. Not with another person in the picture.

She googled the reporter, of course. The flame, the squeeze, the woman with whom Terry had become involved. Professional curiosity, she persuaded herself. She learned Mercedes Rodriguez was a powerhouse. Attractive, accomplished, going places. Brunette, maybe thirty. Not much older than the Wedding Crasher victims.

Don't go there.

Terry's absence meant Sam had more time on her hands. To think. To worry. To dream. But not, apparently, to get a good night's sleep.

She patted a file folder on her desk. Eddie Gould and his people had found it in a safe in Bitsy Newsome's apartment.

"It's a proposal for a multi-use development on Dale Hollow Lake," he told her. "Right on the shoreline. Not one of her colleagues has a clue as to what it's about."

Dale Hollow Lake, with its plentiful stock and unspoiled waters, was considered one of the preeminent fishing spots in the country. The federal government had owned the land for years. The area included a major flood control reservoir and the National Fish Hatchery. All protected and controlled by the Army Corps of Engineers and presumably off-limits to any development.

"Why would she broker a deal that can't happen?" Sam asked, although she realized she knew the answer. Money cleared away most obstacles, whether in Tennessee or D.C.

She searched for a connection to Mark Talcott and found none. The proposal was not a legal document, just an outline of ideas, some of them grandiose, some imaginative, all of them guaranteed to change the area and make a few people very wealthy in the process. If the project moved forward.

Maybe Talcott wasn't leaving his fingerprints, but his move to Washington once again raised a red flag. On a hunch, Sam searched for a connection between Lincoln Charles and Dale Hollow Lake. Other than mentions in a few speeches, she found nothing.

"Why kill Bitsy Newsome?" Terry asked when they spoke by phone the next day. "What kind of power or influence does the facilitator have on a project that isn't likely to happen?"

"Maybe she betrayed a confidence. Exposed a secret negotiation. Got too greedy. Pushed too hard. People get angry when they're deceived."

"You're saying her death was an ordinary homicide staged to look like the work of a serial killer?"

"That's not what I'm saying."

"What is it, then?"

Sam reminded herself to take slow, calming breaths. Not for the first time, she wished she hadn't given up cigarettes.

"Look at the particulars, Terry. Take the stockings or the blue garter. Certain details weren't made public. Who would know about those?"

"Someone with an insider's knowledge of the Crasher cases and a stake in making Bitsy's death look like the work of a serial killer."

"I can't believe it."

"Okay, then you're saying she wasn't killed because of what's in the proposal. And we're back to considering her death part of my ongoing investigation."

"I'm saying I don't know."

"Sam."

"I'm frustrated."

"You sound—" he hesitated. "Tired. Still having nightmares?"

She didn't answer.

"Sam, at the risk of coming across as a nag, I wish you'd—"

"I know. Call Sommers. I will."

"We're only human, Tate. It's not wrong to get a little help, a little outside perspective."

He had a point. She *was* tired. Sick and tired. And confused.

"Cross my heart, Terry," she said. As she disconnected, she could swear she heard a childish voice add, "and hope to die."

Chapter 10

"I'm glad you were able to find the time to see me, Samantha. How long has it been?"

"A while." Sam forced a smile but couldn't meet the eyes of the woman who sat across from her. Instead, she let her gaze travel the office. The decor looked the same, soothing greens and blues. Ocean colors, though the ocean was far from the gritty downtown Nashville precinct where they met. Comfortable couches and chairs, along with a few throw pillows in contrasting colors. Some interesting set pieces on bookshelves and on the walls, interspersed with framed degrees and commendations.

Dr. Jayne Sommers, a slender woman of indeterminate age, still dressed in muted colors, just as she had at their first meeting seven years earlier. She still wore round tortoise-shell glasses, still had her blond hair cut short. She came across as easygoing and accessible, perfect for a shrink connected with the Metropolitan Nashville Police Department.

Sam remembered their first meeting. Her heart sank when she first walked in and spotted the thick file on the table next to the psychiatrist's chair. How much access did the doctor have to Sam's past? Could sealed records be opened? Did they need to be in order for her to be approved to work?

To her relief, the doctor focused in that first interview on Sam's more recent history.

"You majored in criminology and ran track in college. Very impressive, Samantha. Then you came out here to try your hand at singing. I understand the urge to follow one's passion, especially when one is young."

Sam shrugged. "It didn't work out."

"I understand that as well." The doctor smiled. "From singer to soldier. What made you decide to enlist?"

"I met a guy at a bar."

"Who is now your fiancé."

"A very persuasive guy." They both laughed.

In the end, the doctor signed off on the rookie cop. Maybe she decided Sam's distant past would have no bearing on her foreseeable future.

"The door is always open, Samantha," she said as they shook hands.

Sam saw Jayne Sommers twice more. Once just after she shot and killed a suspect who was about to blow away her partner. Another obligatory session. Then, when she decided to leave MNPD for Pickett County Sheriff's Office, the psychiatrist requested a meeting. By that time, Jay was dead, Sam's bad habits had resurfaced, and her restless dreams had slid into nightmare territory.

Though Sam promised to keep in touch, she didn't follow through. She called once, in the middle of the Hooper investigation. Nothing since then. Even though she came to Nashville to bank, shop, drink, or socialize with work colleagues, even though she occasionally visited Jay's parents, she avoided committing herself to a full-blown sit-down.

So, two years.

"Sorry, Dr. Sommers. I guess I let the time get away from me. I've had a lot going on."

"I heard." The response was predictably dry.

"We're getting our fair share of coverage."

"Serial killers make for salacious headlines, don't they? Ms. Newsome was additionally something of a local figure. I'm more interested in how it's affecting you, Sam, especially now that you're the sheriff. You're bound to feel pressure."

"The town fathers and county officials have been nothing but supportive. At least so far. The press, well, that's another matter."

"Less than flattering?"

Sam shrugged. "It's to be expected. Lots of speculation and innuendo. A fair number of reminders about what a lousy job we're doing."

"That must hurt."

"Terry deals with it better than I do."

"How are things with Agent Sloan?"

Sam crossed her arms across her chest, realized she appeared defensive, and dropped them. "We work well together."

"What about the rest of it?"

"There is no 'rest of it.' He's headed back to Tampa, where he has a job and a girlfriend. I probably won't see him again. Unless the killer returns next April."

Dr. Sommers pressed her hands together. "At the risk of sounding like a shrink, I'd say you have a couple of unresolved issues."

"No kidding." Sam put a hand to her forehead. "I'm sorry, Dr. Sommers. I hate that we haven't caught the killer. As for Terry, I don't know what to say. He's professional, focused, and smart. He's also absent."

"Did you talk about—"

Sam cut her off. "Our previous encounter? God, no!"

"Your past relationship."

"If you want to call it that."

"What would you call it, Sam? Two people, each of whom has been dealing with personal tragedy and professional fallout, end up working a homicide whose theatrical elements attract national attention. Emotional responses would have been magnified tenfold. He leaves. Then he returns."

"And leaves again. People do that."

The doctor glanced at her lap. What did she have there, Sam wondered? A tiny notepad? A recording device?

"Why are you here, Sam?"

"I'm—unsettled."

"And how is it manifesting itself?" A careful question, which irritated Sam all the more.

"Besides the dreams? Do you want to know about the half-empty bourbon bottle I keep in my rented room or the one in the bottom drawer of my desk at the office? One good thing about living in Tennessee, there's no shortage of top-shelf booze."

"Samantha—"

"It's not pills, Doc."

"It's an escape. One which I suspect isn't working very well. Tell me about your other nightmares."

"Let's see: I'm singing before an audience filled with unfriendly press people. I'm tracking a killer through a forest. Last night, I was able to make people fall dead on either side of me just by walking through the middle of a crowd."

"Do you blame yourself for the deaths around you, Sam?"

"Death comes with the job, Dr. Sommers. I hate that someone is killing young women anywhere in the world but especially in my county. I might blame myself for not capturing the killer but not for his actions. And I regret Jay's death, but I wasn't responsible. It was a stupid, one-car, no-fault accident."

"What about Afghanistan?"

"No shortage of death in war."

"You acquitted yourself well."

"I didn't do the locals any favors."

"Any American presence would have riled the Taliban, Sam. The fact that you were all women was something they couldn't tolerate."

"Which is why the fanatics decided to execute the villagers, not a week after they celebrated with their new female American friends. Who happened to be elsewhere when the attack took place. Yeah, I know. I saw the pictures. As did the rest of the world."

The uploaded images of bodies baking in the hot sun stayed with her. How could they not? They lay crumbled outside the tent where her squad had broken bread with the villagers just a week earlier. A few men, and children of both sexes, but mostly women. Those who weren't killed or beaten half to death were dragged off to be defiled and subsequently, Sam knew, rejected by their families.

She closed her eyes. "What happened was awful, Doctor. Our unit's morale took a hit. We knew the victims, enjoyed their hospitality. Naturally, some of us questioned the mission. Nothing any of us did could have prevented what happened, though. I know that."

"Then maybe we ought to talk about the massacre you witnessed as a child. When you lost your family."

Sam, who'd been reaching for a hard candy the doctor kept on the coffee table, froze. She sat back. Slowly, carefully, as if she might lose her equilibrium.

"I thought we finished with that subject, Dr. Sommers. God knows I'm done. I am literally all talked out. Between the police and the child psychologists and the adolescent therapists, everyone has plumbed the depths of that particular hellhole."

"We never talked about that day, Samantha."

"Because you've already read about it. Everything you need to know is in that folder you like to keep close at hand." Sam struggled to suppress a sense of panic. "It's not relevant to the here and now."

"You can't believe that to be true, Sam."

Sam folded her arms across her chest. A typically self-protective gesture.

"So, you think the return of the Wedding Crasher has triggered memories of the shooting at my brother's wedding. Isn't that like saying the death of my fiancé in a car accident will give me nightmares when I'm investigating a vehicular homicide?"

"It's more than that. You've seen a lot of death. As you said, it's something of an occupational hazard. Most of the time, though, it's after the fact. Or something you've dealt with as an adult. In this instance, you witnessed these deaths when you were, what, eight?"

"Nine."

"On top of which, you had to testify at the killer's trial. That's a lot of stress for a nine-year-old who's lost her family. Don't you think so?"

"I suppose," Sam mumbled.

"Your nightmares aren't occurring in a vacuum, Samantha. Nor are they the result of your investigation. Rather, your present case is triggering other memories, bringing you back through other traumas you've more or less resolved to the one you haven't."

"Wait a minute. You think I blame myself for what happened? Come on! I was a kid."

"Not blame. Resolution. Something about what happened isn't settled in your mind."

"I—" Sam jumped up, walked over to the window, looked out. "I relive it from time to time. Who wouldn't? It's not PTSD, Doctor," she added hastily.

"I didn't say it was, Sam."

"It's just I have always felt I missed something."

"Missed something how?" The psychiatrist sat forward.

"That's just it." Sam turned from the window. "I don't know. They caught the guy and put him away. The dead are dead, the injured have recovered. Or not. It's over."

Sommers produced a pen and appeared to jot something down. It was the first time Sam had seen her make any notes.

"I'm going to give you a prescription. Something to help you sleep. Better yet, I'll provide you with a week's worth of tablets. No sense in asking you to stop at a drugstore. One pill at bedtime in place of, not in addition to, the bourbon, okay?"

"Absolutely."

"One other thing, Sam. I would strongly recommend a short course of hypnotherapy. Two or three sessions. If you're suppressing a memory, the process might help you access it."

Sam beat back a groundswell of dread. "Sure," she said. "I'll think about it."

"Samantha."

"I'll think about it, Dr. Sommers."

* * *

"Dr. Sommers. Is this a good time?"

Dr. Sommers had been listening to a recording of her session with Sam Tate when the phone rang. She didn't want to answer it. She had no choice.

At first, she found her mouth too dry to speak. She grabbed a glass of water next to the phone and sipped. "Yes, it's fine," she said.

"You had a session today," the man stated. He spoke as if he were a finely tuned engine. Low, quiet, but capable of both power and speed. "With Sheriff Samantha Tate."

I don't want to know how he knows.

"I did."

"The case must be very challenging for her. I would imagine a lot of her past is intruding upon her present. Does it present itself in the form of allegorical dreams or as recovered memories, would you say?"

They might have been two colleagues discussing Patient Z.

"Her dreams at this point are a jumble of impressions. Bits and pieces from here and there. Nothing more than flashes. She's had a lot of trauma in the past few—"

"I'm not interested in her recent history, Doctor, except as it bears upon her distant past. I want to find out what she's feeling about the incident that took place twenty-five years ago. If she's dreaming about it. Talking about it. Remembering it differently or in greater detail than when she was nine."

"You know I can't discuss the specifics." Even as she spoke, the psychiatrist realized she'd crossed a line.

The engine revved a little: stronger, louder, more dangerous. "What I know, Dr. Sommers, is that you have a daughter who studies public policy at Columbia

University. She could be a young woman who makes a difference in the world, given the chance. I imagine you want to give her that chance."

"Please don't—"

"You have access to a version of what occurred at the wedding of your patient's brother. What she thought occurred. What the authorities and the remaining members of her family also believed at the time. I have that as well. So, I'll ask again: Has anything changed to alter that particular narrative?"

"I can't be sure. I've only met with her four times and today is the first time we've even broached the subject. It's just that . . ."

"What?"

"Something about that day speaks to her after all this time. Some recollection is trying to reassert itself. Without a doubt, her nightmares have been activated by the reappearance of the serial killer whose victims are dressed like brides. On that, she and I agree. But is she revisiting her childhood trauma because it offers clues to her present case or because a long-buried memory about the trauma itself is trying to push its way into her consciousness?"

She heard nothing; for a minute, she thought her caller had disconnected. Then he spoke in his unsettling rumble.

"That is something I, too, would be interested in finding out. In fact, that is what I pay you to find out. I expect results, Dr. Sommers. I don't expect to be disappointed."

SUMMER

"When all is said and done, grief is the price we pay for love."

~ E.A. Bucchianeri, *Brushstrokes of a Gadfly*

Chapter 11

The poker game resumed in June. Jerry's idea.

"Best to play when we can these days," he told Sam when he called to reschedule. "For one thing, we all deserve a little recreational time. To take our minds off our troubles."

If only, Sam thought. Nevertheless, she looked forward to the gathering.

As usual, the group played Texas Hold'em. The pot was small, the game easygoing. The pace suited Sam. She'd played in college, continued in the army, and joined in the occasional game at MNPD. Years of keeping secrets had allowed her to develop a reliable poker face. Her mind gravitated to the analytical aspects of play. She took risks, a necessary quality even when the stakes were low. Only her restlessness kept her from being a great player.

Jerry O'Neil and Billy Owens were regulars. So was Brad Goodrich, a county commissioner and developer who hosted the gatherings at his well-appointed home up in Dale Hollow. The house contained the latest in high-end amenities. It boasted a distant view of the lake and a first-row seat to the changing seasons. Billy claimed *Architectural Digest* had approached Brad about a feature spread.

Tom Jackson had been another regular. When Brad Goodrich first invited Sam to take the old sheriff's place, she almost declined. For one thing, Brad had a reputation as a ladies' man. He'd already hit on Sam. Fortunately, her polite refusal and demonstrable lack of interest seemed to discourage him.

She still worried about trying to fill her mentor's seat, both literally and figuratively. Tom Jackson and his late wife had been popular figures in the community.

"That's exactly why you need to accept the invitation," Kaylee advised her boss when Sam mentioned her doubts. "You're continuing a tradition. It's sort of an honor they asked you. Anyway, it might be fun." She shook her head when Sam raised a skeptical eyebrow. Like so many others, Kaylee wondered if her superior even knew what "fun" meant.

Sam had nothing against a good time. Besides, how better to get to know the people to whom she reported than a friendly game of cards?

A rotating cast of public officials occupied the fifth seat, players Jerry or Billy selected. In the two years since she'd started playing with the group, Sam hadn't seen another woman at the table. She wondered when or if that might change.

This game night, she considered what she wanted to wear. Usually she changed into chinos or pressed jeans, a T-shirt, and a jacket. The men showed up after work, which generally meant suits and ties, soon after loosened or removed. Tonight felt different; what she wore carried additional meaning. Her uniform might suggest she was on the job, maybe on her way to nabbing a serial killer. Or her outfit could remind the others that she'd done a lousy job so far of closing either of Pickett County's two homicides.

They don't need reminding, she thought. She decided on jeans and a blazer.

Brad always set up a generous spread. Thick, meaty sandwiches, crackers, chips, and dips of all sorts. At some gatherings, the group fell on the buffet as if they'd been released from prison. Other times the food remained untouched. By prior agreement, no one brought food to the table, only beverages. Sam and Jerry drank beer; the others preferred Maker's Mark.

Jerry, bald and thin-faced, approached the game in a businesslike fashion. A skilled and serious player, he won most hands. Billy tended to settle his bulky frame into the most accommodating chair and light a cigar before he had a look at his cards. Brad was an indifferent player at best. He routinely flouted the no-cellphone rule. Everyone noticed he kept looking down at his lap. No one bothered to call him on it.

At this latest game, he appeared even more distracted than usual. He barely made eye contact with his guests. "Help yourself," he said with a wave at the buffet. Sam figured he was trying to track some deal going through or maybe not going through, judging by his frown. Fine, if he wanted to work while the others played, that was his concern. She only hoped no one else decided to mix business with pleasure.

Billy had invited Tobias Mueller, Thirteenth Circuit Court judge, to sit in. The judge had appeared twice before. Sam hoped he became a regular. Toby could be counted on to bring a little levity to the table. He came across as an affable good old boy, notwithstanding his education at Harvard and Columbia Universities. A gifted mimic and storyteller, he carried with him a collection of anecdotes about visitors to his courtroom.

"I got a guy who's been in for drug possession so many times we're fixing to get him his own chair," he began as Jerry dealt. "So, the man decides he needs a social media presence. He puts up a profile with him posing in his drug lab, all puffed up and proud. Product spread out behind him. He's even wearin' a lab coat. Then he posts a how-to manual for cutting crack cocaine. Very detailed, don't you know?"

He had everyone laughing. Even Brad smiled.

"Naturally, he's arrested," Toby went on. "Now he shows up in my court all indignant, claiming his First Amendment rights have been violated. I tell him he has a right to post whatever he wants, including incriminating evidence the police can use to charge him. Hell, makes their jobs easier." He chuckled.

Billy puffed on his cigar, shooting out plumes of fragrant smoke. "That boy's belt don't go through all his loops. I reckon you find most criminals aren't as smart as they think they are."

"Mostly," Toby agreed. "Although this Wedding Crasher seems to be pretty wily. What's it been, five, six years? And now he's taken up residence in our neighborhood, hasn't he?" Though he didn't look at Sam, she felt compelled to respond.

"Maybe so, Judge. But we've got good people on the case. We'll find the killer and bring him to justice." Her words sounded hollow, almost apologetic.

"You'll get him, Sam," Jerry added. She shot the mayor a grateful look.

Toby took a slug of whiskey. "Incidentally, I hear tell Elizabeth Newsome, the victim, was in on a deal to develop some property right up on Dale Hollow Lake's shoreline. She even lined up investors and presented 'em with a prospectus. It was billed as being strictly exploratory. What do you know about that, Sheriff?"

Game on. "Not a lot, Toby. That seems more an issue for the attorney general's office to investigate."

"Doesn't that land belong to the Army Corps of Engineers?" Jerry asked. "What are we talking, six hundred twenty miles of unspoiled and untouchable shoreline?"

Billy grunted. "The AG might want to start by finding out who's dumb enough to invest in exploring the possibility of a project built on property that isn't for sale and never will be."

"Never say never," Toby said with a smile. "You know Newsome's fiancé Mark Talcott is pals with Lincoln Charles. Our good old congressman even got the boy a juicy job with a top D.C. firm. That sounds pretty cozy, don't it?"

"Charles," Jerry said with a snort. "Figures he'd be in on it somehow, whatever 'it' may be. Anyone know who's ponying up the cash to move this along?"

"Supposed to be some kind of developer-led consortium," Toby replied. "Plan is to build high-end condominiums with a couple of houses, retail, private recreational access, the whole works. Don't mean diddly-squat unless something happens in Washington."

"It could happen," Jerry asserted. "Charles sits on the House Appropriations Subcommittee on Energy and Water Development. They fund the Corps. He wouldn't use his own money, but he might be inclined to use his influence."

"I reckon a project like that could rile people some," Billy observed.

"And enrich more'n a few," Toby replied. He turned to Brad. "You know anything about this fantasy project, Brad? I don't guess your company would have a hand in something so speculative. Still, you must have run into this Newsome woman at one time or another in your line of work, isn't that so?"

Brad went still. He looked up, his phone forgotten. He seemed to apply then discard a range of possible reactions—surprise, puzzlement, anger, fear—before settling on indignation.

"Why don't you go ahead and tell me who or what I'm supposed to know, Tobias? Seeing as you've already formed a set of opinions about my business and my acquaintances, not to mention what goes on right behind my house."

His hostile tone didn't sit well with the assembled group. Jerry shook his head. Billy shifted uncomfortably. Toby frowned. Though small in stature, the normally genial judge could fill any space he occupied with a sort of sanctioned majesty. He had a voice made for handing down judicial pronouncements. Most importantly, he didn't take kindly to being shoved, either physically or verbally.

"You might want to take it down a peg, Bradley. As you know, I make it my business to be aware of what's going on. It helps to be fully informed, whether I'm walking into a courtroom or a poker game. I would also note it is in no way unreasonable to inquire if a prominent local developer such as yourself is aware of a game-changing deal being brokered in his backyard, particularly when the broker herself has just met with a violent death."

"Hold on, Toby." Brad shifted gears; he adopted a placating tone. "I'm not saying it's unreasonable. In fact, I share your curiosity. I heard some rumors. Didn't believe them at first. I can't guess who would get involved with such a risky venture, especially one so tied up with the federal government and D.C. politics. To tell you the truth, it sounds as if someone is pulling a fast one using other people's money."

"Could the Newsome murder be connected to a business deal gone wrong and not a serial killer?" Billy said, tossing a glance at Sam.

"Don't put the sheriff on the spot, Billy," Jerry admonished. "Besides, all signs point to the Wedding Crasher. That makes it mostly the FBI's problem. The other good news is it ain't someone we know."

Sam couldn't be absolutely certain which, if any, of Jerry's observations were true. She wasn't about to contradict the mayor, however. "We're considering all possibilities," she said.

Brad wasn't finished. "If you ask me, it sounds like a whole lotta nothing." That got everyone's attention. "Not Bitsy Newsome's death. That's a terrible tragedy. I mean, any plans for the shoreline. Somebody would have to move mountains to get it off the ground under the best of circumstances. If I had to venture a guess, I'd say the woman's demise put any inquiries into a holding pattern. I wouldn't be surprised if the whole thing has already gone up in a puff of smoke."

Interesting, Sam thought. Bitsy. Not Elizabeth. Maybe nothing, maybe something.

Billy reached for the deck. "Well, there you go. Now, may I suggest we get back to playing cards? I believe it's my turn to deal."

Sam scanned her hand, calculating her bet. When she glanced up, she saw Brad's head had dropped to his phone. She made a mental note to arrange a sit-down with Commissioner Goodrich. She couldn't help but wonder how well he knew Bitsy Newsome. Or Claire

Hooper. Or any one of a number of brown-haired girls, for that matter.

Chapter 12

Emily Upshaw didn't think about being pretty. That is, she accepted her beauty without dwelling on it. Her arsenal of advantages included so much more: She was smart, she came from a loving family, and she wasn't afraid of hard work.

True, good looks conferred a certain status. People deferred to her. They went out of their way to help her. Unfortunately, some tried to attach themselves to her, as if her good fortune could somehow rub off on them. She made a point of avoiding people like that.

Despite her efforts, she couldn't get away from periodic entanglements. Girls who texted, emailed, left handwritten notes. Boys who hung around her locker or did her favors she never asked them to do. Those who took advantage of any and all opportunities to publicly affirm how tight they were with Emily Upshaw.

"Ignore them," her friends advised. Mostly she did. Or she sent what her bestie Anna called "cease and desist" orders. Most of the time, these measures ended the harassment and Emily only had to contend with hurt feelings for a week or so. Other times she needed an adult to intercede, a teacher or guidance counselor. Never her parents or the offender's parents. That was a bridge she wouldn't cross.

Mostly, Emily stayed on her best behavior and dreamed about letting loose. She didn't really like parties, though it wasn't something she wanted to advertise. She'd tried pot and hated how weed made her feel. She went out an d made out with a couple of boys here and there. She always stopped short of what she called "the danger zone."

Her virginity wasn't a point of pride, not going into her senior year. She knew what some of her classmates said about her, that she was an "ice queen" who thought she was too good for Pickett County. She would have been willing to be deflowered if only to unburden herself before college. She just hadn't found the right moment or, more importantly, the right guy.

The man she'd been dating over the summer was different. Patient, kind, older, a grown man with a grown-up's self-control. Handsome, strong, and smart. He made her feel protected and safe. He didn't push her to sleep with him.

June slid into July, which melted into August. She loved the clandestine nature of their romance. With classes starting in a few weeks, she didn't think she could keep him a secret. She wasn't sure she wanted to. Her choice of boyfriend would set tongues wagging for sure. She liked that.

Absent pressure from her boyfriend, Emily felt her own urges grow. She alternated between feeling restless and dreamy. She was ready to move affairs along, make her needs known. So, she set a time and place in her mind. Then she set her plans in motion.

She began with an announcement to her parents at breakfast on Friday. More like a comment tossed off in casual conversation.

"A group of us are going to Dark Skies tonight, if that's okay," she said. "To look at the night sky for a class project." A section of Pickett State Park had recently received an official designation as an ideal location for stargazing.

"What a great idea," her father replied, his enthusiasm on full display. Andy Upshaw, a dedicated amateur astronomer, belonged to the Upper Cumberland Astronomical Society. The group met monthly to watch for meteor showers or exchange information on the latest advances in telescopes.

"August is a good time, Emily. Although it's a little early to see the Perseids, isn't it?"

"We'll have plenty to look at, Daddy. It's the new moon stage."

"Andy, did you forget we're going to stay over in Nashville this evening?" Sue Upshaw interrupted. "Emily, sweetie, we're leaving early this afternoon and returning late tomorrow night."

Even better, Emily thought.

"It's just one night away, Sue," Andy replied. "Emily's a big girl. She'll be fine."

Emily held her breath. She didn't want them to deny permission. More importantly, she didn't want to be the impetus for another disagreement. Her parents had been arguing a lot lately, as recently as last night.

"Is it safe?" her mother asked.

Before Emily could launch a response, her father provided one.

"Sure, it's safe, Sue. Dark Skies is a very popular spot with families and such. Hell, they cosponsor all sorts of events up there. I have no doubt the park rangers keep a sharp eye on visitors."

"They do," Emily interjected. "We couldn't be safer. Plus, Gina is driving and she can't drink because of her diabetes. Not that the rest of us will be. It's really all about stargazing."

"Do you want to take the NexStar, honey?"

Emily felt a pang at her father's generous offer. The Celestron NexStar was his prized possession, a computerized telescope that ran about $1,200. At one point in her life, she would have jumped at the chance to look at the stars through such a sophisticated lens and imagine life on other planets. No more. Life on this one was just dandy.

"Daddy, thanks. I don't want to worry about such a valuable piece of equipment. I have a couple of classmates who will bring their scopes tonight. We'll use the NexStar when you and I look at the sky together."

"All right, then. Have fun, honey. Take notes."

"I will."

"Don't forget to feed Suki and change the litter box," her mother added. "Oh, and don't forget to turn on the alarm when you leave the house. Text if you need anything."

"Mom, I will."

Emily's father winked at her. "You haven't even started your senior year, but your poor mom already has empty nest syndrome."

"I do not!" her mother protested.

"Daddy, don't tease Mommy."

They all laughed. Emily realized how much her family meant to her, how she depended on them. Would she feel differently after tonight? Separate? Distant? "I love you guys so much!" she blurted out.

"We love you, too, Ems." Her mother gave her a hug. "I worry too much, I know. That's what moms do. Have fun."

Emily spent the long drive home from work that afternoon thinking about what she'd wear. It was plenty hot in the summer, but nights frequently cooled down, even in the foothills. Not that she'd have trouble staying warm. She giggled.

She hadn't come right out and announced to her boyfriend that she'd chosen the date of her deflowering. When he asked her to dinner and told her to pick the place, she suggested a romantic evening outdoors with a blanket. He seemed amused.

"You're not worried about mosquitoes or nosy park rangers?"

"We'll have bug spray. And I know a couple of places off the beaten path at Dark Skies where we can see the stars without seeing anyone else."

"You sound like you've had some experience with the night sky."

Damn. Had she blown it, come across either as too geeky or too experienced?

"I just like the idea of spending time in a beautiful place with a beautiful person."

"What a nice thing to say. Tell me, Em, how romantic do you want to get? Music? Wine? Neither is technically allowed in the park, but we don't care about the rules, do we? Maybe you have something else in mind? Something that may not technically be permitted?"

His voice flowed over her like warm honey. She shivered and flushed, grateful he couldn't see her.

"I'll leave it to you. Whatever we do will be absolutely lovely." Emily hoped she sounded sophisticated.

She arrived home by six thirty, relaxed in a bubble bath, then spent a half hour rummaging through her mother's clothes. As expected, the pieces were more conservative than she preferred for her special evening. At least the two of them were about the same size. She pulled out a sheer lilac low-cut blouse and held it in front of her. Sue Upshaw usually wore it over a camisole. Optional, Emily decided with a smile.

She took several selfies, adjusting herself in the light so the absence of a bra was more implied than obvious. When she had a shot she liked, she posted it on Instagram with the words, “Special outfit for special night. #hotenough.” She decided the hashtag made her sound knowing and clever.

Finally, just before nine, she heard his Mazda Miata pull into the driveway.

“You look gorgeous,” he said as she climbed in. “I thought we’d drive with the top down. Do you mind? I hate to see that beautiful hair all mussed up.”

Emily had prepared for this just as she’d prepared for everything else leading up to tonight. She grabbed a barrette out of her bag and pinned up her hair, letting a few tendrils tumble around her face.

“There we go. All set. Oh, and I brought a blanket.”

“You are a wondrous woman. And impossibly sexy. Are you hungry?”

“Famished.”

“Good.” He brushed her cheek. Gently, lovingly. Suddenly, food didn’t seem so important.

By the time they reached the viewing area, the western sky had dimmed. Emily counted a dozen cars in the lot. She squelched her disappointment.

“It’s busier than I expected.”

“Never fear, my princess.” He opened the door with a flourish. “I did my reconnaissance a few days ago and found a secluded area just up the trail. Most of the park closes at sunset, so we should have enough privacy.”

“It sounds perfect. As long as you promise to protect me from wild animals.”

He held the flashlight up to his face and smiled. Something moved behind his eyes. "I'll do my best, lovely Emily," he said.

He took her hand and led her to the spot, well away from any prying eyes. Under a stand of trees, Emily spread out the blanket while he unpacked cheese, crackers, olives, and a bottle of wine, along with flatware, plates, and stemmed glasses. To Emily's delight, he'd even brought along battery-operated candles.

They sat in a circle of flickering light, surrounded by shadows. Though a night chill set in, Emily felt warmed by the ruby-red wine. The alcohol made her light-headed. She barely touched the food. Time passed. She didn't know or care how late it was.

Her name on his lips felt like a caress. "Kiss me," she demanded, because it seemed like a bold thing to say. He did, and the heat spread from her mouth to her groin. She groaned.

"What are you really hungry for, sweet Emily?" he crooned as he nibbled at her ear. One of his hands found its way under her blouse and onto her bare back. The other reached her waistband and slid inside her panties. She was already damp.

He kissed her bare shoulder as his finger circled below, an unhurried tease that made her whimper. When he brought his mouth to her breast, she gasped.

"Wait," she commanded as she pulled off her mother's blouse. She straddled him, her arms around his neck. They kissed again. Then it was his turn to pull back. He began to unbutton his shirt in a slow striptease that made Emily swoon. His unzipped jeans revealed a full-on erection.

Emily had never seen a naked man below the waist, except for one furtive and accidental glance at her older brother through the bathroom door. Anxiety gnawed at the edges of her desire.

As if reading her mind, he pulled her to him and held her. She lay against his bare chest and inhaled the scent of him. He ran his fingers through her hair.

"If you're not ready, Emily, we can slow down or stop."

He tipped her face to his and kissed her as deeply as she'd ever been kissed. Her body responded of its own accord. He stroked her up and down her body. Without prompting, she touched his erection and he gasped. Emily felt powerful, womanly.

"I am ready. Readier than you'll ever know."

He lowered her gently to the ground and pushed himself into her willing body. Her hips rose to meet his. She lay on her back and let herself imagine she flew among the stars, a queen, no, a goddess both loved and in love.

I will never know a moment like this again, she thought.

She never would.

Chapter 13

The call came in on Sunday midmorning. As usual, Sam was at her desk. The week had been busy, what with the influx of tourists enjoying Pickett County's natural beauty. "More like ruining it for the rest of us," Cob Atkins complained. No one paid him any mind.

Sam wasn't alone. Most of the staff worked at least one weekend day a month. The sheriff had a problem not common to most bosses: Her employees seemed happy to put in the extra time. She often had to remind them to go home to their families.

Abdi stuck his head in. "We got a report of a body, Sheriff."

"What? Where?"

"Out by Pogue Creek. Backpacker found it. The call went to Fentress County Sheriff's Office. Their ME is on the scene. Doc Holloway is on the way."

"Pogue is in Fentress County. Why'd they call us? Never mind. Let's go."

Fentress County contained nearly four times the population of neighboring Pickett. The demographics had remained stable over decades. Over ninety-seven percent of the residents were Caucasian, the remainder either African American or Hispanic, with less than one percent of the census classified as *other*. Fordham Collins, the county sheriff, fell into that last category.

His dark eyes, black curls, light olive skin, and nose that managed to be both broad and long suggested Southern European roots. He was often asked about his ancestry. The question didn't bother him. Everyone always asked about everyone else. Where are you from? Who are your people? Which is your church?

"I'm a regular melting pot as far as I can tell," he once told Sam. "The anthropologist from Duke University who came around when I was a kid told my folks we belong to some unclassifiable subgroup called the *Melungeon*. Portuguese, Spanish, and Scotch-Irish immigrants, Native American mixed in there. Some free black ancestors, though you'd be hard pressed to get my kinfolk to admit to that part of it. You name it and it hangs on my family tree. That and two bucks will get me a cup of coffee."

He peered at Sam. "What about you? You must have some Mediterranean blood in you. Where are your people from?"

She ducked her head. "Everywhere, I reckon."

Ford accepted her evasion with his usual equanimity. "Well, there you go. I'm not any one thing, and you ain't from any one place. Guess we got that more or less in common. Besides being the sheriffs of two backwoods counties, that is."

Today Sheriff Collins waited for them beside his cruiser, his shirt rumpled and sweat-stained. The temperature had neared 90 degrees by ten o'clock and was accompanied by a saturating humidity. Typical for August. No one could be expected to smile, even without a homicide to process. Nevertheless, Sam had a bad feeling about this one.

"Sorry to bother you on a Sunday. I guess we share jurisdiction, seeing as this portion of the park belongs to both our counties. I suspect you're going to want this all to yourself."

Sam's stomach tightened. She didn't like the sound of that.

"The body was found up a trail leading away from the Dark Skies viewing field," Collins continued. "No events scheduled last night, but we've always got people here. Amateur astronomers and the like. The rest of the area closes at sunset, which is about nine this time of year."

"Don't you have cameras in the parking lots?" Abdi asked.

"I'd say they cover ninety percent of the area. And one was on the fritz."

"Who found the body?" Sam asked.

"Couple of hikers. We took their statements. If you want to interview them—"

"No need."

Two Fentress County cruisers sat in the parking lot, engines off but lights flashing. Sam, Abdi, and Ford climbed an uneven path past one of the cliff-lined river gorges and ducked under a multicolored sandstone arch. They followed a hiking trail that overlooked Pogue Creek Canyon. The view from the top was stunning. No one even glanced.

The group left the canyon loop road. At the beginning of a more out-of-the-way trail, they came to a forest thick with hardwood trees. Even from a distance, Sam recognized the ash-gray bark. *Quercus alba*. The oaks, tall and prepossessing, shaded the mix of dense growth and clearing. In the middle, she could make out a prone figure. She compressed her lips to keep from cursing aloud.

Four people worked the area. Ranger Travis Green looked up, nodded, and returned his attention to the ground beneath his feet. Last year, he and Sam dealt with overenthusiastic members of an off-trail riding club. The officers defused the situation, although not before guns were drawn.

She caught a glimpse of the forensic detective Fentress County Sheriff's Office recently added. Gary, that was his first name, Sam remembered. He snapped still pictures from various angles while a young woman she didn't recognize operated a video camera. Roberta Edelstein, the Fentress County coroner, knelt on the ground, her ample back to the new arrivals. A solid cube of a woman, she'd dressed in sensible shoes covered with throwaway booties, stretch slacks, and a colorful cotton blouse damp with perspiration. A strand of salt-and-pepper hair escaped the makeshift bun she held in place with a number two pencil.

Sam steeled herself and walked forward, Abdi by her side.

A young woman lay with her head on a pillow. No, not a woman, a girl, no more than seventeen. Long hair, dark blond, expertly highlighted, which suggested money. Even here in the eastern mountains of their rural state, high school students with generous parents could mimic big-city style.

The dead girl wore a flouncy chiffon dress the color of daffodils. The cut was modest, the hem to the knees. Nothing a young woman in this century would choose for herself. Blood from an ugly wound at her neck had stained the neckline. Another rust-colored patch formed a half-circle on the front of her skirt. Stockinged legs ended in white shoes with straps across the instep. Wilted daisies rested in her right hand.

"We know her," Abdi said flatly.

"Sheriff Tate," Edelstein said, hoisting herself to a standing position. "And you are . . ."

"Detective Abdi Issen, ma'am."

She shook his hand. "I'm sorry we have to meet under these circumstances, officers. I've already called Dr. Holloway. He was under the impression it was his day off."

"No such thing," Sam said.

Edelstein sighed. "That seems to be the case more and more these days, doesn't it? Should we wait for him?"

"No need."

"The victim . . ."

"Emily Upshaw," Abdi said. "Only daughter of Andy and Sue Upshaw. He's an engineer and a builder, she's a teacher. They've got an older boy over at Tennessee State. Emily is—was—going into her last year at Pickett County High School. Cheerleader, captain of the soccer team, member of the student council. She also interned at the county paper last semester."

"You know a lot about her," Edelstein remarked.

"It's a small community," Sam said. "Emily wrote about our office, spent some time getting to know us."

With a pang, Sam recalled the pretty girl whose presence brightened everyone's day. Emily proved to be observant and insightful. She wrote with tact and sympathy about the toll Sheriff Jackson's death took on the department. She avoided melodrama. She described the new sheriff as inspirational, which surprised Sam. What mattered most was that the finished piece credited the deputies and reflected well on the department.

"Was she reported missing?" Edelstein asked.

"No," Sam replied, "but it's a weekend. Her parents might think she's staying with friends. They might even be out of town. Was she killed here?" Out of the corner of her eye, she saw Abdi pull out a pad and begin to take notes.

"Doubtful. The scene is remarkably clean, almost scrubbed. I won't know more until—"

"Until you get her on the table. I know."

"We'll need to move her very carefully. She's still at the stage where we could do some real damage."

"I suppose it's too soon to call TOD."

"I won't make it official until I've done a more thorough exam. My findings then need to be corroborated by Dr. Holloway, the ME's office, TBI. We have a process."

She paused for a minute. "Body temp and the presence of rigor around the face and neck suggest she died between twelve and thirty-six hours ago. She's young, which affects my calculations. We're outside and it's hot, two more factors. The temperature last night moderated somewhat. That may further alter my timeline."

"Okay, forget the precise 'when' for a minute. Cause of death?"

Edelstein looked askance, as if she'd been asked to make a prediction on an election or place a bet at the track. Did medical examiners find common ground in their struggle to deal with impatient detectives who tried to rush the science?

"As I told Sheriff Collins, it's complicated."

"Make it simple, please."

"I'll try. The victim ingested a near-fatal dose of something toxic. Look at her fingernails. Underneath, where the polish's been chipped off, you can see they've turned blue. Same with her lips. The color is consistent with symptoms produced by certain benzodiazepines."

"Rohypnol?"

"It's certainly possible."

"What about the cut on her neck?"

"It must have hurt." Like Holloway, Edelstein had an arid sense of humor.

"But it didn't kill her?"

"I'd say no."

"Then the Rohypnol killed her."

"No."

Sam kept her voice level. "Dr. Edelstein—"

"Look." Edelstein lifted the girl's skirt to reveal a deep three-inch wound running lengthwise down one leg. "Cut to the femoral artery. She could have bled out in three to, say, ten minutes. A messy, nasty way to die, except, I suppose, if you're unconscious."

"You're saying someone overdosed her, dragged a knife across her neck, and then sliced her femoral artery?"

"I'm pretty sure the last injury is the one that killed her. If I had to hazard a guess, I'd say she was first dosed with Rohypnol, too much to guarantee compliance and too little if the goal was death. Someone then tried to cut her throat and botched it. That cut was made right to left, by the way."

"Right to left? A left-handed person?"

"That may well be. After which the femoral artery was severed, albeit with far more skill. The last cut would have worked instantly."

"Same blade as the other cuts?" Sam asked.

Edelstein gave the sheriff a hard stare. "Possibly."

Sam struggled to contain her impatience. "So, the killer's first efforts are sloppy and ineffective. Then he, what? Steps back, gets hold of himself, and uses a second weapon to make a cut worthy of a surgeon?"

"I can't answer that, Sheriff. I can't even say that Ms. Upshaw died here. The area around her body is immaculate. All I can tell you is the victim was more or less cleaned and dressed postmortem."

"Anybody want to talk about how she's dressed?" Ford Collins had his arms folded across his chest. Sam recognized the pose. It was one she assumed many times, as if the simple act of crossing two limbs one over the other would make the grisly reality easier to process.

"Kids wear that kind of stuff, don't they?" Abdi said. "I mean, they dress up in vintage clothes."

Ford shook his head. "I have two daughters. They love old clothes. They combine them with new stuff, though. A frilly dress with combat boots. A tuxedo jacket with a nose ring. That kind of thing. This girl is fixed up like she was going to a spring prom maybe seventy years ago. No makeup, frilly dress, stockings. Shoes my grandmother could have worn to church."

Sam glanced at Abdi. "Sound familiar?" she asked.

"How about yes and no?"

"How about the same and not the same?" Ford chimed in. "Close enough to your ritualistic murders but with a couple of elements off."

Your ritualistic murders. As if she'd deliberately imported a serial killer rather than inherited one. Either way, both the victim and the murderer belonged to her.

"Doctor, does she have all ten fingers?"

"She does."

"What do you think, Sheriff?" Abdi asked.

"I think we're looking at a homicide which is both like and unlike our previous homicides. The same and yet not the same."

An obvious conclusion, not to mention a conundrum with which Sam Tate was all too familiar.

Chapter 14

"The shit is fixin' to hit the fan. Sorry, boss."

Abdi wasn't given to cursing, even around his irreverent superior. Not that Sam would have blamed him for letting loose with a bucketful of blasphemous phrases. Another homicide just months after the first one, which remained open. A murder that hit hard in more ways than one.

While Abdi drove them back to the office, Sam called her assistant. "We have another homicide, Kaylee," she began without preamble. "I need you to come in. And would you get hold of whoever's off today and see if you can get them to come in as well?"

She then telephoned Karen Polk, the DAG lawyer. The woman promised to alert her boss. Finally, Sam reached out to Nate Fillmore.

"What the hell?" he exclaimed. "Is there a run on dead bodies no one told me about?" He agreed to send over his top investigator. "She's the best, Sam," he declared. "If something's there, she'll find it."

She disconnected just as a text came in.

"We have to call Emily's parents," Abdi reminded her.

Sam looked at her phone. "Dispatcher says they just called in, wondering if they could file a missing persons report."

"Convenient."

"Doesn't make it any easier."

Most of the staff had assembled at the station by the time Sam and Abdi returned. Sam filled them in on the horrific discovery at Dark Skies. They reacted with predictable shock and anger, not to mention concern. Several deputies had teenagers about the same age.

"I know this is an awful thing to contemplate, people," Sam told them. "Abdi and Ralph will be at the high school tomorrow morning. Before then, we need to—"

"Are we looking at another victim of the Wedding Crasher?" Dana Wilkins asked. She was one of only three female deputies, an employee ratio Sam wanted to change.

"I'm not sure. Feels more like an imitator. Our job isn't to trade in feelings, though, but facts. This might be a copycat or something else entirely."

"Do her parents know yet?" one of the dispatchers asked.

"All they know is their daughter went missing. They're coming into the office. I will tell them in person behind closed doors. We're trying to rush the pre-autopsy photo."

Everyone in the room knew that none of Tennessee's regional forensic centers allowed direct viewing of the body. Identification had to be made via an image, usually just the head and taken post-autopsy. In this instance, the ME's office had moved to expedite the county sheriff's request.

"We're not going to be able to keep this murder quiet," Sam continued. "Which means we've got to stay with the evidence and ignore the conjecture. Those of you with high school students in your family should let your kids know Emily was killed. No details but we don't want them caught by surprise or pulled into the rumor mill."

Andy and Sue Upshaw arrived forty-five minutes later. She ushered them into her office. Kaylee followed to offer coffee, tea, or water. The Upshaws declined.

Before they sat down, she returned, not with beverages but with the expected fax. She looked shaken. Understandable. She was a mother. Her son was in Emily's class.

Sam placed the image on the desk. Andy Upshaw picked it up, gave a tense nod, and put the picture back facedown.

Sue Upshaw did the same. "That's Emily," she whispered. Sam was prepared to deal with histrionics, but the woman seemed more catatonic than anything else. It hadn't sunk in yet.

"I know this is a difficult time, Mr. and Mrs. Upshaw. Perhaps, though, if you'd be willing to talk with me a few minutes, we could—"

"We came in to make an identification, Sheriff, not to sit here and answer questions." Andy Upshaw's tone was barely civil. "My wife is in shock. We need to get home and contact our family members, beginning with our son. Then we have to make funeral arrangements. I'm sure you can start your investigation without our help. Unless this is part of an ongoing hunt for a serial killer that should have been concluded long before now. In which case, my only daughter would still be alive." He glared at Sam.

"Andy, please," Sue said.

Upshaw stood. "Excuse me," he said. The man wasn't offering an apology, only an exit line. He put his hand under his wife's elbow and gently guided her to a standing position. On the way out, she whispered, "I'm so sorry, Sheriff Tate."

Sorry for what? Sam wondered. She would soon find out.

She called Terry Sunday night. She'd already decided to approach the murder as a local matter. Smaller task force, area experts. She didn't believe the FBI would get involved. She simply wanted to bounce her ideas off of someone looking at the case from the outside. A colleague. A friend.

"We're treating this as a separate homicide, despite the bits of ritual that look like our serial killer," she told Terry. "That's probably an attempt to mislead us, or maybe this new killer admired our serialist but couldn't manage to quite match the MO."

"I agree. Whoever did this tried three times to kill her. Two messy and one neat. That's not how the Wedding Crasher operates."

"And yet the site was clean as a whistle." Sam considered a moment. "Serial murderers don't generally change their methods, do they?"

"It depends, Sam. A true psychopath might try to mix things up just to confuse us. Our serialist is pretty dedicated to routine. From what you've described, this murder is messy, impulsive, almost thrown together."

"The killer may be left-handed."

"There you go. Not our serial killer." He exhaled. "Unfortunately, I have a hunch it won't make any difference to the principal players."

"I expect it'll be rough, Terry."

"As long as you don't expect it to go as you've planned."

Sam thought she understood. She and her officers would need to keep their passion in check. Follow the evidence. Stick to the process. Stay laser-focused. Stay clear of the emotional churn at the periphery: the grief, the anger, the fear. Expect the unexpected. Ignore the hustlers, the attention-seekers, the busybodies. Hadn't they gone through this not five months earlier? They were prepared.

No such thing, she soon learned.

By midday Monday, *Pickett County Press* had released online and special print editions of its paper. The stories focused on the Upshaw murder. There was plenty of maudlin prose about Emily, along with several unsubtle broadsides about the failure of local authorities to curb the "rising tide of violence."

Here we go again, Sam thought.

Twin hashtags began to trend on Twitter: #PickettCountyMurders and #TheWeddingCrasher. Instagram users shared photos taken with long-range lenses of "the most recent murder sites" (the *only* murder sites, Sam wanted to protest). National outlets began to pick up on the more salient details. Those stories, a mix of truth and supposition, went viral.

"This is insane," she told Nate. "My deputies are tied up on phone calls trying to reassure callers we don't have a serial killer roaming the streets. We have to get out in front of this."

"We might be a little late for that."

"Terry Sloan said the same thing. What's with you guys?"

"We're jaded. Or maybe we have more familiarity with the politics."

"Politics?"

"All I'm saying is, if it can get worse, it will."

Sam tried to schedule an interview with Andy and Sue Upshaw, only to be directed to their attorney, who explained he also served as the designated family spokesperson. He also told Sam the Upshaw family would be happy to cooperate once they'd been over certain details with other officials. Sam refrained from asking which officials they wanted to consult.

She considered Terry's and Nate's admonitions and Sue Upshaw's whispered regrets. Sam had had some experience with what her superiors called "the politics of grief" during her time at MNPD. Her commander cautioned that police officers would never work a corner as treacherous as the intersection of pain, power, and publicity. She vowed to stay even more alert for complications.

Abdi reported on his interview with Emily's friend, Anna Fleishman, whom he interviewed after school with her parents present. In between sobs, she'd revealed that Emily had been seeing someone special. Someone she met just after she started working her summer job in Nashville. Older, she'd confided to Anna. More experienced. A man, not a boy.

"Did Anna meet this man?" Sam asked.

"No. Never got a name, never saw a picture."

"Does the friend think Emily was sleeping with him?"

Abdi shook his head. "Maybe not. Anna couldn't seem to address the topic of sex with her parents sitting right there. But from the texts Emily sent and the photo she posted on Instagram, I got the impression she planned to lose her virginity that Friday night."

He showed Sam the picture. Bare shoulder forward, head tilted back, streaked blond hair worn loose and messy. The girl's idea of a sexy pose, no doubt copied from any of a hundred images she'd seen over the course of her young life. Typical teen selfie, right down to the hashtag. Sad and now, in retrospect, tragic.

"One more thing, Sheriff. Anna received another text at midnight on Friday. 'Dirty deed done!' Definitely from Emily's phone."

"Find that phone, Abdi. Call the phone company if you can't. I want to know who was on the other end of any texts she sent or received."

"Can Dr. Edelstein tell if Emily died Friday or Saturday?" Abdi asked.

"She's waiting on the report from Nashville."

"So, Friday's lover isn't necessarily Saturday's killer."

"Maybe, maybe not. He's still a person of interest."

More surprises. Terry called in the afternoon to say he booked a night flight and would meet her at the office bright and early the next morning. She quashed the pleasure she felt at his imminent return. *Keep your head on straight, Tate,* she warned herself.

"I thought we agreed this isn't the FBI's case, Terry."

"Doesn't matter. This situation is about to go pear-shaped. You can thank Lincoln Charles. Andy Upshaw called his office. Charles called my director. Just now, the congressman announced he would make a special trip to Byrdstown on Tuesday to address his constituents."

"What?"

"That's not all. Mark Talcott, newly relocated to our nation's capital and apparently taking his bereavement in stride, also promised to appear."

"They're linking the two cases before we've had time to process the evidence," Sam fumed. "What the hell does Charles think he's doing?"

"Given how few people reside in Pickett County, I'd say Congressman Charles is playing to a much larger audience."

Chapter 15

Terry, Sam, and Calvin Jakes met the next morning and walked over to the town hall. They avoided the scrum of reporters surrounding the makeshift platform at the front of the building. "National outlets," Jakes grumbled. "Again."

With the hollow-eyed Upshaw family by his side, Charles inveighed against serial killers in Tennessee as if they'd taken over the state. He promised the full investigative power of the federal government would be brought to bear on this homicide. Never mind local law enforcement hadn't tied Emily's murder to the Wedding Crasher—and might not.

Jerry O'Neil was asked to say a few words. Sam was not. She couldn't help but view the decision as a slap in the face.

"Andy Upshaw is heartbroken," the mayor told her afterwards. "He's also connected. He did the only thing he could think of. Charles is using him to score political points or maybe raise his national standing. That's obvious to anyone with half a brain. But we're between a rock and a hard place, Sam. I need to know you're on top of this."

"We're on top of it and ahead of it, Mayor," she replied. "We've got a release going out today about our own press conference, at which we'll express our gratitude for the congressman's interest and emphasize that we're keeping *all* lines of inquiry open. I've already called together the task force."

The relief on his face almost made her feel guilty. "Just remember," she added, "we don't have any proof this is our serial killer."

"Never mind all that. I knew I could count on you. This ain't gonna be easy. Maybe the FBI can take the heat. Hell, their PR guy can manage Charles and the press so you can do your job. You're still in charge. People around here trust you."

Her sunglasses hid her eye roll. "Good to know."

Within hours of the Charles press conference, Sam had Calvin Jakes send out a release on Pickett County Sheriff's Office letterhead announcing the formation of a task force to investigate Emily Upshaw's murder. Included were acknowledgments about the importance of the case, oblique references to ongoing investigations, and an expression of profound appreciation for help from local, state, and federal agencies.

At the next day's press conference, Terry deferred to Sam, who hammered home the same message. The Upshaw family attended with their lawyer. They stayed in the shadows and deflected all press inquiries. Congressman Charles was notably absent, as was Mark Talcott.

"I suggested to the congressman's office that he might not want to push so hard for federal involvement," Jakes reported after the conference. "I reminded him the optics of D.C. interference in county and state business wouldn't look good."

"Good Lord, we have to worry about optics?" Sam exclaimed.

"That's what you have me for, Sheriff."

The expanded task force met Wednesday. Ford, who'd joined them, was characteristically blunt. "Let me get this straight. We gotta pretend to mount a federal investigation in order to satisfy the victim's relatives and their powerful political friends?"

"We're not pretending anything, Ford," Sam replied. "We're investigating with assistance from our state agencies, as we always do. TBI, state police, the district attorney general." She coughed loudly. Polk raised her head to find everyone staring at her.

"We're available to help in any way we can," she said, and went back to her phone.

"The FBI is here in response to a request from the family and Congressman Charles," Sam continued. "They're in a 'wait and see' mode."

"Wait and see if this is the work of their serial killer?" Captain McHenry spoke up from the far corner.

"Wait and see if we can be of any assistance." Terry looked around the room. "Although I doubt you'll need us."

"Aren't you all here for the extra-robust coffee?" The room erupted in laughter at Abdi's faux innocent question. Most everyone had experienced Kaylee's brew firsthand.

"Nice save," she mouthed at her detective.

Andy and Sue Upshaw finally agreed to see Sam late Wednesday afternoon. She worried they would ask to meet at the station and arrive with an entourage. Instead, they invited her to their house. Terry offered to accompany her. She almost accepted; the two of them hadn't spent any time alone. She decided against it.

"Let me handle this, Terry. You can manage the circus for a couple of hours."

His smile almost broke her heart. "I am the consummate ringmaster."

The Upshaw residence stood on four acres at one edge of Rankin Ridge Lane. Sam ordered away a news van, which led to a brief conversation about free speech and constitutional rights to cover important stories.

She drove up a gently sloping driveway, parked, and knocked on the elaborately carved front door. Andy answered and motioned her to come in, then turned away. She remained in place for thirty awkward seconds before Sue Upshaw appeared and brought her inside.

The main floor could best be described as open-plan masculine. Wood accents and oversized furniture dominated the two areas visible from the hallway. An inviting leather sectional faced a massive stone fireplace. No dead animals with glass eyes adorned the walls. Instead, the owners had mounted a sixty-five-inch flat-screen TV just above a mantle that held family pictures.

Sam pulled her eyes away from the framed photograph of Emily and followed Sue to a room off the kitchen. A large glass table sat under an ornate wood-and-crystal chandelier that made her think of an elk with his head stuck in a water glass.

Andy pulled out a stiff-backed chair, his face set in a scowl. “Sit,” he ordered Sam.

His wife stood, unable to decide what to do with herself. “Sheriff, would you like some sweet tea or a cookie?” she asked. “I’ve got some of each.”

“She’s not here on a social call, Susan.”

Sam turned her attention to his wife. “Thanks for your offer, Mrs. Upshaw. Some tea would be nice.” Her words sent Sue into the kitchen for three glasses and a pitcher. The act of doing something seemed to revive her somewhat. Andy continued to glower at Sam until his wife returned.

Might as well jump right in, Sam decided.

"Mr. and Mrs. Upshaw, my goal is to find the person who killed your daughter. I don't care if it turns out to be a serial killer, a stranger, a high school student, or a family acquaintance."

"You're not suggesting—?"

"I'm not suggesting anything, Mr. Upshaw. I'm here to bring you up to date and see if you can provide me with any further information." Sam chose her words with care. "It's clear you want to help and we welcome that help. As you know, we're considering whether Emily's murder"—she saw Sue Upshaw flinch—"is connected to the ongoing FBI investigations."

"You mean the Wedding Crasher. I thought that was obvious."

"I'm afraid it's not, Mr. Upshaw. We need to consider other possibilities, if only to rule out anyone acquainted with Emily or members of her family."

"Tyler told me there were state troopers snooping around campus."

"Not snooping, Mr. Upshaw. Investigating. We simply wanted to determine if any of your son's friends had ever expressed an interest in Emily. Apparently, she began seeing someone at the beginning of the summer. He wasn't a classmate of hers and he might have been older."

Andy turned to his wife. "Did you know about this?"

Sue looked chagrined. "I didn't. She never said anything to me. She seemed happy, but who wouldn't be at her age? She had so much to look forward to." Tears derailed her.

"Sheriff, are you saying that some boy—some man—my daughter may have dated this summer killed her?"

“We don’t know. We need to locate the person in question and then work out the timeline. Emily died on Saturday night. We know she met someone on Friday night.”

“At Dark Skies. She told us she was going with friends.” He made a fist and repeatedly punched the palm of his other hand. Sam doubted he felt the blows.

“Believe me, Mr. Upshaw, we will find this person. I also want to widen the net. Do you or your wife have any enemies, someone who would want to cause you pain by killing your daughter?” She remembered to add, “I realize how difficult it must be to even think along those lines.”

Sue put her face in her hands. Andy took a breath through his nose and huffed.

“Tennessee has a reputation, Sheriff Tate, mostly deserved. Public corruption, racketeering, extortion, forgery, counterfeiting, fraud, and embezzlement. You name it. We’re at or near the top of a list of the most morally bankrupt states in the union. Any corporation willing to grease the wheels can expect a mega-subsidy. We got highway construction projects padded out the wazoo and politicians lining their pockets.”

“Andy.” Sue lay a hand on her husband's arm. “Sheriff Tate doesn't need a lecture on Tennessee governance.”

He shook her off. “My point is, a lot of people are dipping into that well, but I'm not one of them. I don't offer kickbacks or bribes. I retain a full-time staff of skilled architects, engineers, and tradespeople who are dedicated to their craft and loyal to me. Most of my work comes through competitive bidding. If I lose out, I lose out.”

He shrugged. “That might very well earn me enemies around here. Maybe someone who wants to hurt my business. Hurt me. But I can't imagine anyone would want to harm my Emily."

He coughed to cover a spasm of grief and dropped his gaze. Sam waited. She had no intention of pushing. She could drill down more deeply later on if necessary. She hoped she wouldn't need to. Digging into the relationship between politics and business in the state was akin to jumping into a fetid sinkhole.

"Did Emily have any interests outside of school? Maybe a part-time volunteer position?"

Sue managed a faint smile. "She interned at the county paper last year. Volunteered at the clinic the year before. She got her first real job in Nashville this past summer. Four days a week. We thought it was too far to travel, but she insisted. She really wanted the store discount."

"She worked at Nordstrom, correct?"

"Yes, behind the perfume counter. She enjoyed the experience."

Sam thought about that. Tennessee law allowed sixteen-year-olds to work retail. Emily could have easily attracted the attention of a potential suitor. Someone older and wiser in the ways of seduction. And possibly murder.

"Everything you've shared is appreciated. One more thing. I'm afraid I'll need to take a look at her room, if you don't mind. Or we can put it off, although it's best not to wait."

Sue Upshaw looked at her husband.

"Do it now," he said without looking at her. Sue touched her husband's shoulder. His head came up.

"Look, Sheriff Tate." He cleared his throat, struggling to make eye contact. "About that media circus with Lincoln Charles the other day. We just wanted—"

"You wanted justice for your daughter, Mr. Upshaw. That's what I aim to give you."

Chapter 16

Two days later, Sam was back at her desk, rubbing her eyes and alternating between store-bought coffee and Kaylee's potent brew. Sleep continued to be an iffy proposition. She'd long since used up the pills Dr. Sommers had given her. Not that they kept her dreams away; they simply kept her from remembering them when she woke, muzzy-headed and angry.

Meanwhile, she had at least half a dozen messages from the psychiatrist. Most of them inquired about her health. A few urged her to consider hypnotherapy. She ignored them all.

Emily's room and car had been searched. Not a single clue, nothing that gave any indication she had a paramour. No diary, no pictures, no unfamiliar articles of clothing. Maybe Romeo wasn't the gift-giving sort.

So here she was, back to criminal detective work. Trying to keep a promise she didn't know if she could keep. Missing Terry, who spent most of the time in the Cookeville office. Sam assumed he was staying out of her way so she could work the Upshaw murder as a local homicide. At least she hoped that was why he'd made himself scarce.

She gnawed on her pencil and reviewed the notes she'd made. They contained little in the way of specifics. Emily had a summer job and an older mystery boyfriend who may or may not have murdered her. She might have picked up a stalker. Maybe she attracted the attention of a complete stranger. Someone she passed on the road. Someone she served at Nordstrom's perfume counter. Someone who went to her school or lived down the street.

No names, no real leads. Only a promise to a dead girl's parents, both members of the community she'd pledged to protect and serve.

On another page, Sam created two side-by-side columns. Under "not the same" she wrote:

- younger
- blonde
- student
- killed in August, not April
- dressed in yellow, not white (not a "bride")
- different (messier) death
- no missing digits

The second column, labeled "the same," read:

- postmortem ritual (objects, dress)
- objects themselves (silk pillow, flowers, votive candles)
- no blood at scene (meticulous killer?)
- lying under oak trees (*quercus alba)*

For some reason, she circled the last line.

Kaylee appeared at the door. "You got a call. Line two."

"We have a working intercom, Kaylee." Sam tried to sound amused rather than annoyed. "You don't need to get up from your desk just to announce a call."

"I know, but this sounds like it might be more personal. I asked if it was a police matter and she said not exactly, but that it couldn't wait. I didn't want to advertise your personal business out in an open space."

Sam almost laughed out loud at that. She doubted she got two personal calls in a year.

"Anyway," Kaylee went on, "now that I'm here, I can check on your coffee supply." She headed towards the desk.

Sam covered the mug with her hand, softening the gesture with a smile. "I'm fine, Kaylee, thanks. Mind telling me who's holding on the phone?"

"Your aunt Gillian from Delaware. Did I even know you had an aunt Gillian? Or that you were from Delaware?" Faintly accusing.

"I'm sure I mentioned her, Kaylee. My life is an open book." *With missing pages.* "She's my mother's sister. I don't get back there that often, but we're in touch. I promise."

"You gotta do better, Sheriff. Family is important."

"You're absolutely right. Could you put her through?"

"Samantha?" Her aunt's voice, with its lyrical inflections that two generations away from County Kilkenny couldn't erase, sounded uncharacteristically tentative. "I'm sorry I didn't call you on your cell phone. I know you prefer I not use your work number, but I felt I ought to get in touch as soon as possible. I would have called your personal number, but it's on my cell phone, which I'm not using because I'm not sure where I've put it."

Gillian Murphy Walsh, one of the liveliest yet most level-headed women Sam knew, a professor of English literature, a woman who'd taken over the arduous task of raising her traumatized niece, babbled like a frightened child.

“Aunt Gillian, slow down. What’s going on? Are you all right? Is Ma?”

She heard her aunt draw a breath. The exhale whistled through the phone.

“I’m fine, Sam, and so is your mother. Or as well as can be expected under the circumstances. Which is to say, no change.” Another breath, slower. “I’m sorry if I frightened you. I didn’t think this could wait.”

“What happened?”

“They released Arthur Randolph three days ago.”

Sam’s mind went blank for a second. “Randolph? How do you know?”

“Irwin Hoffman’s son called. He was our lawyer during the trial. The father, that is. Do you remember? You must. The son—Doug—is also a lawyer who took over when his dad passed. Someone at the state facility in New York called his office and he got in touch with me. I asked him to do that. He doesn’t have your forwarding information.”

“That’s how I wanted it.”

“Now that you’re in the news, though —”

“What else can you tell me?”

Gillian cleared her throat. “As I understand it from Doug, Randolph is still subject to some sort of constraint. House arrest, an ankle bracelet, armed guards outside his mother’s mansion. I’ve asked Doug for details. I’m not obsessed, mind you. I just want to know where he is. I’m glad Kevin isn’t around to see this.”

Sam’s uncle had died five years earlier. She’d attended the funeral and spent time with her mother. Was that the last time she’d gone back to Delaware? Could she have been that busy? That thoughtless? Yes, Jay died. Then she left MNPD for her new job. The

Wedding Crasher made the first of two appearances. She took over as sheriff. Still, she could have made more of an effort. For her own mother. For the sake of the woman who became a second mother.

"I must have forgotten the terms under which that man could be released," her aunt was saying.

Twenty-five years. That's what a mass murderer could get if he had money, standing, and a brilliant lawyer who entered a diminished capacity plea. Never mind that Randolph's actions should have earned him a mandatory life sentence for murder. Never mind the dead, the maimed, the invisible scars left on the living.

His lawyer sold it as a tragic one-time event perpetrated by a disturbed young man. Now the supposedly rehabilitated killer had been released to the care of his wealthy mother. Did anyone believe he'd tamed his uncontrollable impulses? Not Sam, not for a minute.

"Do you feel threatened, Aunt Gillian? Do you want me to come home?"

"No, dear." Her aunt had regained her composure. "I'm not afraid of Mr. Randolph. Nor do I believe he or anyone else knows or cares about your mother or me at this point."

"What do you mean 'or anyone else'?"

"Nothing. I worry about you."

"I doubt Arthur Randolph is looking for the adult version of the nine-year-old whose testimony helped put him away, Gillian. He admitted he pulled the trigger. He didn't fight a guilty plea. It was twenty-five years ago. And let's not forget, I'm not that easy to find, given that I'm living out in Tennessee under a new name."

"You're newsworthy, my dear. Even back here, we've been following the story of the methodical killer whose victims look like brides and the pretty sheriff and handsome FBI agent who are trying to bring him to justice."

Sam groaned. "Do your friends know?"

"Do they know my niece Sophia is now Sam Tate, the intrepid sheriff of Pickett County? No one has come to me with an old high school yearbook and asked outright. Besides, people have doppelgangers, which is the position I'm taking."

"I'm sorry to put you through this, Aunt Gillian."

"I can handle things from my end." Gillian sounded more like her old self. "I'm simply concerned certain tenacious reporters could start digging into your past. If they do, who knows what they'll find and what they'll do with the information?"

"It won't happen and maybe it doesn't matter after all this time," Sam said with more bravado than she felt. "Meanwhile, I am more than protected from any nut job or journalist who comes for me. I'm ex-army, a decorated cop, a sheriff. I've got a pretty ferocious woman standing outside my building. The FBI's got my back."

"And how is Special Agent Sloan?"

"Smart, steady, and unavailable, Aunt Gillian."

"Things change, dear heart. For the worse but also for the better."

Sam laughed. "Ever the optimist. I need to get back to work. I'll see if someone can keep an eye on Arthur Randolph. I don't expect him to hop the Amtrak, but it's best we all stay alert. You did a smart thing, calling me."

"Samantha—"

"Kiss Ma for me, okay? I love you." Sam disconnected.

Jesus, Arthur Randolph.

She flashed back, just for a second: pink and white and red and black. A man with a gun. A second—

The image shut itself off, as if someone with a remote had changed the channel. *A second what?* she wondered. Then even the question disappeared.

She went back to her list and spent the rest of the day working to discipline her wobbly concentration.

About five thirty, Terry showed up. "Interested in dinner?" he asked.

"What do you think?"

"I think I want dinner and you look like you need it."

"Absolutely."

His company was exactly what Sam needed. The conversations with her aunt and then with various individuals in New York unsettled her more than she wanted to admit. Sam had no plans to share her worries about vengeful murderers or buried memories with Terry, however.

They went to the Dixie Café, an iconic Byrdstown bistro with friendly staff and above-average food. As usual, the place was crowded. Weekends featured live music that made talk nearly impossible. Even that evening, the soundtrack was jacked a little higher than Sam preferred.

Before they'd even settled into their booth, he asked, "What's wrong?"

"What do you mean?"

"You look perturbed."

Sam shook her head. She made a point of keeping her thoughts and feelings hidden. She'd been teased as far back as college about her poker face. Terry, though, was unusually attuned to the slightest alterations.

"Nothing we're going to discuss over dinner," she told him with a smile. "Per your regulations, I might add."

Terry Sloan had one rule at dinner: no work talk. "Better for the digestion," he insisted. Though curbing her impatience proved challenging, Sam came around to his way of thinking. Food tasted better unaccompanied by thoughts of death.

They chatted over pork chops and fried apples for him and steak with green beans for her. Like two long-time colleagues. Or old marrieds. At one point, she looked up from her plate into his tawny gaze.

"What?"

"This is nice," he said. "Not the circumstances, of course, but the working together part. The being together part." He put down his fork. Was he going to reach across the table?

The longing hit her like a two-by-four, immediately followed by a surge of panic just as forceful. She wanted to jump across the table. Pull off his shirt. Curl up in his lap. Hang on for dear life. Hide. Run.

"Sam, are you—?"

"Oops, my cell phone is vibrating. I got a text. Hang on." Sam checked the small screen. It was a feint and Terry knew it.

"You're not that good at lying, Tate." Terry pushed back his plate. "Talk to me."

She put down her phone. "I've been making lists until I'm blue in the face, Terry. All the ways the Newsome and Upshaw murders are the same. All the ways they're not."

"Go on."

"The differences first. This victim was younger. She died in late summer. She was dressed up but not like a bride. She had all ten fingers. The death was messy, poorly thought out, and torturous, although that last may not have been deliberate."

Sam took a pause, then continued.

"Now, what's the same? The staging, the locale, the neatness of the site, the knockout drug, the slit throat, the fact that the killer used a knife of some sort."

She sat back, frustrated. "I don't even know how to classify the second cut, except to note its efficiency."

"They still might have been made by the same person."

"A schizophrenic left-handed killer?"

Terry's rollicking laughter drew several smiles. Most people wouldn't have guessed the sheriff and her nice-looking friend were discussing such grisly matters.

"Glad you find my theory so amusing, Terry."

"Sorry, Sam. Look, you may have a disturbed killer trying to pay homage to his idol, the Wedding Crasher. I won't even discount the possibility that they've been in touch. On the other hand, maybe Emily's killer deliberately set the scene and made a mess to confuse us and get noticed. It worked. The media is here. The FBI is here."

"Not for long."

"I promise you, Sam, you will get whoever did this. And I will help, regardless of what official procedure tells me I can and cannot do."

"I will hold you to that promise," she said.

Even if I can't keep mine.

Chapter 17

She walked him to his car. There was a moment before he took off when his amber eyes lit up. He leaned in, made a beeline for her mouth, turned at the last minute, and bussed her left cheek. They parted like awkward teens.

Sam went back to the office to think some more. She could have done that anywhere. Sitting at her desk at least made her feel as if she were getting something done.

She had company. Though the night deputy patrolled the county in a cruiser, one of four dispatchers manned the switchboard. The dispatchers connected the sheriff's office to the community day or night. The job required someone with endless amounts of patience and a clear voice. Sallie Mae Davenport fit the bill. When Sam peeked into the small room, she saw the short, apple-cheeked woman perched in front of her monitor, a pillow at her back, her head of dyed brown curls bobbing ever so slightly as she busied herself with her knitting.

Sam sat down at her desk and spread out everything related to the homicides. Pictures of the victims, her lists, notes, and printed reports about the cases. Then she talked to the collection as if she might somehow connect with the elusive killer or killers.

"Are you grooming someone, Wedding Crasher? A junior killer to follow in your footsteps? An apprentice to carry on your name? Or have you spawned a bunch of crazies in my county?"

No answer.

She scanned a couple of articles about dresses worn by teens in the mid-twentieth century. She studied the old case files. She considered how Emily saw herself and how someone else might have viewed her. Maybe it didn't make any difference. Her killer could be unconcerned about whether she was the right age with the right hair color. Maybe what mattered was the act. Kill a young woman. Ritualize her murder. Confuse the investigators.

At 1:00 A.M. she threw down her pencil and left the building. The temperature had dropped into the seventies after reaching ninety-five. The moist air smelled of dead leaves and gasoline. A light breeze rattled the old maple tree out back, peeling off stray leaves. Autumn was more than a month away.

Sam took the sheriff's car and cruised Main Street. Byrdstown shut down early; even the bars closed at midnight. Once she got out of town, streetlights and sidewalks disappeared. The area was mostly farmland, flat and exposed except for spots of dense tree growth here and there. Sam drove cautiously, on the lookout for slow-moving, low-to-the-ground, night-dwelling creatures.

The Granville cottage sat just off the road, thoroughly hidden behind a mix of pines, poplars, maples, and oaks. As usual, Cora had left the front porch light on. The rest of the house was dark, to Sam's relief. She wasn't in the mood for chitchat with a well-meaning, conversation-starved woman.

She had the key out when she heard a noise. Not an animal and not the wind.

Fortunately, Sam had exceptional hearing. She caught the whisper of a trigger pull on a barely audible exhale a millisecond before the first bullet zinged past her head. Two more followed,

The shooter was likely using a semiautomatic rifle known as the Bushmaster Predator. Ideal for hunting. Tonight, she was the prey.

She hit the ground before bullets four and five came her way. A flowerpot on the porch exploded. Sam rolled over her right shoulder and ended up crouched at the corner of the cottage with her Smith & Wesson pulled. She threw a well-aimed stone at the front light and knocked out the bulb.

In the silence, she made rapid-fire calculations. One shooter, probably prone, working with less light, unless he'd brought night-vision goggles. She needed to draw his fire away from the house.

Cora Granville, a light sleeper, would have heard the shots. Her landlady had a weapon, a Sig Sauer P238 she'd bought without a permit. Guns and rifles were as ubiquitous in Tennessee as moon pies. The last thing Sam needed right now was a feisty but inexperienced woman barreling out the front door with a gun.

Sure enough, a lamp came on inside, then another. Sam remained in shadow but not for long. Cora opened the front door a crack and yelled, "What's going on? Who's out there?"

Bullet six hit the porch.

"Close the door and turn out the lights, Cora," Sam ordered. "We've got a sniper situation."

"Sniper? At my house? No, sirree. I'm coming out."

"Cora, stay put, goddammit!"

Sam fixed all her senses on a particular spot in the darkness and pulled out her military grade flashlight. Its beam could temporarily blind a person.

"Shit!" The voice might have been male or female; Sam couldn't tell. What she heard in the exclamation was surprise but not pain. That meant the gunman wasn't wearing the goggles. At most, whoever lay behind the rifle might see spots for a couple of seconds.

A couple of seconds was all Sam needed.

She sped to the rifleman's hiding place. As fast as she was, the shooter managed to get out of the way. Since he didn't disappear into thin air, Sam assumed he rolled just out of sight behind a tree or into a hollow. She trained her flashlight on the area.

The front door of the cottage crashed open and light flooded the porch. Cora Granville stood backlit in the doorway, clad in her nightgown and holding her gun in both hands. "I've got a gun!" she yelled.

"Get down!" Sam yelled, as bullets seven and eight sailed in the direction of the house. The shots went wild, maybe because the shooter had changed locations. Sam tore across the path to the house and up the porch to tackle her landlady, none too softly. They both fell to the floor. Cora's gun skittered under a table.

The gunman took off, crashing through the underbrush and away from the cottage. Sam, torn between giving chase and securing the safety of her landlady, chose to stay with Cora. She helped the older woman to her feet, located the Sig, and emptied the chamber.

"Are you all right? Nothing bruised, strained, or broken?" She remembered to add, "I'm sorry I had to knock you over."

"Don't be silly," Cora replied. She straightened her nightgown and fluffed her hair. "You acted quite professionally, all things considered. Now, where did I put my gun?"

"Don't think about that right now." Sam put an arm around the woman and led her to the tiny kitchen table. "Come sit down. Have some tea. That was quite a scare we just had."

"Have they gone?"

"I think so."

"But who would want to shoot at me?"

"Not at you. At me. I can't tell you how much I regret bringing this trouble to your door."

Cora patted Sam's hand. "Really, Sheriff, it's no problem. Shouldn't we call the police?"

"I am the police, Cora. Don't worry. I'll let my colleagues know."

As if to remind Sam of that obligation, her car radio crackled.

"That's my dispatcher. Let me answer her and then have a look around. Are you sure you're okay?"

"I'm fine."

Sam went out and grabbed the receiver through the car window. "Hey, Sallie Mae."

The dispatcher sounded calm, as usual. "Sheriff? We got a report of a 10-38 out by Mrs. Granville's place. Are you there? Did you hear anything?"

"I heard gunfire. Now it's quiet. Who made the call?"

"Dorothea Corbett."

Sam knew the resourceful woman; she owned and operated a nearby farm. Dorothea was nobody's fool. Sam thought quickly.

"It's possible she heard a recording. Don't some of her neighbors play those to scare off the crows?"

"In the middle of the night? I don't think so, Sheriff."

Another smart woman. Sam waited a beat.

"It could be Bill Gibbons went and fired off his rifle again," Sallie suggested. "He might be too drunk or ashamed to let us know." Gibbons had a well-documented history of inebriation, often coupled with disorderliness or reckless endangerment.

"Call Miz Corbett and tell her I'm checking it out right now. I'll do a sweep of the area and I'll drive by the Gibbons place."

"Okay, Sheriff. Y'all take care. 10-4."

Sam hated to withhold information from Sallie Mae. The sheriff had a responsibility to report an incident, same as her deputies. She needed to tell Abdi. And Terry. No one would consider this attack, coming in the middle of two homicide investigations, to be a coincidence. On the other hand, her aunt's call reminded her she might have more enemies than she knew. She just needed a little time to work out what it all meant before she worried anyone else.

Sam retrieved an evidence kit and a clean pair of latex gloves from the car and set her flashlight's beam so it lit up the area like a used car lot. Crushed leaves and spent cartridges marked the spot where the shooter lay on the ground, probably behind a tripod.

She picked up five casings with her pen and loaded them into a plastic bag. They were 5.56mm NATO bullets. Originally designed to be used with military rifles, they were as common as the weapons that fired them and as easy to purchase. She also recovered two bullets from the front porch, carefully digging out one that was lodged in a support beam. No need to bring the house down. Tomorrow she would look for the rest of the cartridges. For now, she had what she needed.

Cora, who had been sipping tea and smiling, initially resisted Sam's request to turn in. At last she began to pick up on the sheriff's impatience and agreed to lie down. Within minutes, she was fast asleep. Sam turned out the lights and went back outside.

How had the suspect escaped? She hadn't noticed any tire tracks except her own at the edge of the property. She jumped in the car and slowly drove back the way she came in, training her searchlight, looking for clues.

Nothing moved on the stretch of road she traveled. The lights were off at the Gibson place. Dorothea might still be up; Sam caught a shaft of light at the back of the house. She hoped the old woman would accept Sallie Mae's assurances and get some rest. She wasn't likely to. The women of Pickett County could be single-minded. Just like their sheriff.

She came back to the house and pulled a rifle out of her trunk. Then she scanned the area once more near the hollow. She found a set of footprints that led into the woods and disappeared. A popular style of boot that could have belonged to a large woman or a medium-sized man. She listened, her senses on high alert, and heard nothing out of the ordinary.

Satisfied, she went back to sit on the front porch with the weapon in her lap. Locked and loaded. She settled into the sturdy rocking chair and patted the scarred wood. Cora told her it had been in the Granville family for generations. She rocked and thought. The movement soothed her, but only a little.

Who would take a shot at her? Arthur Randolph? No, he was miles away. Emily's killer? Possibly, but why now? No suspect in his or her right mind could possibly think killing the sheriff would solve anything. The Wedding Crasher? The action didn't fit any known profile.

Perhaps the shots were meant to warn her, not kill her. Sam didn't care. Threats against her constituted threats to her colleagues and her friends. Cora, Abdi, Doc Holloway, Nate, Terry. The idea that any of them might be hurt didn't so much frighten as infuriate her. Nobody with a rifle and a grudge was going to bully her. Not by a long shot.

Chapter 18

Sam had attended several memorial services during her time with MNPD. Mostly for other cops. Police presence at a civilian funeral was a dicey proposition, she soon learned. The department waited to be invited. They usually weren't asked.

She managed to get through the services by imagining herself removed, an observer. Her earliest memories of family wakes featured boisterous displays of emotion, copious amounts of food, a lot of being pressed to smoky chests and perfumed bosoms. She never got used to it, even before the funerals for her father, brother, and cousin sent her into a self-imposed silence that lasted for months.

Today she stood at the back of the First United Methodist Church in Livingston as a representative of the county in which Emily Upshaw's body was found. At least she got to wear her uniform, which she found far more comfortable than the requisite black dress.

The service had been moved from the chapel to the larger sanctuary to accommodate the many guests. Sam estimated some two hundred people showed up. Families with children around Emily's age. Colleagues of Andy Upshaw. Local officials, including the mayors of Byrdstown, Celina, and Livingston, not to mention commissioners from three counties. Emily was the popular daughter of a well-liked and well-established couple.

A few mourners filed past the closed casket; no one lingered. Unlike the Baptists, Methodists tended to eschew emotional displays of any kind. Most everyone remained in the hard-backed pews. The women dabbed discreetly at their eyes. The men clenched their jaws.

Lincoln Charles and his stunning blond wife joined Andy, Sue, and their son, Tyler, in the front row, ahead of more distant relatives. The man certainly knew how to be in the right place at the right time. Mark Talcott joined them.

"Does Charles have a private jet or is he using taxpayer money to get back and forth?" Abdi whispered.

"He does seem to be ever-present," Sam replied.

Kaylee Simpson sat with her husband and three sons halfway up the aisle. She wore a subdued knee-length black dress. She looked exactly like what she was, the middle-aged mother of three. Her face was pinched with the effort of holding back tears. Empathizing with Sue Upshaw, if Sam had to guess.

Jeff Simpson pulled at his collar and shifted uncomfortably. Probably wanted to be anywhere but at a funeral. All three boys wore jackets and ties. The younger two, closer in age, fidgeted and occasionally shoved each other, only to be admonished by their mother. The eldest sat at the edge of his seat. Head down, he leaned almost into the couple in front of him. Praying or thinking of something entirely unrelated; Sam couldn't tell. Maybe he grieved. He was a high school senior, which put him in Emily's class.

Across from the Simpson family, Brad Goodrich sat alone and stared straight ahead, his mouth set in a tight line. Like most of the men, he'd chosen a navy blazer, which he'd paired with a starched pinstripe shirt, custard tie, and gray slacks. According to Billy Owens, Goodrich owned four such blazers, an assortment of starched shirts, and a collection of pastel ties. All custom-tailored in Nashville by the same man his father had used.

Brad had earlier walked to the front row to offer his condolences to the Upshaws. Perhaps Brad attended not only in his official capacity but also as a business acquaintance. Maybe even a family friend, although one relegated to a row farther back.

He offered his hand to Andy and then tried to pull free when the man held on a little too long. Sue Upshaw also clung to him. By contrast, his encounter with Charles seemed perfunctory and Mark Talcott shifted so that he faced away.

What that's all about? Sam wondered.

A man Sam didn't recognize stood at the end of the row of police officers. In profile, he looked like a model: light eyes, chiseled jawline, straight nose, groomed one-day beard, small stud in one ear. His cotton shirt was turned up at the collar. He'd stuffed his hands into his well-worn jeans. A fitted leather jacket kept him just north of underdressed. She made a note to speak with him later.

The service lasted a half hour, which seemed to relieve the crowd of mourners. Most of them passed out the door and through the receiving line. Then they bounded down the steps and into the bright sunshine like schoolchildren at recess. Duty done, they were ready to shed clothes and sadness for a more familiar Saturday routine.

Sam and Terry walked out together. Each was preoccupied, Terry with his own thoughts, Sam with trying to find the handsome stranger who'd attended the memorial service. Before she had time to widen her search, Kaylee buttonholed her boss.

"Beautiful service, wasn't it, Sheriff? So unbearably sad. I feel for Sue Upshaw. Losing a child upsets the natural order of things. Most people can't understand how important our children are to us. Their pain is our pain. Their loss is our loss. It's like having your insides torn out." The strength of her empathy took Sam by surprise.

Kaylee suddenly shifted gears. A quick shudder, a flip of the hair, the tiniest of smiles. "Ah, well. It's too bad, that's all. I need to get back to my family. Excuse me, Sheriff Tate, Agent Sloan." She turned and walked away.

"She must have an on-off switch," Terry observed.

"Hello, Special Agent Sloan. Sheriff Tate, may I have a word?"

Sam turned to find Mark Talcott at her elbow. As usual, the man was impeccably dressed, in a navy custom-tailored suit with a marine-blue tie. On closer inspection, Sam took in his sallow complexion and the thin sheen of perspiration on his forehead and upper lip. The attorney did not look well.

"Go ahead," Terry said. "I'll be by the car."

Sam and Talcott moved out of the stream of mourners and stood under a shady tree. "I didn't expect to see you here, Mr. Talcott," she said.

"Andy Upshaw knew Bitsy. The family was very kind to me after her funeral. I thought this was the least I could do." He coughed. "Besides, I wanted to talk with you."

"Why don't you make an appointment?"

"Quick turnaround. I'm headed back to D.C. after the internment."

"With Lincoln Charles."

Impatience flickered in his dark eyes. "You have a problem with him, don't you? Lincoln Charles has been good for our district and he's been good to me. Loyalty counts for a lot in my book."

"And how do you feel about disloyal people?" Sam asked.

Talcott's pale face darkened. *Bull's-eye*. "I don't kill them, Sheriff," he began. He staggered and caught himself with a hand to the tree trunk.

"Mr. Talcott? Can I help you?" Sam went to touch his elbow, but he yanked his arm away.

"You're not the sort to let anything drop, are you?" Talcott hissed as he pushed away from the tree. "Yes, I have a new job in D.C., thanks to Lincoln Charles and, if I may say so, my own damned hard work. That's not why Bitsy and I were relocating, though. Congressman Charles also got me into a clinical trial program at Johns Hopkins. I have a rare blood disorder, Sheriff, a piece of information I trust you'll keep to yourself. This is my best—my last hope."

Sam knew her mouth had dropped open. "The trips to D.C.—"

"Were literally for my health. Including the one I took the weekend my fiancée was murdered."

He blinked, stood up, straightened his tie. "I don't know who killed Bitsy, Sheriff. Or the Upshaw girl. Maybe they were separate incidents. Maybe Bitsy really was the random victim of a psychopath with a hang-up about brides or brunettes. Or maybe it just looks that way. Real estate is a killer business around these parts."

He glowered at Sam. "You want to help, Sheriff Tate? Do your job. Look around." He flung out his arm. "You've got all the suspects you need. Pick one."

He turned and headed to the line of black limousines that waited for those invited to the internment. Lincoln Charles, wearing an expression of studied sorrow, waved him over. The congressman seemed to be many things. A businessman with financial ties to the district he now served. An opportunistic, power-hungry politician. And, apparently, a good-hearted friend to a man in need of one.

Neither she nor Terry had been asked to the cemetery. She didn't mind. She preferred not to watch someone lower a body in a box into the ground. Her predecessor would have been invited. Different time, different kind of sheriff.

Brad Goodrich stood near the line of cars. His tense stillness had been replaced by a case of the nerves. He bounced on his toes and looked around with an air of jittery anticipation, then locked eyes with Sam. Goodrich dropped his head, slipped on a pair of sunglasses, and ducked into the last car, the very picture of guilt.

"Abdi," she said, turning to her deputy. "Did you happen to notice the man standing in the back with us? Jeans, leather jacket?"

"I did. Who was he?"

Sam shook her head. "No idea. Maybe I'm suspicious of everyone I don't know." *And more than a few I do know.*

"Understandable. Are we headed back to the office?"

"Hang on. Eddie's called me a couple of times. Let me see what—"

"Why don't you go ahead, Detective Issen?" Terry said. "The sheriff and I have some business to discuss. I'll give her a lift back when we're done."

Abdi looked at Terry and at Sam. "I'll see you back in Byrdstown, Sheriff."

"Shouldn't be too long," Sam told him.

Terry grabbed her by the elbow and steered her to his rental car, tucked almost out of sight away from the building. He stopped just short of shoving her into the passenger seat. He squeezed behind the steering wheel, took off his sunglasses, and stared out the windshield for a minute.

"What angers me, Samantha," he began, "is that I had to hear about the Thursday night shooting from your detective. Who didn't hear it from you first but from your dispatcher. Meanwhile, your landlady, who found the entire experience thrilling, was busy informing everyone else in town."

He was going with a formal lecture. She decided not to match his tone.

"You know Cora Granville, Terry. The more dramatic, the better. I filed a report the next day. I filled Abdi in. No, I didn't tell you. For one thing, you have enough to worry about. For another, I couldn't say whether what happened has a direct bearing on our work."

"Sam, your life was in danger—"

"Not really."

He slammed his palm on the steering wheel. "For Christ's sake, Tate. Stop parsing this. And by the way, when were you going to mention that Arthur Randolph was out?"

Sam felt herself go hot. "How did you know that?"

"I've had Randolph on my radar for some time. One of the advantages of being FBI is access to all sorts of records."

"You shouldn't have—"

"Bothered? Cared?"

Sam whirled on him. "Either. Both. You're not my husband, or my boyfriend, or my caretaker. You're not even a steady colleague." She blinked back unexpected tears. "You show up in search of the Wedding Crasher and leave when the trail goes cold. I'm the one left to deal with two homicides, a murky suspect pool, and a mass murderer from my past who may still be a threat to my family. You're the one who retreats to warm breezes, cool drinks, and a pretty woman."

"Sam, if I could change—"

The old-fashioned ringtone broke through the tension like a bucket of ice.

"Darryl, go ahead," Terry said. "Our phones were off during the Upshaw service. Yeah, we're still in Livingston." He listened for half a minute. "No kidding. Wait, today? Why are we just hearing about this? Okay, tell Detective Gould. Never mind, we'll call."

"What's going on?"

"Eddie Gould called Darryl when he couldn't reach you. MNPD is in the middle of a stakeout to capture a sexual predator they've been after for a while. Thought we might like to observe."

"Why?"

"He's been hunting his victims at Nordstrom's perfume bar."

"They're just telling us?"

"Better late than never. You up for a short road trip?"

"What, now? Well, damn." She looked down. "At least I'm in uniform. Okay, let's go."

Terry saluted. "I live to serve." He started the car. "Wouldn't it be something if a Nashville stalker is your killer? Or mine."

Sam didn't respond. She was focused on squashing the fluttering sensation in her stomach, as if she'd swallowed a kaleidoscope of butterflies.

Chapter 19

Terry got them to the Mall at Green Hills in under two hours. Record time, considering the heavy traffic on a Saturday. He cut through most of it, thanks to a portable police siren he tossed on the dashboard. Between the alternating blue and red strobe lights and the low *woot woot* sound, he was able to clear a path.

Eddie had texted a suspect profile sheet to Sam. She read aloud as Terry drove.

"Not much of a description. Medium build, medium height, young to middle-aged, Caucasian. Blue-gray eyes. Sometimes glasses, sometimes not. He poses as a high-end perfume salesman scouting the competition for his company. Carries a small vial that he invites his marks to sniff. Whatever he's concocted makes his victims compliant but not unconscious. He's then able to get them to his car and drive them somewhere to do whatever he does to them."

"Unlikely he's using Rohypnol." Terry couldn't hide his disappointment.

"That doesn't mean he isn't committing one crime to mask an even bigger one, Terry. Or maybe this is what he does off-season. We can't be sure."

Eddie texted them again to look out for a van marked PANERA.

"If only," Terry said with such longing Sam burst out laughing.

"Don't worry, we'll get you fed. I'm hungry, too."

They found the van parked at some distance from the mall entrance. Eddie slid open the panel door and waved them in. A policewoman sat up front, a sniper rifle on her lap. She turned her head and smiled. The van's driver didn't; he kept his eyes forward. In the rear, a red-headed technician perched in front of a split screen. Two more uniformed officers crouched behind him.

"Tight fit," Sam observed.

"You get used to it after a couple of hours. Agent Sloan, Sheriff Tate, meet Andrea Shiner and Todd Lord. She's the one with the weapon. Back here we have officers Booker Milton and Anaya Patel, and our tech is Officer Sean O'Keefe."

Everyone nodded except the taciturn driver. Milton, stocky and solid, held out a box. "Help yourself before I finish them off," he said, patting his midsection. "Cops plus stakeouts equal donuts. Talk about a stereotype. Bet the FBI doesn't indulge."

"Trust me; we do," Terry replied, his hands around a glazed pastry.

"Thanks for getting us onto this sting, Eddie," Sam said. She indicated the woman in front. "SWAT? For a sexual predator?"

Eddie shrugged. "Who knows what we have, right? Better safe than sorry."

"Where's the undercover officer?" Terry asked, pointing at the screen.

They turned at the quick double knock on the door.

"You ask, we deliver," Eddie laughed.

Outside stood a small woman, slender and perhaps five foot two. She appeared to be in her twenties. Nicely dressed in expensive jeans and a soft green blouse that reminded Sam of the underside of a leaf. High-heeled peep-toe sandals brought her height up. Her long hair, brown with blond highlights, tumbled in waves past her shoulders. Good jewelry, real gold by the look of it. A tasteful-looking engagement ring on her left finger. The weekend wardrobe of a confident young professional woman.

She looked like just the sort of victim the Wedding Crasher would favor.

"Time for a quick break, then back to work," she announced, reaching for the bottled water Eddie offered.

"FBI Special Agent Terry Sloan, Sheriff Samantha Tate, this is Detective First Class Elaine Marsh. She is both the mark and the officer in charge. It's a little unorthodox, but who's gonna tell her that?"

"Pleased to meet both of you. Eddie filled me in. I hope our guy is your guy."

"It would make everyone's lives easier," Terry replied.

Detective Marsh's voice was a surprise, rough and low. Closer inspection put her at ten years more than Sam had guessed. The woman was well into her thirties with the no-nonsense demeanor of a seasoned cop.

Eddie looked at his watch. "Okay, my work here is done. I gotta take off."

"You're not part of this operation?" Terry asked.

"Nope. Midtown Hills is not my precinct. There seems to be plenty of talent on site. I think you've got this." He grinned at Elaine. She responded with an affectionate pat.

Maybe long-time colleagues, Sam thought. *Maybe more than that.*

After Eddie took off, Elaine faced them, no nonsense. "Let me make sure I understand why you're here, Sheriff Tate," she said.

"Call me Sam."

"Okay, Sam. I understand you've got an open homicide—the high school girl. Our guy preys on women at the Nordstrom perfume counter, which is where the girl worked last summer. Do I have that right?"

"You do."

Elaine turned to Terry. "I have to admit I didn't understand at first why the FBI would be interested in our suspect for a murder that took place in Pickett County. Eddie tells me it may be connected to that serial killer you're chasing."

Terry nodded. "The Wedding Crasher. The woman found last spring—"

"The Nashville woman dressed up like a bride."

"That's the one. She'd been shopping at this perfume counter weeks before she died. Now it could be a coincidence—"

"But you have to follow up. Makes sense."

Sam looked at the screen. "How do you know which part of the weekend your suspect will appear?" she asked. "Does he come at a specific time or on a specific day?"

"We don't because he doesn't. From what information we've gathered, we now believe Perfume Man shows up once a month or so to scout or score. We've been on stakeout over the past three weekends. Nothing so far. Who knows? Today might be your lucky day." The detective yawned and stretched.

"Time to go back to playing Brittany."

As she walked off, they saw her posture change, and with it, her entire demeanor. She went from world-weary cop to eager young shopper in seconds.

The picture and audio from the concealed videocams were surprisingly clear. The shot angles implied a camera on the perfume counter, probably hidden within a display, one on the opposite counter, and one in the ceiling fixture.

Elaine came into view carrying an oversized Kate Spade bag. The sales clerk, a substantial-looking woman likely undercover, bustled over to help her "customer."

They watched for about an hour. Traffic to the counter was moderate and turnover fairly brisk. Nearly all the visitors were women. Sometimes a customer would linger. Elaine/Brittany would make herself scarce at those times, appearing only after the individual left. At one point, Sam's gaze was pulled to the upper right-hand corner of the screen. An obscure figure—male? female? — seemed to hover just out of camera range.

"Is this a trick of light?" Sam asked the technician.

"It looks like a human being. Maybe a shadow of someone passing by."

At fifty-nine minutes, a man in tan slacks and a nut-brown blazer appeared onscreen. Average height, weight, and coloring. A suburban dad, a little dressed up for a Saturday? Or someone else?

One camera caught him casting sideways glances at Elaine, who was in deep discussion with the clerk. His expression, both shrewd and malevolent, caused Sam to shudder.

"I'm sorry," Elaine as Brittany said to the clerk. "None of these fragrances work for me. They're too insubstantial, if you understand me. Not worthy of a special occasion. I mean, I'm almost positive my boyfriend is going to propose to me tonight. I need everything to be perfect, right down to the perfume I wear. It's got to be a unique scent, one he can't get out of his head."

The man in the blazer reacted. He frowned, his eyes on the perfume bottles in front of Elaine rather than on her. *Smart,* Sam thought. He shook his head and added a shrug. The gestures were small, one after another. Enough to draw Elaine's notice.

"Excuse me, sir, do you have a problem?"

"The fragrances you're looking at seem a little, ah, immature for you. More like something my niece would want to wear. She's twelve."

Elaine turned her full attention on him.

"Really?" Halfway between haughty and insecure, as if she knew her choices were inadequate. "What do you suggest?"

Perfume Man assumed an apologetic air. "I'm sorry. I shouldn't intrude. I'm in the business, that's all."

"The perfume business?"

"Right. Mostly high-end fragrances that I market to stores that cater to a selective clientele, like Nordstrom's." He looked for confirmation from the salesclerk, but she had apparently moved off to help another customer. He had impeccable timing.

Elaine seemed to engage in a brief internal struggle about continuing the conversation. Then she rolled her shoulders back, tossed her impressive mane of hair, and smiled.

"Is this new product of yours available here?" she asked.

"It will be. It's called 'Sensual Delight.'"

She wrinkled her nose. "Isn't that a little cliché?"

"We'll probably change it," he assured her. "We're releasing in a month. Even then, the fragrance will only be available through a very few outlets."

The guy was a born salesman.

"Terry, the person I saw earlier is back," Sam whispered. She pointed at the monitor. "It's not Perfume

Man, obviously. It's someone different. Wearing a hoodie. In August."

"What does your fragrance smell like?" Elaine asked Perfume Man.

"The women in our test group mentioned vanilla, sandalwood, and jasmine." He leaned on the word *women*.

"That sounds nice. I read somewhere those are the scents men love." Elaine stepped to him. Flirting. "Do you need any more testers?"

"I'm afraid not. We're beyond the testing phase. Too bad. You obviously have something special going on tonight, Miss—"

"Brittany."

"Brittany, I'm Doug." They shook hands. Sam noticed Elaine positioned herself so that the man was facing the camera.

Perfume Man appeared to be struck by an idea. "You know, maybe I could slip you a small sample. It's completely irregular."

"Could you?" Elaine sounded delighted. "Would you?"

Terry whispered back to Sam, "Do you think that other guy is an accomplice?"

"I don't know."

On camera, Perfume Man was making his pitch. "I've got two sample bottles in my car," he said. "I could probably spare one. Would you like to try a little first, see if you like it?" He reached into his pocket, withdrew a small purple bottle, and pulled the stopper.

Elaine bent to the container and inhaled. "Whoa," she said as she staggered. "It's like I clicked my heels and landed in Oz."

Terry turned around to one of the officers. “Is she wearing plugs?”

The officer chuckled. “Peppermint-soaked and shoved up her nose. A trick she learned in narcotics.”

“It’s him,” Sam insisted. “He’s been there almost the whole time.”

“What are you talking about, Sam? Who’s been where?” Terry asked.

“Let me get you the other bottle,” Perfume Man suggested onscreen. He put an arm around Elaine and started to lead her to the exit.

“Got him!” exclaimed the tech with satisfaction.

“Go!” ordered Milton. The officers sprang to life. They piled out of the van and took off at a run.

“We’ve lost him! Come on!” Sam yelled and tore after them.

“Sam, wait!” Terry called out as he scrambled to follow. “They’ve got their guy!”

“Not our guy!”

Chapter 20

The perfume counter was just inside the entrance. Terry saw in passing that the three undercover cops and two more with impressive-looking weapons had surrounded the Perfume Man. A small group of bystanders watched the arrest. Most of them had their phones out. The man at the center of all the activity no longer looked confident, especially as Elaine pulled his arms back and slid on a pair of zip restraints.

Terry refocused on Sam. She circled wide of the police activity in pursuit of the hooded figure. No one noticed her tear down the aisle and crash through a door marked NO EXIT. He charged after her into a small parking lot adjacent to a loading dock, thankfully empty.

"Stop! Sheriff's office!" Sam yelled as she gained on her quarry.

"FBI!" Terry added for good measure.

To Terry's surprise, the runner turned to them and raised both hands.

"Gun!" Terry bellowed. "Sam, get down!"

Sam ducked and rolled as the gunman shot twice. She yanked a small pistol from the small of her back and returned fire. Terry pulled his weapon and followed suit.

"Shit!" yelled the gunman. Male voice, young. And fast; he disappeared around the corner like a jackrabbit on steroids.

"Sam!" Terry called out. "Did he hit you?"

"I'm fine. Get him!"

Terry rounded the corner and looked out at the mall's ring road and the multiple lots filled with cars and people. Shoppers out for a relaxing Saturday moved briskly or ambled along to and from their vehicles. A few had stopped to look around, as if puzzled by distant sounds they hadn't identified as gunshots. He didn't see anyone in a hoodie.

Terry returned to find Sam on her feet, dusting herself off.

"He disappeared," she said flatly.

"I couldn't—"

"Sloan! Tate! You okay? We heard gunfire." Elaine Marsh moved fast for someone in heels. Right behind her were all three cops from the van, with weapons drawn.

"Where's your suspect?" Sam demanded.

"Hold on a minute." Elaine planted herself in front of them, hands on hips. "I'm the one who should be asking the questions. Starting with the obvious: What the hell just happened?"

"Terry fired after the suspect fired on us," Sam said before Terry could reply.

"What suspect?" Elaine demanded. "Obviously not mine. I've got him in custody."

"Someone else was hanging around the perfume counter during your sting, Detective," Sam told her. "A man. I'm not sure the age; he moved quickly, though. He had a hoodie pulled up, so I couldn't see his face. But I'd seen someone dressed like him before."

"What? When?"

"In a video our first victim made at the same perfume counter last spring."

Elaine looked as if she might spit nails. "Let me get this straight. You took off after a guy in a hoodie, a guy whose face you couldn't see, because he was dressed like a guy you saw in a video made months ago. All because your Mr. Hoodie happened to be at the counter at the same time as the man we were after. What do you suppose this mystery man was doing there?"

"Maybe scouting for prospects."

"Not for Perfume Man. He works alone and without weapons."

"No," Terry said. "For the Wedding Crasher."

"Christ Almighty," Elaine said.

* * *

The events of the afternoon put a bee in MNPD Commissioner Kelly's bonnet, to put it mildly.

"On the busiest shopping day of the week, the busiest mall in the area, hell, maybe in the entire state, turns into the O.K. Corral. The shooters are an unidentified male and two law officers with no jurisdiction but plenty of face time in the news. This all takes place on the heels of an operation that took our department a hell of a lot of time to set up. An operation funded with taxpayer dollars. Am I missing anything?"

Sam and Terry stood in front of the portly, white-haired, and obviously none-too-pleased commissioner like students in the principal's office. The man strained to keep from yelling. Sam kept her eyes on his throbbing neck vein and prayed he wouldn't stroke out.

"I've got calls to return from the mayor's office, the regional DAG, and most likely the governor's office," the commissioner continued. "We're already getting hassled by the press." He turned to Elaine Marsh. "You got an idea how I'm supposed to explain this shit show to any of them, Detective?"

"I invited Sheriff Tate and Special Agent Sloan along, sir," Elaine told him. "They've been pursuing leads related to the death of two young women in Sheriff Tate's county."

"Commissioner Kelly, if I may." Sam stepped forward. "Detective Marsh was generous enough to allow us to observe her sting. There was—is—a strong possibility Emily Upshaw, our most recent victim, was killed by someone she met while working in Nashville, maybe even at the perfume counter at Nordstrom. There was a reasonable expectation it might have been the target of the sting."

Terry shot Sam a look. She was stretching the truth six ways to Sunday.

"I can assure you the sting wasn't compromised," Elaine said. "The, uh, activity in the parking lot occurred after we'd read the perp his rights, handcuffed him, and turned off the tape."

Kelly looked only slightly mollified. "Thank the Lord for small favors. I still don't understand what prompted the shoot-out."

Terry spoke up. "We saw a second man at the perfume counter. Someone we thought we recognized from an earlier video made by Bitsy Newsome, the dead bride from last spring. We gave chase and he opened fire."

"Did you hit the son of a bitch?"

"It doesn't appear so, sir," Terry replied. "We didn't find any blood at the scene."

"Bitsy Newsome hails from Nashville," Elaine added.

The commissioner's face, already tinted the color of pallid beets, turned nearly crimson. "I'm aware of that, Detective. The family reminds me on a regular basis. I'd guess you're also catching a fair amount of flack, Special Agent Sloan."

"Comes with the territory, sir."

Kelly smacked his hands on the desk in front of him and pushed himself to standing. "I'm still gonna have a lot of explaining to do. I'll talk with the mayor's office, see if we can keep your names out of it. Call it an unrelated incident that had police officers chasing a suspected thief. Emphasize the guns were fired in an empty parking lot. Last thing any of us needs is a jurisdictional pissing contest."

"I can assure you, nothing that happened outside was seen by lingering observers. We cleared out the mall pretty quickly."

"Doesn't mean there won't be questions, Detective Marsh. Your own captain might want to know who gave you permission to invite these two along. Meanwhile, you still haven't determined if this guy is connected to the homicides investigated by Pickett County Sheriff's Office or the FBI, have you?"

"I'm going to interview the suspect within the hour."

"You interview, your guests observe. Special Agent Sloan and Sheriff Tate can feed you questions through an earpiece, but they will not be in the room. Is that clear?"

He addressed Sam and Terry. "I'm a fan of transparency, officers. I may be pushing against the current cultural tide, but I don't like dissembling to the press, not to mention to the people to whom we report. In this instance, however, we may need some discretion when it comes to your activities. I don't need to spook the constituents. And I sure as hell don't want the FBI up my butt. Is that understood?"

"Yes, sir." All three of them spoke at once.

The interview turned up no surprises. Sam and Terry watched and listened to the "woe is me" tale of the Perfume Man, a pharmaceutical rep named Clayton Volk. It took Elaine no time to pierce Volk's thin skin and release his potent emotional cocktail of resentment, envy, anger, and entitlement.

"He believes women are to blame for all his troubles," Sam told Abdi on the phone as she and Terry drove back home. "Guy's got a misogynistic streak a mile wide. He hates his successful older sister. He hates his parents for presumably favoring her. As far as he's concerned, women are all bitches, every last one of them. Uh-huh. Yeah. Oh, we've definitely seen it before."

She glanced over at Terry; he nodded, his eyes on the road.

"Volk's been at Nordstrom maybe ten or fifteen times over the past two years," she continued. "He traveled quite a bit, probably hunted elsewhere. Elaine Marsh—the detective in charge—thinks the victim list extends to other perfume counters in other states. What's that? No, his MO never varied. He used a homemade cocktail on his victims. He took them to a deserted spot. He raped or sodomized or in some other way degraded them. Then he brought them back to where he picked them up."

She listened a couple of seconds.

"A real sweetheart. Unfortunately, he doesn't profile as either of our killers, Abdi. He disabled his victims, but he kept them conscious. He wanted them to remember what he did. He wanted them humiliated. What's that? You're right. Dead people feel no shame." She saw Terry look at her. "I know. We're disappointed, too."

She disconnected and they rode the rest of the way in silence.

They got to the Dixie Café around seven thirty to find the place jammed. Saturday night. They walked in past a table of reporters, one of whom half-rose out of her chair. Terry glared at her and she sank back down.

Sam snagged a booth in the back. Terry stopped a busy waitress with a smile and ordered a burger with the works, sweet potato fries, a salad, and a beer. Sam requested a bourbon and Coke along with a slice of apple pie.

"You sure that's all you want, hon?" she asked.

"I'm good, thanks," Sam replied, and caught Terry's look.

"What? It's been a stressful day."

"Far be it from me to deny you a sugar high." Terry's expression said he'd like to do just that. "While we're waiting for our food, where do we begin?"

"With the obvious. The sexual predator is not our guy."

"Let's start with the man you thought might be our guy. The one we chased out of a busy store. The one who fired at you. The episode that caught us a truckload of hell from the current MNPD commissioner. All of which you failed to mention to your lead detective just now."

Sam ducked her head. "I'll tell Abdi in person. Why have him worrying about me? It's not like I got shot."

"You hesitated out there."

"I did not," Sam protested, but she had, literally for a second. Nothing anyone would notice except Terry.

"When the gun came up, I had an image—"

"Like a vision?" he asked.

Sam pulled at her drink. "Nothing like that. I didn't hallucinate a cleaver-wielding crazy or see a dead bride."

She stared into her glass. "More like something from my past I couldn't quite remember."

"Will you please call Sommers?"

"Twice in six months. She's going to be impressed."

"I mean it, Tate."

"I will, promise. Meanwhile, I'm still trying to figure out why our stranger, who may or may not be the same guy I saw in Bitsy's video, picked today to visit Nordstrom."

Terry sat back. "Maybe Mr. Hoodie wasn't looking for just any brown-haired woman."

"What?" She watched him watching her. "You mean me?"

"It's possible he followed you—followed us—to Nashville."

"Why?"

"Not sure. To keep an eye on you, find out what you were up to. I don't think he intended to end up in a gunfight. Oh, and by the way, even though he held the gun with two hands, I have a feeling he was left-handed."

"God Almighty." Sam drew in a ragged breath. "Do we think Emily's killer trailed us to Nashville in broad daylight right after her memorial service? He's got to be insane to take a risk like that."

"Not necessarily insane. Impulsive. Incautious. Inexperienced. Maybe even high."

"A risk-taker, nonetheless."

The food came. Terry ate with gusto. Sam stabbed at her pie. The warm filling oozed from the hole she'd made and she lost her appetite.

When Terry pushed back his plate, she announced, "You're leaving Monday."

"I have to. Notwithstanding today's incident, which I can't report to my superiors, there are no credible Crasher leads and no reason for me to stay. Is there?" His amber eyes searched hers.

Just two unsolved homicides in the space of four months, a killer who might be a copycat or a personal assistant to a notorious serial murderer, and a county sheriff with multiple targets on her back and an urge to grab the man sitting across the table and hang on for dear life.

"Nope," Sam said, as Terry signaled for the check. "No reason at all."

AUTUMN

“This is what rituals are for. We do spiritual ceremonies as human beings in order to create a safe resting place for our most complicated feelings of joy or trauma, so that we don't have to haul those feelings around with us forever, weighing us down.”

~ Elizabeth Gilbert, *Eat, Pray, Love*

Chapter 21

After so many years in Tennessee, Sam had learned not to equate the advent of the equinox with an obvious change of seasons. Spring and fall in Pickett County were lovely, without a doubt, but those seasons arrived and departed according to their own timetables. Fall proved especially reluctant to make an appearance, often waiting until well into October.

Nevertheless, Sam felt September 21 to be particularly portentous. Fall meant cooler temperatures and even cooler trails. The murder and the attacks—it's how Sam thought of the two shoot-outs—had occurred a month earlier. Nothing since. Emily was buried, the news media was onto another story. Terry had decamped to Tampa and Sam had nothing to look forward to except the poker game.

She certainly wasn't prepared for Abdi's announcement, delivered that morning with his characteristic understatement, nor for the jolt of adrenaline that followed.

"Got a visitor who might interest you, Sheriff. Remember the mystery man from Emily's funeral? Well, his name is Rory Franklin, and he's waiting in the conference room."

Sam jumped up from her desk. "You've got to be kidding me. He just walked in? Is he alone?"

"He is alone. No friend or relative or lawyer. Get this: He identified himself as Emily's 'special friend.' Says he wants to help."

"Son of a—" Sam muffled her excitement. "Please offer Mr. Franklin some of Kaylee's atrocious coffee. That should make him feel welcome. I'll be there in a minute."

Rory Franklin sat in the conference room, legs crossed, arm draped across the back of his chair. He examined his manicured nails, the very model of well-crafted ease. A lock of his carefully styled brown hair tumbled across a forehead that over time would move back. Close up, his thin face, angled cheekbones, pointed nose, and prominent chin struck Sam as generic. He wore loafers without socks, a fitted shirt, and jeans that were clean and tight. A small stone twinkled at his left ear; a gold ID bracelet dangled from his right wrist.

The stranger from the funeral.

As soon as Sam and Abdi entered the room, he stood, all polite attention. He beamed; his white teeth gleamed and his blue eyes crinkled at the corners. He looked closer to thirty than twenty. A seventeen-year-old girl might find him attractive.

"Mr. Franklin, thanks so much for coming to see us. I'm Sheriff Tate. This is Detective Issen."

"Call me Rory, Sheriff. I just want to help in any way I can." He spoke with a light drawl. It didn't sound natural to him or the region. His voice was deeper than she expected, a quiet purr. A voice made for seduction.

Sam extended her hand. He took it and made a point of stroking her palm with his thumb. She kept herself from pulling away. Instead she delivered a forceful squeeze and held on a little longer than he might have wished. He sat down, momentarily nonplussed.

"You live in Gordonsville, is that right?" Abdi asked, looking down at his iPad.

"It is."

"But you were born in San Diego. Under the name Ronald Fackler."

Rory/Ronald flashed his gleaming smile.

"Impressive detective work. Yes, I legally changed my name and moved out here last year to pursue my music career. California felt too false."

Abdi glanced at Sam. The irony was not lost on her, though Rory didn't seem to notice. He sat forward, radiating sincerity, his hands spread on the table.

"I know I should have come in earlier, Detective, Sheriff. Honestly, I was too broken up. Then, what with the funeral—"

"You were at the funeral?"

He lowered his eyes briefly. His long lashes brushed his cheek. "Ah, just briefly. I didn't talk with anyone, though. Andy and Sue—Mr. and Mrs. Upshaw—had plenty of other people to support them. I didn't want to intrude."

"Andy and Sue? Emily's parents. So, you've met them?" Abdi posed the question as if he were genuinely curious.

"Well, no, not exactly. I never got the chance, sadly. It's more like I feel as if I know them."

"Because you knew Emily. How long had you two been dating?"

"I'd say a couple of months. But a lot can happen in that time. I can tell you it was much more than a summer fling. We cared for one another. Now, I realize"—he clasped his hands together in front of his heart—"there was a bit of an age difference. We didn't notice, but some people are narrow-minded when it comes to things like that."

"You mean her friends? Or her parents?"

"Parents are supposed to be protective, Detective. I respect that even if I didn't think Emily needed protecting." Rory realized his gaffe and assumed a chagrined expression. "I was mistaken. And as for her friends," he went on, "they were children."

"You met her friends?"

"Actually, I didn't. She wanted to hold off a little longer. I think she worried they'd be jealous, you know? People were always jealous of Emily. Or they needed something from her. One guy decided she was his soul mate. She tried to be nice to him—that was so like Emily—but I could tell he creeped her out. Couldn't get it through his head that she didn't feel the same way and never would."

"You know this how?"

He opened his eyes wide. "She confided in me. What I'm trying to say is, Emily was too mature to date someone her own age. Less girl, more woman, if you know what I mean." He seemed ready to wink at Abdi but changed his mind.

"Where did you meet Emily Upshaw?" Sam asked.

She'd surprised him. He looked like a deer caught in the headlights. "Where?"

"It's a simple question, Mr. Franklin. It wasn't through her school. You aren't a student and you don't teach there. You don't coach sports or teach Sunday school. You don't have a job at the department store where she worked this past summer. I'm not sure exactly what it is you do."

"I'm a model. And a musician. Lead singer with a country rock band. I write some of my own material." He pushed out his chest, just a little.

"Working the Nashville scene, are you?"

"I do all right."

Sam leaned so far across the table Rory jerked his head back. One of the first things she'd learned as a detective was how practiced interrogators deliberately disrespected the personal space of certain witnesses. Nothing intimidates quite like proximity.

"Let me rephrase my original question for you. Where does a man who is nearly thirty and is working at the edges of the music business encounter a high school senior? You did know she was seventeen, didn't you? Do you make a habit of looking for young women, Rory?"

He looked shocked. "I'm not a stalker, Sheriff."

"Do you buy your cologne at Nordstrom's perfume counter in the Mall at Green Hills?" Abdi asked.

Sam could see the back-and-forth questions were beginning to pierce Rory's carefully constructed façade.

"What? No. I mean, why would you ask that?" Rory swiveled his head back and forth between Sam and Abdi, trying to locate the chink in their united front. Which of them was the good cop? Which one could he charm?

After a couple of seconds, he gave up the charade. Or appeared to. Appearances were Rory Franklin's stock in trade.

"Okay, look. Now and again, Emily came over to the Bluebird Café at the end of her shift. I've been working there for pocket change, mostly waiting tables. Oh, and my group plays some late afternoons. It's a great opportunity. I'll tell you what; we're about to bust out. One of the owners is a friend. He's all but promised us a regular prime-time spot this winter."

Sam remembered the Bluebird Café as a legendary venue that had launched a number of bona fide artists. Established songwriters came to perform their own material. She'd played open mic, even booked an afternoon gig. Well before this twenty-first-century version of a rhinestone cowboy got to town.

Sam had no idea whether Rory or his music were any good. He possessed the requisite looks, right down to the unnaturally smooth skin and even features. He had ambition. He also had a very small window of opportunity. Pretty men didn't always age well.

Abdi picked up the questioning. "You met Emily at the Bluebird and you two started, what, dating? In a group or alone?"

"Always alone. It was Emily's choice. She said she didn't want to share me. I never pushed her. About anything. She decided when she was ready. To become intimate, you know? She chose the time, the place, all of it. Believe me, she was in the driver's seat the whole way."

Sam couldn't claim expertise on the subject of teenage girls or their hormones, but she recognized a grade-A manipulator when she saw one. Something else about him bothered her. Her fist clenched in her lap. She brought her hands up, rubbed them lightly, and folded them on the table. "Do you own a gun?" she asked.

He looked genuinely surprised at the question. "A gun? What? No. I know it's part of the mystique around here, but I never thought I needed one. Hold on, why are you asking about guns when Emily was"—he gulped like an endearingly befuddled romantic hero—"when she was stabbed. Which was in just about every media account of the murder, by the way."

"I'm simply asking, Mr. Franklin. I assume you went back to Nashville after the service. Did you drop by the mall?"

Abdi was peering at her, his expression as puzzled as Franklin's.

"Sheriff, I have better things to do with my time. In fact, I was escorting a certain lady to an afternoon wedding." He smiled triumphantly.

Sam sat back, a signal to Abdi to continue.

"Let's get back to the matter at hand. Was Friday night the first time you became intimate? Or were there earlier sexual encounters?"

"Friday was the first time."

"You went to Dark Skies Park?"

"We made love under the night sky. All very romantic." Rory looked pleased with himself.

"And did you make a date for Saturday night as well?"

Rory hesitated. "Uh, no. I'd already made plans."

"And what did these other plans involve?" Sam asked.

"Hanging out with friends." Rory watched the two of them, his perfect face a perfect mask. "I see what you're doing here, Sheriff. I read that Emily died on Saturday night. You want to check my alibi, don't you? You're trying to see if I hooked up with her. Well, I didn't. I've got, what do you call it, incontrovertible proof."

Neither Sam nor Abdi responded.

"You can check with my friends. And with the bartender at 3 Crow Bar. I can give you names and numbers. Hell, I even snapped a shot. Time-stamped and everything. Here you go." Rory held out his cell phone and pointed the screen at the two officers.

In the picture, he had an arm around each of two young women. They were dressed in what Sam's former MNPD partner called "hooker lite." Maybe professional, maybe out for a good time. Fine with a free drink or two rather than money, although who knew anymore? The clothes they wore could have been combined to make one outfit. Heavy makeup, expertly applied. The provocative body language and the suggestive looks made her think they were at least special kinds of friends with benefits.

Rory identified them as Kittie and Rita and named Mike as the bartender. He even offered up contact information and the number of the bar. Then he smiled and yanked the phone back.

"You might have done me the courtesy of letting me know I was a suspect." He'd dropped any pretense of amicability along with his phony dialect. "I came in because I wanted to help. I feel really bad about what happened to Emily. I sure as hell didn't drag my butt down here to be harassed. If you're going to continue to question me in this fashion, I might need to contact a lawyer."

"I think that's a good idea, Rory," Sam said. "Please stand up."

Abdi cuffed the man.

"What the hell is this? You have no right to hold me. I just gave you an alibi for Saturday night. I can prove I had nothing to do with Emily Upshaw's murder."

"Rory Franklin, you are under arrest on charges of aggravated statutory rape." Abdi recited him his rights. Sam noticed the man's face had gone ashy, then blotchy. Neither shade flattered him.

"I didn't rape anyone!"

Sam came around the table and got right in Rory's face.

"In case you don't know Tennessee law, Mr. Franklin, aggravated statutory rape is defined as the unlawful sexual penetration of a victim by the defendant when the victim is at least thirteen but less than eighteen years of age and the defendant is at least ten years older than the victim. Fits you to a T."

"I told you, it was consensual! Besides, the bitch is dead!"

"Right. And some other 'bitch' is going to be safe from you for the time being. You will be processed. Then you can have that phone call you were going on about. Abdi will escort you out."

The interview had lasted fifteen minutes.

Abdi handed off the suspect to Ralph and came back moments later. "Okay, he's being booked," he said. "Kicking up a royal fuss, too. The guy's a sleazebag, a slime ball, an out-and-out predator. But he's not Emily's killer. By the way, what am I missing?"

"What do you mean? I'm disappointed, of course, but it may clear up a couple of things."

"Why did you ask Rory about having a gun? Or where he was the afternoon of the memorial? Is this about the Nordstrom shoot-out?"

Sam grimaced. "I wish you wouldn't call it that."

"You think the man you chased was Rory Franklin?"

"Not if his alibi checks out."

Abdi's shoulders slumped. "So, we're back to square one."

Sam shared her detective's discouragement. She felt as if she were grasping at straws. Nevertheless, she put a hand on Abdi's shoulder.

"This is a distraction, Abdi. Nothing more. I'm not about to let either the Wedding Crasher or his imitator make the next move. Not when I still have a play."

Chapter 22

The FBI's Tampa field office is one of three in Florida, each with its own set of smaller offices. Tampa alone has more than 120 agents working in the local headquarters and six satellites in Brevard, Fort Myers, Lakeland, Orlando, Pinellas, and Sarasota.

There's plenty of crime to go around in Florida. While special case agents are trained to work on any case to which they're assigned, they tend to build expertise in a particular investigative area, like counterterrorism, cybersecurity, or violent crimes. During a major case, though, all available agents will be tapped to assist.

Terry spent the autumn months on a multiagency sting operation that dwarfed previous efforts to lasso crime in the Sunshine State. At first glance, it appeared a gang local to the Miami-Dade area was running drugs up and down Florida's east coast. The DEA agreed to help out Miami Metro and the Florida Bureau of Investigation. A couple of mid-level busts yielded additional players from Central America responsible for several execution-style murders. Homeland Security jumped in to assist.

Then a sharp-eyed analyst discovered the Central Americans had been taking meetings at the Tampa home of Michael "Mickey" Civella. The Philadelphia-born Civella was newly relocated to Tampa, along with his wife, grown children, and several other relatives. Many suspected he had also shifted a significant portion of his business to Florida. While his move followed a pattern common to mobsters from the Northeast, Civella drew the Bureau's focus.

Despite presenting as a semiretired businessman, the man held a high-ranking position within the single most organized criminal enterprise in the United States, La Cosa Nostra. Most of the public assumed the Mafia had gone out of business. The FBI knew better. The crime syndicate had become leaner and far more discreet but no less sinister.

The Organized Crime Unit had been watching Civella for years, trying to build a case against him. Now, thanks to a couple of incautious Panamanian drug dealers, they'd found another way to break the Mafia's stranglehold on criminal activities in Florida.

Terry spent part of his time in meetings in Miami and almost none of his time with Mercy. She noticed. "Between the murders in Tennessee and now this operation, you haven't had time to breathe," she protested over the phone. "Can't you take a little time off?"

"Honey, I would like nothing better. But this presents a huge opportunity for us. We're building a major case against the mob in Florida. A crime-fighting coup. Wouldn't you want me to be part of that? We're talking about a big story, Mercy."

"Can you promise an exclusive?"

He mentally kicked himself. He had no business promising anything to this wonderful woman. Not professionally and not personally.

"I can't make any guarantees. Let me see where we are and what I can share."

"Okay. But you're going to be exhausted. I can be at your place when you get home from Miami tonight. I'll cook you something to eat."

"How about tomorrow, babe?" He tried not to sound impatient with her.

"That's fine, Terry. Sleep well."

He knew he wouldn't.

He finally carved out some time to call Sam. They hadn't talked for weeks. He missed her and their easy camaraderie. He wanted her to know he hadn't bailed on her. He didn't want her to be disappointed in him. Maybe he wanted more, but he had no right to even think along those lines. Terry could argue with himself about the purpose and value of guilt all he wanted. It still threatened to capsize him.

To his relief, she seemed glad to hear from him and genuinely curious about his work.

"What's it like?"

"This is so much bigger than anyone could have predicted, Sam," Terry enthused. "I'm talking drugs, murder, prostitution, money laundering, the works. I can't remember the last time I saw so many agencies in one room. We're throwing everything we've got at it."

"You sound excited."

"I'm running on too much caffeine and too little sleep." He laughed. "And maybe a fair bit of anticipation. At this point, I'm in meetings or reviewing videotapes. Some stakeouts. Boring stuff but we've got to do everything by the book. The Mafia knows how to lawyer up. Not only that, they're burrowed so deeply into legitimate enterprises they're almost invisible."

"I bet you're ready to jump away from the computer, strap on your weapon, and go hunt down the bad guys. Maybe get in a little back and forth gunplay."

"You're saying I'm a man of action?"

"I'm suggesting you be careful if it comes to that, Terry."

"I will."

"Do you think you're going to be tied up a while? These kinds of operations can take months or years."

"They could, but that doesn't mean I'll be on the task force the entire time. The case agent is a guy out of Philadelphia named Applebaum. We'll see how he wants to proceed once we've collected the information. Besides, I can still work our cases. I'm not about to turn my back on the Wedding Crasher. Anything new on that front?"

"Nothing on this end. I'm just trying to work Emily's murder."

"No suspects?"

Sam hesitated, just long enough for Terry to wonder what she was keeping from him.

"They pop up, only to disqualify themselves."

"Do you still think Emily's killer is tied to the Wedding Crasher?"

"Yes. No. Maybe. There's a connection I can't quite grasp."

"You can't see the forest for the trees."

"What?"

"It means—"

"I know what it means. It jogged something, though. Damn. It's gone."

"It'll come to you."

"No doubt. Maybe I'll decide Emily's killer and the Wedding Crasher are both working for a mysterious someone from my past. Wouldn't that make things easier?"

"Sam, you don't even know that anyone's trying to—"

"Terry, I was kidding."

He guffawed. Too much for the modest joke but he was trying to stall while he figured out how to ask his next question. He went for an off-handed approach.

"Speaking of assassins, has anyone shot at you lately? Fired rocket launchers? Slipped poison into Kaylee's coffee, not that you'd be able to tell?"

"Funny, Terry. No, no one has made another attempt on my life, not that I know of. Then again, it's only been, what, two months. Give it time."

"Are you having more bad dreams?"

"Occupational hazard."

"Have you talked with Sommers?"

"Last summer."

"Not since then? Come on, Sam."

"Terry, I'm fine. I'm not about to freeze or faint or fall into a fugue state. I'm eating more and drinking less. The shooting was a clumsy attempt by an amateur killer who I will find. I haven't received any further threats. Besides—"

"What?"

"Sommers wants to try hypnotherapy on me. She thinks I need to remember more details about the day of the wedding. She thinks it'll bring up something I'm suppressing. I want to remember if it will help me sleep at night, but I—it's not a good time, you know?"

He did. The idea that someone would reach into his unprotected mind and pull out his long-buried thoughts on his father's death, or those of his wife and unborn son, made him physically ill.

"I get it, Sam. As long as you're otherwise taking care of yourself."

"I gotta go to Nashville next week. Maybe I'll make an appointment."

"Good." He waited a beat. "Take care, okay?"

"Absolutely. Keep in touch."

"You, too, Sam."

Terry stared at the phone and then into space. He understood her need to retain tight control of her feelings. Emotions informed and often encouraged impulsive action. For instance, he felt compelled to do something to assure Sam's safety and peace of mind. The logical portion of his brain listed all the reasons not to. He wasn't her guardian. He didn't even know if she was in danger. He had no business in her past.

She'd shared quite a bit of personal information several years earlier, during a particularly intimate and vulnerable moment in time for both of them. The Hooper case. He didn't get the impression she suffered from PTSD. Neither, apparently, did Sommers.

Yet something about the twenty-five-year-old incident remained unresolved, despite a year's worth of visits with a child psychologist right after the massacre. Something that fed the bad dreams, which themselves were triggered by the serial killer known as the Wedding Crasher.

Terry rubbed his temples. He once saw Sam do it and thought it might work for him. His post-caffeine headache was amplified by concern. He'd left Sam to handle a serial killer who might have sheltered in place in Pickett County. Now there'd been a second murder, this one sloppy and careless. Inspired, aided, or even perpetrated by the Wedding Crasher; perhaps planned as a feint. And what about Arthur Randolph? Was he a threat?

He had to know. Time to organize his own operation.

He called Paula Norris.

Paula, with her elfin features and large gray eyes, had an uncomfortable relationship with the world. When she'd attended the police academy with Sam, no one believed she had the necessary aptitude for police work. She alternated between being bluntly outspoken and withdrawn.

"I'm on the barely socialized end of the spectrum," she once confided to Terry.

She was brilliant, though, especially when it came to cybersleuthing. Her far-above-average skill set had attracted the attention of several police departments around the state, who competed for the talented young woman.

To his surprise, she'd buttonholed Terry with a plan to join the FBI. Sure enough, she suffered through a couple of interviews and a year of training so she could end up inside the Cyber Crimes Division in Washington. Her superiors agreed she was one of the most proficient specialists the FBI had ever encountered, and that said a lot.

Life as a computer whiz suited her. Paula preferred machines to humans. She enjoyed small physical spaces coupled with the wide-open plains of the Internet wilderness. She felt at home in cyberspace and relished the cat-and-mouse aspect of catching the criminals who occupied it.

"Agent Sloan, what can I do for you?" She sounded both amused and preoccupied. "Does Violent Crimes need the services of Cyber? Wait, you're in Tampa. Is this to do with the mob sting?"

Terry couldn't be sure if Paula was using her lightning-quick skills to review his file or whether she pulled the information off the top of her head. Cyber agents tended to be on top of everything going on in the FBI. Sooner or later, every division turned to them. Virtually every crime had an online component.

"Neither. This is a, ah, new investigation. Off the books, for now. I need everything you can get me on one Arthur Randolph. Mass murderer who went to jail twenty-five years ago. Released from Central New York Psychiatric Center last August into the care of his mother."

"New York? Seems a little far afield in terms of your usual turf." Paula was being her usual direct self.

"It may or may not be relevant to my current investigation."

"Okey dokey. Anything else?"

He told her. Her surprised intake of breath reminded him how far over the line he might be headed.

"So, you not only want eyes on this material, you want to know if anyone else has been looking, perhaps employing the clandestine services of his or her own super cyberdetective."

"I realize this is unconventional, Paula."

"I thrive on unconventional, Agent Sloan," she replied and clicked off.

She called him back in three hours. He'd been half-watching a surveillance tape. He had to go back to the beginning several times to adjust for his wandering attention.

"What took you so long?" he asked with a laugh.

"I had to set a slew of traps and alternate pathways in order to work around FBI firewalls and its security, which is formidable, as you well know."

"I was teasing you, Paula. Were you able to get what I requested?"

"I was. You might be surprised at who's seen this information. I guessed 'sealed' means different things to different organizations and individuals." A pause. "There are photos."

Terry considered how a mind like Paula's might operate. For all her challenges with interaction, she made connections far more quickly than most people.

"Don't jump to any conclusions, Agent Norris. Best not to express or share any suspicions you may have about any of this, either. Can I count on you?"

"As to the first, no," Paula answered. "I'm going to jump where I jump. But I can keep a secret. Especially if I think you've got everyone's best interests at heart. You do, don't you?"

"Always, Paula."

Chapter 23

Sam fought to keep her spirits up. Homicide investigations weren't solved as quickly as film and television led people to believe, she reminded herself. Still, she felt the pressure of two unsolved murders as a great invisible weight she carried throughout the day and into her bed.

She struggled to keep the task force going even as its members began to disperse. First Eddie withdrew. "Official word is the Emily Upshaw case doesn't concern us," he explained. Then Karen Polk announced that she had better things to do. Both Captain McHenry and Ranger Watson followed suit.

"I'm here if you or TBI make any progress," the captain assured Sam.

Nate Fillmore showed up for two more meetings, more out of loyalty or pity, Sam decided, than because he'd made new discoveries. Abdi reported on interviews with Emily's employer, her classmates, her parents' friends, her brother's friends, and anyone her father had ever worked with. No one had anything substantive to add.

Sam reviewed the footage the DAG's office got her from the cameras on Nordstrom's main floor. After several hours, her eyes burned and her enthusiasm flagged. What was she looking for, anyway? An accomplice, a copycat, a stalker, or an ex-boyfriend? Maybe a ghost.

As October drew to a close, summer's heat finally left. Other police matters began to intrude. Though Sam stayed in touch with the Upshaws, she had nothing to offer them. Congressman Charles had moved on to other pursuits. About Mark Talcott, she heard nothing.

One morning, Sam sat across the table from Abdi, a plate of muffins between them, and acknowledged defeat.

"Much as I enjoy your company, Detective, I think it's time to suspend these task force meetings."

"We can still work the case, Sheriff." Abdi sat forward, his face eager. "We've made some real progress. For instance, we can proceed on an informed assumption that Emily Upshaw was not killed by some random psychopath."

"You think she knew her killer?"

"I do."

"Motive?"

"Jealousy, absolutely." Abdi stated. "Or envy. I know, that sounds like a fellow student."

"Or more than one." Sam rubbed her forehead. The idea that a group of scheming teenagers murdered the Upshaw girl gave her a headache no amount of coffee could chase away.

"Could be an adult with a sick fixation," Abdi added.

"What's your theory concerning the Wedding Crasher references?"

"Someone who admires the Wedding Crasher. Or the little touches might be the killer's or killers' idea of a sick joke." He put a hand to his head. "Damn, I guess it's not quite as narrowed down as I thought."

"This is how it works, Abdi. Like you said, we're making headway."

She went back to her office, wondering why she couldn't be straight with her second-in-command. Headway? More like headwinds. Were they dealing with one killer or more? Strangers or close friends? She had both too many and too few suspects to consider for Emily's murder.

Sam hadn't ruled out Brad Goodrich. He'd hosted another poker game a week earlier. If he felt any stress, he kept it well hidden. He played the part of jovial host, even going so far as to decorate the table with pumpkins and orange crepe paper. Jerry invited a DAG lawyer named Carla Evans to the fifth seat. Besides being an able player, the woman entertained with hilarious stories of various colleagues using inventive pseudonyms. Sam suspected a cell phone–dependent coworker known as "Apple-Addicted Annie" was none other than the estimable Ms. Polk.

As much as she enjoyed herself, the game served as a reminder that she still wanted to look into Commissioner Goodrich. Gut feeling or desperate attempt to shake loose a clue; she couldn't say. Nothing tied him to Emily Upshaw's death. He even had an alibi for the night of the girl's murder, some summer charity function he attended in Knoxville. He could have hired someone to kill her. But why? Any disputes with Andy Upshaw could be dealt with in court.

Did Emily stumble upon some piece of information that might harm Brad? Something about his part in a speculative scheme that involved Bitsy Newsome? What about his relationship with Newsome? Had anyone considered Brad as a suspect in the serial murders?

Stop, she warned herself. The Wedding Crasher cases weren't hers to investigate. She simply couldn't shake the feeling that everything connected. She could take her concerns to the DAG. She ought to at least check in with Terry.

No, she needed to get her ducks in a row. Which meant a deep dive into the Dale Hollow Lake business.

Armed with the usual cup of bad coffee, she sat down to review what she had on Brad Goodrich. He'd been born and raised outside Nashville to Leonid Popov and Darlene Goodrich. The father legally changed his name just after marrying. The man must have decided a bland all-American moniker would better serve him in business and in life.

Brad enjoyed a cossetted childhood. Private prep school. Four years at Tennessee Wesleyan University. Two failed marriages and one engagement that didn't end with a wedding. No children. Images of all three women indicated a type: lovely, young, and brunette.

She turned her attention to his business ventures. Brad joined Cumberland Development, his father's company, just after graduation. While the elder Goodrich invested in or partnered on projects in Florida and Georgia, the bulk of his development centered on the Beltway region around Nashville.

Within a few years of the old man's death, Brad expanded the business. He landed contracts for work in the northern and eastern parts of the state. A mixed-use development with faculty townhouses near Tennessee Wesleyan. A skyscraper in downtown Knoxville. Most recently, Cumberland Development had worked on a proposed project with Town and Country Realty, a small real estate company that specialized in high-end homes. Bitsy Newsome's employer.

Brad never denied he knew the Newsome woman. He simply failed to mention he had business dealings with her. An honest omission or something more troublesome?

What had been planned for Dale Hollow Lake? It must have been highly speculative, given the near insurmountable constraints. Had Brad invested? Had he persuaded others? Bitsy Newsome or Andy Upshaw? And where did Lincoln Charles figure in all this?

She logged on to search for corporations newly registered with the state of Tennessee. The research was tedious. Sam sucked on a lemon drop and tried to limit her visits to the coffee pot. She began with a list of LLCs, which offered some liability protection but also tended to be more lightly regulated.

Two hours later, she'd found the company. DHL, LLC had been formed just last December. Less than a year old, which meant no annual report. Nothing on initial capitalization or expenditure. The CEO was listed as Alexi Popov, Brad's never-used middle name, paired with his birth surname. A handy alias for a speculative venture. Sam also discovered an account in that name at a Knoxville bank called Appalachia National.

Sam sat back, hands laced behind her head. She had two ways she could check the corporation's bank statements. One, get a court order and see how and when it played out. Two, find a way to break into password-protected accounts or bypass firewalls. The first method would alert Goodrich. The second was undoubtedly illegal and certainly beyond her capabilities.

Sam wasn't a hacker, but she knew someone who had those skills. Paula Norris, now with the FBI's Cyber Crimes Division.

"Sam Tate!" Paula sounded almost cheerful. "How long has it been?"

"Too long," Sam admitted.

"Never mind; we've both been derelict. How is Pickett County's gutsy female sheriff, as the news accounts call you?" She laughed; Sam didn't.

"That's me. Church picnics and serial killers are all part of a day's work. How about you? Saving the world from cyberterrorism one basement-dwelling slacker at a time?"

"I like to think so. I'm sure having fun trying. And I never have to deal with cameras or microphones shoved in my face."

"It's not what I wanted, Paula."

"I'm sure you didn't." She grew serious. "When I heard you'd left MNPD, I meant to call. I just—"

"Yesterday's news, Paula. We're reconnecting now. Frankly, I could use your help."

"I'm in demand this week."

"What do you mean?"

"Never mind. Let me call you back." She hung up.

Two minutes later, Sam's cell phone rang. "Private line, accessible only to me," Paula announced.

"You can do that from wherever you are?"

"You'd be surprised what I can do from where I am. How can I help?"

"It's related to a local homicide but also an FBI case. I ought to call the agent in charge to get the ball rolling."

"Terry Sloan?"

Sam began to regret the call. "You can say no. No sense in mixing you up in my investigation."

"Nothing wrong with acting independently, Sam. For instance, I work for the FBI, but I'm my own person. Even better, I'm in a dimly lit room with a dozen computer screens. What do you need?"

Half an hour later, Paula texted encryptions with instructions to Sam's phone. Sam opened the documents and sent them to her laptop. Paula had sent over bank statements for DHL, LLC and for another account under the name Mountain East Holdings. The mysterious entity had opened six months prior to DHL's inception and closed when papers for the latter were filed.

Mountain East began with a fourteen-million-dollar investment. Over half a year, checks went out to Shale Ridge Lodge in Celina, a hotel in Nashville, an upscale catering outfit, a high-end printing company, and a group that conducted an environmental study. The biggest check, for ten million, went to the owner of a twelve-acre property set far back from Dale Hollow Lake's shoreline and well away from federally controlled land.

Mountain East's last check, for three million dollars, went over to DHL. A generous sum from a New Jersey company helped build the new company's reserves, along with several sizeable deposits made up of smaller checks. Individual investors, Sam surmised. In short order, the total in the account reached fifty million, a decent amount against which a reputable developer might borrow.

The money that left that account over the next few months raised a number of questions. More than half went to a nonprofit organization based in D.C. Payments were made to the printing company and a group that conducted a design study. Twelve million went back to the unknown company in New Jersey. Sam noted that several checks were written to individuals, possibly repayments. The account balance dropped precipitously. Nothing was coming in.

Sam decided she could look at the information in either of two ways. Maybe Brad was proceeding, after a slow start, to develop his little twelve-acre property. He returned some capital to the investors because the new project cost less. Other investors stayed on because any land in the vicinity of Dale Hollow Lake had the potential to increase in value.

Or maybe, having raised money for the development of land he didn't own, Brad was trying to swap in a different project altogether and pull a fast one on the investors expecting lakeshore property. Sam didn't want to think of all the ways that might be dishonest, not to mention criminal.

Paula called a half hour later. "Got what you need?" she asked.

"You've uncovered a veritable treasure trove of questionable, shady, iffy transactions. I can't be sure if any of it is illegal. I wish I knew more about the New Jersey company that made the big loan. I could trace it—"

"Hang on." Sam listened to a series of rapid keystrokes. "Okay, it's—get ready for the stereotype—a waste management company owned by a Russian businessman named Oleg Popov. Perfectly legal from what I can see, although it might be a cover for a new variation of the old Mafia. Popov. Family loan?"

"No doubt. I wonder how insistent the family was on prompt return on investment. I don't suppose you can come up with a list of the individual checks that made up the initial deposits to DHL, LLC?"

"Not off the bat. I could dig a little more, but I've got this thing I'm supposed to do."

"You've done plenty. Can you just tell me the name of the signatory on Mountain East?"

"Let's see. Yep, the short-lived Mountain East was a DBA—Doing Business As, albeit not registered as such. Uh-oh, that might be a misdemeanor under Tennessee law, although some banks are a little lax about paperwork. I see two signatories. Alexi Popov and Elizabeth Newsome. Does that help, Sheriff Tate?"

"You have no idea."

"Excellent. My work here is done. Don't be a stranger. And stay out of the limelight."

Paula hung up. Back to tracking down far-flung evildoers, no doubt. Which left Sam to ponder exactly how she wanted to play her hand.

Chapter 24

"Turn around and around in a circle and see what happens."

"It's not that kind of dress, Ma. And I'm not a little girl."

"No, of course you're not. Well then, move as if you were dancing. Please. Do it for me."

The girl stood on one foot and executed a single twirl. The hem lifted, then drifted back to her body with a contented sigh. She swung her arms and swayed side to side as if to music. Her mother clapped her hands.

"I love this dress," the girl declared.

She turned her back to the mirror and looked over one shoulder, then another. She wore a customized version of the same frock the bridesmaids wore. The rose-colored, cap-sleeved silk dress rustled when she moved. With it she wore a real gold necklace and matching filigreed hoops that had belonged to her mother's grandmother.

"You are nothing less than stunning," her mother announced. "An example for future maidens of honor."

When Stefan and Nicole had invited her to be part of the wedding party, she'd alternated between excitement and concern. How would a nine-year-old fit into a wedding party? Too young for a bridesmaid, too old for a flower girl.

"We can make it work," Nicole told her. "My maid of honor is a matron. Stefan's best man is a she, which, trust me, sent my parents into a tizzy. Why not a maiden of honor?"

Why not? Especially one that got to dress as an adult, right down to the stockings and shoes with kitten heels.

Her cousin Johnny might easily be persuaded she was the best-looking girl in the bridal party. She could see his lopsided smile, his bright hazel eyes, his nod of approval at how adult she'd become.

She giggled, then put a hand to her mouth. Johnny was twenty and her first cousin. Older and family. Not only that, he was constantly on the edge of trouble, or so her father said. Dropping out of college. Moving in and out of the house and driving his parents crazy. Hanging with some shady characters.

No, she didn't really want Johnny Russo as a boyfriend. She'd settle for having him admire her. She giggled again.

"Sounds like fun in here. Am I allowed to enter?"

She turned at the deep voice, both authoritative and reassuring. "Daddy," she protested. "You know only the bride hides before the wedding."

"Just wanted to make sure. I don't know what the rules are when it comes to maidens of honor."

A tall, broad-chested man with ebony hair and a strong nose stepped into the bedroom. A raft of emotions washed across his face: pride, love, surprise, even sorrow. He covered them all with a wide smile.

"Lucky me. I've stepped into a room with the two best-looking women around," he said as he brushed aside his wife's auburn curls and lightly kissed her forehead.

"Don't exaggerate, Petey," her mother said. She looked pleased.

He turned his gaze on his daughter, already inching past five feet tall. "You certainly look grown up," he told her. "I would hug you, but I don't want to mess anything up."

"Thanks, Daddy. I just need to be perfect."

"You already are," her parents said together. They all laughed. The girl hadn't heard laughter around the house for some time. More a low level of bickering, a nonstop hum of disquiet. Notwithstanding her brother's upcoming wedding, something had strained her parents' relationship. Whatever it was, Stefan, long out of the house, couldn't or wouldn't tell her.

The wedding would repair the rift between them or drown it in a sea of love and possibility. Only later would the girl recall the day as the last time she believed in happily-ever-afters.

"Are most of the guests here?" her mother asked.

"They better be," her father grumbled. "The garden is overrun already. There must be two hundred people down there."

"Between our family and Nicole's family, especially with her father being a judge—"

"I'm just glad I'm not paying. Holy crap, Antun's charges a fortune. And why the ceremony is outdoors instead of inside a church, I'll never know."

"Pete, language. Remember, it's not our day, it's theirs. Times change."

A breathless bridesmaid with thick platinum waves, ruby lips, and dark arched eyebrows stuck her head in. "Excuse me, Russo family, but we need our maiden of honor. Ready for your star turn, honey?"

The girl had instructed her parents to take pictures with her brand-new Instamatic. She also planned to fill what she called her mental scrapbook. Not that she had a photographic memory. She simply saw everything as a snapshot in time.

So, she "photographed" it all, and committed it to memory, beginning with the petal-strewn wooden aisle that cut through the lawn and led to the gazebo. Ahead of her, five bridesmaids and a very pregnant matron of honor lined up to one side of the priest. Behind her handsome brother, his groomsmen preened or squirmed in tuxes and dark pink bow ties. All except Wyn, whose folded arms, wide stance, and impassive gaze gave away nothing.

All eyes came to rest on the girl as she performed a measured glide down the aisle, alone for a moment in the spotlight. As if the day belonged to her. Her brother gave her a thumbs-up, which almost caused her to laugh out loud. Johnny grinned appreciatively, which pleased her to no end.

The group of guests buzzed with anticipation, all except the serious man with the square chin in sunglasses and a drab brown suit and the harried mother with the three bickering kids.

As she made her way to the gazebo, the girl passed an unkempt young man in a rumpled blue jacket who sat in the fourth row on the bride's side. A shock of greasy blond hair fell across his forehead. He patted his chest and fidgeted with his tie. His blue eyes moved everywhere. Crazy eyes, her brother would have said.

The music changed and the bride appeared in a cloud of lace and satin on the arm of her father, the judge. He left her at the bottom step as Stefan reached out a hand to help her up. *Handed off from one man to another,* the girl thought, but that was what everyone expected.

She looked out at the crowd again. Funny: Both the rumpled man and the one with the sunglasses had half-risen from their seats. She wished she could order them to sit down.

Then she turned her attention to the bridal party.

Stefan looked slightly dazed, as if he couldn't believe his good fortune. That expression remained for a second on what was left of his face after the *boom* went off in front of her. The girl tore her gaze from the hole in her brother's head and took in the chaos created by the blond man with the gun standing on his chair, yelling and spraying the gazebo and the surrounding rows of people with bullets.

The wedding party fell, one by one, like flat targets at a firing range. "Down!" her father yelled as he launched himself out of his chair and up the steps. He tackled her to the ground, his weight all but smothering her.

"Pete!"

The girl turned her head to see her mother try to reach across the fleeing mass of guests. Then a blossom of red appeared at the side of her head and she disappeared beneath the human wave like a drowning victim.

After what felt like forever, several male guests rushed the blond gunman and knocked him off his perch. They fell on him, kicking and pummeling and shouting and then kicking more until he lay still.

The girl struggled out from under her human shield and to her feet. Lying in the grass between overturned chairs, people moaned and called for help. Elevated on the platform, she stood alone in a pocket of eerie calm. No one cried or moved or struggled. Bodies lay scattered like discarded socks. Blood ran all around her, coating whatever it touched: the satin dresses, the crisp white shirts, the gauze draperies, even Nicole's snowy veil. Her mental snapshots blurred and shredded until they were nothing but jagged slashes of red, white, the blue of the sky, and the brown of her father's lifeless eyes.

* * *

Terry closed the file with a shudder. He felt as if he'd been put through the ringer. While he didn't believe in comparing experiences, particularly traumas, he couldn't imagine going through what Sam had, especially at such a young age. He'd extrapolated from the dry yet detailed court reports and added his empathy for a child terrorized by the bloodshed around her.

He recognized some of the players. "Crazy Eyes" was, of course, Arthur Randolph, the madman who brought a gun to a wedding because the bride, Nicole Wozniak, never returned his love, never even noticed he existed. He'd killed or injured fifteen people, including most of the wedding party, using a German-made semiautomatic pistol.

Who was the man in the brown suit? Probably a guest whose somber attitude stuck with the young girl.

Thanks to Paula, he had eyes on the full transcript without having to go through official channels. Previously, both the army and MNPD had looked at the transcripts. A short list, available to only a few. How much information would show up on routine paperwork for a driver's license or a credit card or even a college application? Probably not much. Requests for sealed juvenile records, especially witness testimony, came with plenty of restrictions, at least theoretically.

What interested him was a recent request made within the past year by an individual attached to the New York court system. Someone who used a bogus account that went nowhere, according to Paula. Which suggested research on behalf of an unknown entity with a fair degree of clout. And a desire to remain in the shadows.

He wanted to know who was interested; he also wanted to know why. What prompted anyone to review a twenty-five-year-old case? The release of the perpetrator? Sam's heightened public profile? Even if someone could tie Sophie Russo to Sam Tate, who cared? An inquisitive reporter? Or someone whose curiosity might be dangerous for Sam?

Terry studied the grainy photo. The adult woman looked different than the girl in the headshot, the girl who wore a rose-colored dress on the worst day of her life. But those wide eyes that reminded him of soft moss in sunlight, those hadn't changed.

You should at least warn Sam, a little voice told him. *Not until you have more information*, an equally insistent voice countered.

I hear you both, he told them.

Chapter 25

Deputy Tara Fence couldn't shake her disappointment. Even at the beginning, when the Upshaw murder occupied the office nearly full-time, she'd felt sidelined. Per Abdi's request, she'd followed up on Rory Franklin's alibi for the time of the girl's murder. It checked out, she was sorry to discover. At least the sheriff and her lead detective had made mincemeat of the sleazy predator. He would spend time in jail, an outcome that satisfied Tara.

Her pleasure didn't last. She had other more mundane duties. Mostly paperwork for traffic mishaps. She'd helped rescue two honeymooners trapped in their car by an angry bear. She and Ted Ralston from Animal Control had a laugh over that one. Then there was that domestic disturbance call she'd answered with one of the older deputies. That was rough. Mostly, she dealt with the calls that involved runaways or rowdy teenagers.

Tara understood why the teens looked for trouble. They were bored or angry. They didn't fit in. They found social situations challenging. Home didn't always provide a refuge, either.

The daughter of a long-haul trucker with an erratic temper, Tara had put up with plenty of ill treatment at home until she grew almost as tall as her father. Boyd Fence, suddenly unsure about his strapping daughter, replaced physical with verbal abuse. That stopped when he perished in a multicar pileup north of Lexington when she was fifteen.

Tara had several more years of teasing to endure, though. She was statuesque, a Viking warrior with flaming red hair and broad shoulders. She was also, perhaps paradoxically, bookish. Her classmates couldn't see her virtues, only her differences. Moreover, everyone seemed to have an opinion about her gender preferences except her.

The day after she graduated, she applied for a part-time job with Pickett County Sheriff's Office and registered to study at the Tennessee Law Enforcement Academy. To her surprise, she moved off the waiting list and into class within two months. By November, she'd become a full-fledged full-time deputy, thanks to Sheriff Samantha Tate.

Tara admired the woman more than she could say. Sheriff Tate was even and measured, a fair boss. She'd served time in the military and with two police departments. She'd seen death up close and worked with squads made up primarily of men. She took flak from no one. Tara aspired to her superior's brand of confidence and cool.

Abdi Issen functioned as her big brother and guide. Like Tara, he was an outsider. Like his boss, he appeared unflappable. She relied on him to steer her through the ins and outs of forming and maintaining reliable relationships with her colleagues.

Tara remembered Emily as a pretty girl who turned heads. For all her attractiveness and popularity, the younger girl appeared kind-hearted, as if her beauty bestowed a responsibility towards those less fortunate. She once complimented Tara on her hair, of all things.

Tara wanted to help catch Emily's killer. She believed her youth could work in her favor. She knew the territory and the population. She remembered the fears, the hopes, the hormonal surges that colored every interaction and decision. If she could strike out on her own, she might be able to extract more information.

She decided to put herself on the line. She walked right into Sheriff Tate's office one day and offered to take on an expanded role in the search for Emily's killer. To her relief, her boss reacted positively to the offer.

"I'm more than happy to have your perspective, Tara," the sheriff said. "I suspect you'll be more effective talking with Emily's peers, especially now that the shock is wearing off."

The sheriff sat back and steepled her hands. "Here's what I want you to do. Approach Emily's classmates away from school. Keep it informal. You're listening; you're not conducting interviews. You can't do that with a minor except in the presence of a parent or responsible adult. I'm not certain you're ready for that role in any event."

Tara's shoulders slumped.

"We do need your help, Tara. I'm glad you want to be involved. Just make sure you report regularly. Find Abdi. Find me. Okay?"

Tara nodded and got ready to leave, but Sheriff Tate wasn't through. She stood to make her point, her startling eyes wide and unblinking, her voice low.

"One more thing: It doesn't matter if whoever killed Emily is a copycat, a one-off, a hired gun, or the Wedding Crasher himself. We're dealing with a stone-cold killer. Never imagine your training protects you and never assume you can't be surprised. If something feels off, back away immediately and come to us."

"Yes, ma'am."

The first thing Tara did was pull out the handwritten notes she'd made during the Rory Franklin interview. Something he'd said near the beginning stuck with her, something he claimed Emily told him about a kid mooning after her. Classmate? Neighbor? She figured Sheriff Tate and Abdi had made note of the comment. It seemed like a major clue. Yet no one had brought it up.

Maybe Emily had exaggerated for effect. No doubt she'd had plenty of admirers. Tara just needed to figure out who she could ask.

She tried to remember where she and her classmates spent their free time. The jocks went out for multiple sports throughout the school year. A few students busied themselves with youth-oriented church activities. The juniors and seniors all had driver's licenses. They had cars or friends with cars. They took off to Dale Hollow Lake, or they went over to Bowling Green to mingle with the college kids. Or they drove to Nashville to be around real excitement.

Did Emily meet her killer in Nashville? Or was he waiting for her when she returned to the area?

Some of the students went to Bobcat Den over on Route 111 after school. Though technically a breakfast, lunch, and dinner kind of place, the owner had no problem with kids who came in between three thirty and five o'clock, as long as they ordered something. Since the restaurant had plenty of Pepsi and a killer chocolate cream pie, that was never a problem.

Tara decided to start there.

Dressed in jeans and an olive field jacket, she pushed open the door of the diner and took a booth facing the door. Just behind her, a gang of laughing youngsters entered and plopped down at a group of tables. They shed coats and backpacks and grabbed menus. Neither the most nor the least ambitious, Tara decided, casting an intuitive eye at the group. Maybe an athlete or two, possibly a smart kid hiding his or her scholastic abilities. Primarily lower-middle-class teens with parents struggling after the latest recession. Most of them might want to leave Byrdstown someday. Some of them never would.

Tara noticed one boy wedged into a booth opposite her and facing the back of the restaurant. She had a clear view of his hollow cheeks, tired eyes, and pierced ears. His turned-up collar barely hid the tattoo on his neck. Another one peeked out from the sleeve of his army jacket.

She knew him. He must be a senior by now, although she recalled he'd missed several months at the end of his sophomore year. Pneumonia, according to his family. Hard drugs, according to the town gossip machine. Heroin had made significant headway in the state, especially in the rural areas. The boy had other issues, she'd heard. A semester at a rehab facility didn't seem out of the question.

She'd seen him at Emily's funeral, along with almost the entire town. How well did he know the girl? Enough to want something from her? Friendship? More than that? They were an unlikely match, she so sunny and he so dark. Maybe they had interests in common. Maybe not.

Tara looked down at the menu. The pies tempted her; they always did. Her height didn't license her to stuff herself, she decided, especially on a fact-finding mission. Fact-finding, not fat-finding. She smiled at her joke. When she looked up again, the tattooed boy stood at her table.

Tara nearly jumped out of her skin. How the hell had he crept up on her like that?

"Sorry, didn't mean to startle you." He sounded perfectly pleasant. His voice was low, more man than boy, and with a slight drawl that owed more to the South than to Appalachia.

"Tommy, isn't it? I remember you. How's it going? I mean, how are you feeling? You were sick, right? You look good now." Tara pinched herself under the table to keep from babbling. Something about this boy unnerved her.

"It's TJ now. Yeah, I'm all better. Almost caught up. Easy stuff. I'll probably graduate with my class."

"Well, that's great, Tommy. I mean, TJ."

"Mind if I sit down?"

Tara gestured at the bench across from her. He slid in, pushing his long legs underneath the table so she had to scoot her feet back. Pewter eyes glowed under heavy brows and thick lashes. It wasn't oxycodone that lit his fire, she decided. A stronger drug. Heroin. Combined with something that had nothing to do with pharmaceuticals.

"Tara Fence. I remember you, too. You became a cop." A declaration, not a question.

"I did."

"Lifelong ambition?"

"You could say that."

"Do cops usually visit old high school hangouts?"

Had to hand it to him; he was sharp. She decided to be straight with him.

"They do if they're trying to pick up information."

"On Emily Upshaw, you mean?" He looked around and dropped his voice to a whisper. "Or maybe her murderer?"

Tara tamped down her rising excitement. "I'm open to anything anyone might have to offer."

He sat up so he was closer to her. His eyes raked her like shards of glass. She willed herself not to pull back.

"I can tell you she was a very popular girl, Deputy Fence. Very beautiful, smart, and with a generous spirit. Very gracious to losers, strays, and other lesser beings. Not like most of the bitches, excuse me, girls at our excuse for a school. You must know all this from talking with her friends. And the people who claimed to be her friends." His voice remained neutral, yet something in his delivery chilled Tara.

"She sounds too good to be true," Tara replied. "She must have made some of her classmates jealous."

"Maybe, although they were more likely to fall in love with her."

"Did you?"

He glared at her. "Do I look like an idiot?"

"You tell me."

He rested his elbows on the table, folded his hands, and propped his chin. She could see his tattoo more clearly. It looked like the top of a tree. She couldn't tell if it was part of a bigger drawing that ran down his back or possibly his chest.

"You don't know anything about my relationship with Emily. Or if I even had one. Let me provide you with the inside story. We talked before and after school or between classes. Mostly about poetry. Sometimes politics or history. She favored Emily Dickinson. I preferred my poetry a little edgier. She was an intelligent girl, something few of the idiots at school realized. I enjoyed our little chats. Then I went away for a while and when I returned, we'd both moved on. As for what she did outside of school, I couldn't tell you. Our paths never crossed."

"So, not a close friend."

His voice hardened. "I know where you're going with this, Deputy Fence. You figure she was out of my league. Maybe she was, but then why would I waste my time on someone like that? Or are you, what do they call it, projecting? You went to school with her not so long ago. Just a couple years ahead, weren't you? Tell me: Did you fall in love with her? Did you wish she were playing for your team?"

Tara felt her face sting and redden as if she'd been slapped. *Do not react,* she ordered herself. She imitated the boy's position, stared directly at him. They looked for all the world like two young people having a serious discussion. In this case, deadly serious.

"I'm not sure what you're after, Tom. Why don't you help me out? You approached me. Do you have something you'd like to share? Some new tidbit that might help us find Emily's killer? Do you have anything meaningful to contribute, or would you like to continue wasting my time? Because if you're trying to provoke me or impress me with how clever you are, it's not working."

He sat back, eyes narrowed. Tara thought about the gun in her car, locked away in her glove compartment.

Then he smiled, one of those expressions that rested between a sneer and a smirk. It made her want to reach out and smack him.

"You've got your work cut out for you, Deputy Tara Fence. I don't envy you. Happy hunting."

He walked out, which is when Tara Fence discovered blood on her hand from where she'd dug her nails into her palm.

Chapter 26

Early one rainy November morning, the Pickett County Sheriff's Office received a report of a serious single-car accident on Route 325, less than ten minutes away. Sam was already at her desk, along with a good many of her regular staff members. She called Abdi, Ralph, Ken, Dana, and two others over and ordered Rhonda, the dispatcher on duty, to contact the state police and put Doc Holloway on standby.

"You sure you want all of us on a traffic accident?" Ralph sounded skeptical.

"Just a hunch, Ralph."

Abdi said nothing.

As they rounded the bend, they came upon lingering plumes of smoke. A ten-year-old Toyota Corolla rested in a ravine, its rear bumper angled up almost vertically. The firefighters had already doused the engine. At least they would avoid the possibility of a gas explosion or an errant spark that might jump into the dense undergrowth and start a major conflagration.

Sam ordered barriers set up. Traffic was relatively light and the stretch of road about as rural as it got. Still, she wanted to prevent any rubbernecking, which would block access.

As soon as she got out of the car, she looked for and failed to find skid marks. Odd. Low-hanging fog clung to the trees. Rain pelted the road. Maybe the moisture had already done its work. While the curve in the road scarcely constituted a hairpin turn, the driver should have noticed the yellow warning signs and prepared to slow down. Then why go off the road? It seemed a dramatic accident for this location.

"We got a body," a firefighter called out.

Sam shut out all of the noises—the wailing sirens, the slamming doors, the voices barking orders or murmuring in her ear, the quiet drumbeat of the late-fall shower. She shut her eyes to any sights but the person strapped into the car. A gray shirt underneath a black parka. A milky-white, unlined face lightly dusted with freckles. A thick strand of long red hair that clashed with the dripping blood.

Tara Fence.

A scream formed in Sam's throat. She swallowed it. Instead, she knelt, reached into the car, and scanned for a pulse. Nothing.

"No!" Abdi wailed. He stood just behind her as the rain streamed off the back of his coat. He looked shocked, bereft, even vulnerable. The young woman in the car had been his pupil and his friend.

Sam touched his arm. "Abdi," she said quietly, "get Ken and look around back at the road. Make sure he takes pictures of everything, from the approach to the bend to the point where the car went off. You're looking for debris, skid marks we missed coming in, signs of a fuel leak, anything. See what you can see. It'll be a mess what with the rain, but do your best."

"It's Tara." He choked on the words.

Sam looked straight into the eyes of her trusted second. "Abdi, listen to me. Tara is dead and it's gonna hurt even more later on. At this moment, I need you to help process the scene before anything else gets washed away. This appears to be an accident. On the other hand, we're in the middle of at least one murder investigation.

We have to check everything very carefully. Do you hear what I'm saying? I'm counting on you. Send Ralph over, please."

He straightened his shoulders. "I will, Sheriff."

Sam turned back to look at the young woman for whom she'd had such high hopes. Tara wasn't burned; the fire had been short-lived and relatively contained. If it weren't for the peculiar tilt of her neck, the head wound, and the thread of blood along the corner of her mouth, she might look as if she'd fallen asleep at the wheel. Sam considered and rejected the possibility.

"Sheriff, did you need me to—shit! Is she . . . ?" Ralph stopped just behind Sam and made the sign of the cross. Sam recalled that Ralph and his sizeable family attended St. Christopher Church in Jamestown. She pictured him lighting a candle for Tara.

"She's gone, Ralph, and we've got work to do. Can you handle it?"

He gulped. "Yes."

"This car has to be thoroughly examined. Willy's on his way."

"Dana just let his tow truck through."

"Good. Take a car and follow him back. Someone from TBI will meet you at his shop. Don't start poking around until the investigator gets there. Then make sure you keep track of everything the investigator does. Remember, that person works for us, which means he or she works for you. I want real-time reporting. This is a top priority. And Willy better not keep any of us waiting, either. I don't give a goddamn if some hotshot from Dale Hollow wants his BMW yesterday. We clear?"

Her no-nonsense approach worked like cold water to the face. "Got it, Sheriff. Just so I understand, what is the investigator—I mean, what are we looking for?"

"Anything other than driver error that might have caused the car to go off the road. For instance"—Sam peered into the driver's side—"I'd like to know why the airbag didn't deploy. There may be a mechanical or electrical explanation. Find out everything there is to know about this make and model. Have the investigator check the engine, tires, steering, brakes, fan belt, fuel line, even the interior air-conditioning and heating systems. Your dad was a mechanic, wasn't he? You know something about cars?"

A look of purpose crossed the deputy's face. "I do."

"Okay, then, you're the man for the job. Don't interfere, but watch like a hawk. Take notes. Nothing gets by, okay? Nothing."

Ralph trudged up the gentle slope, passing two firefighters carrying the equipment they needed to get Tara's body out of the crumpled car. Cutters, spreaders, rammers, and a heavy-duty drill. The Jaws of Life. Not for poor Tara. Up at the edge, the paramedics waited. Sam shook her head. They went back to their trucks to replace their life-saving equipment with a black body bag.

She resisted the inclination to help and followed her deputy up the hill. She was about to punch in Holloway's number when she saw him standing by her car.

"You're keeping me busy, Samantha."

"Not by design, Doc."

Sam called Nate to request that TBI investigators be sent to the auto body shop and to the scene of the accident. She tried to guess what he was thinking by the tone in his voice. Nate played it close to the vest.

"I'm guessing you don't consider this an unfortunate accident, Sam. They do happen."

"Not lately they don't. But I'll try to keep an open mind."

Abdi came up in time to catch the tail end of her conversation. "You have a feeling about this, don't you?"

The question she found so difficult to answer.

"As I always say, Abdi, we're not going to speculate." *At least not yet.* "We'll come at this from every possible evidentiary angle. For all we know, the brakes failed. Or poor Tara had an aneurysm. Right now, I need to talk with her mother."

"Do you want me to come with you or stay here?"

Sam looked up at the sky, then all around her. "We have enough people here. Let me tell Ralph. You come with me."

Tara lived with her mother in an unincorporated community called Moodyville, which featured one convenience store and little else, not even a postal code. Sam had visited the Fences one other time. Home was a modest ranch with an attached carport, an ample front lawn, and a small shed in the back. Nothing seemed changed, except for a ramp over the two steps leading up the front entrance.

Vivian Fence answered the door dressed in an oversized sweater and baggy jeans. She held a cane. Sam estimated her to be a well-worn forty. Pain and disappointment had aged her. Her wispy gray-blond hair reached to her shoulders. The lines across her forehead and along the sides of her mouth suggested a permanent state of defeat. Only her large cornflower eyes belied her air of weary resignation.

"Sheriff Tate, Detective Issen. What a surprise. Come in, please. Take off your coats and sit. Would you like some coffee? Tara's on her way to work." She moved towards the kitchen, trying for a moment to sustain the flow of animated chatter. When they didn't reply, she turned back to them, her blue eyes on fire.

"Did something happen to her?"

Most law officers consider death notification to be the worst part of the job. Delivering what is likely the most horrific news a family will ever hear requires finesse. Sam made sure her staff went through notification prep. Even before the recent homicides, Pickett County had had its share of violent or unexpected deaths to report. People in the area tended to know one another, which made most of the notices personal. It had to be done right.

"Mrs. Fence, we do have some news to share and yes, it's about Tara. Do you want to sit down? Please?"

Vivian sank heavily into the cushions and Sam sat next to her, not quite touching the woman. Abdi stood nearby, respectful and attentive.

Sam described the situation in a calm and straightforward manner. Not once did she use the word "accident," a decision she made on the spot. Vivian closed her eyes and shook with silent sobs. Sam laid a hand on her shoulder. The abiding sorrow in the room soaked into her skin and etched itself on Abdi's face as he approached.

"We have to ask you a few questions, Mrs. Fence, just to help us make sense of what has happened," he said. "Do you mind?"

"Of course not. Please take a seat, Detective. I can still get you that coffee."

"We're fine, truly." He sat in a worn corduroy chair across from the couch. "Did Tara have any health issues that you know about? Had she ever fainted or seized?"

"Nothing like that. She had all the usual childhood diseases and all the shots, too. I'm not one of those anti-vaccine people. I had Tara tested for autoimmune diseases twice, when she was ten years old and just last year. I wanted to make sure she didn't inherit my rheumatoid arthritis. The results were negative. We felt like we dodged a bullet."

She put her hand to her face. "She did everything around the house. How will I manage?"

Sam took the woman's hand. "Please don't worry about that right now. Tara was a Pickett County deputy. We take care of our own, okay?"

Vivian sniffed then squared her shoulders. "Okay."

"How about her mental state?" Sam asked.

"Tara and I both survived my husband. High school might have challenged her, but once she joined the sheriff's office, she woke up happy every morning. She loved her job, Sheriff. I can't tell you how thrilled she was that you made that happen. She seemed even more excited than usual." Her eyes opened onto a bottomless well of sadness. Sam felt hollowed out.

"Tara made it happen, Mrs. Fence." Sam waited a beat. "Do you have any idea what had her feeling so enthusiastic?"

"She said she was involved in some sort of investigation. Interviewing, taking notes, and working up theories like a real detective. I asked her if it had to do with the murders. She wouldn't tell me. Said it was too early to speculate. Said she had a lead she was following. I was a little worried. I wanted her to be careful."

"You said she took notes," Abdi said. "Do you know if she used a computer or a notebook? Would she keep anything in her room?"

"She used a notebook. She liked how Sheriff Tate wrote everything down. You're welcome to look in her bedroom, but I think she left everything locked in her desk at work."

"Thank you, ma'am. We'll check both places."

"Where'd they take her, Sheriff Tate? When can I see her?"

"Someone will put you in touch with the ME's office. We might need to order an autopsy, just to rule out anything unusual. Not that we have any expectations in that regard. We all want to know what caused the death of a healthy young woman."

Vivian stared. Her face was wet with tears, but her jaw was set. "Just get at the truth, Sheriff. My baby girl would expect no less."

Chapter 27

They buried Tara Fence the Sunday before Thanksgiving. The funeral competed not only with the beautiful weather but also with a couple of college and professional football games, not to mention morning services. It didn't seem to matter. The modest brown brick church could scarcely accommodate the many who came to pay their respects.

Unlike Emily Upshaw's relatively sedate funeral, Tara's service at Moodyville Mission Baptist Church included plenty of fire and brimstone. The parishioners' emotional outpouring contrasted with the silent "blue wall" at the back of the church. More like gray and black and khaki and white and green. The various uniforms represented officers from not only Pickett County but also five surrounding counties. In addition, a handful of mourners showed up from area fire and rescue units.

Vivian Fence had family for support. A sister from Illinois, a couple of cousins. Only a few local officials were in attendance. Jerry O'Neil and Billy Owens made an appearance, although neither addressed the congregation. None of the other commissioners made it to the service, no doubt thanks to more pressing leisure-time activities.

Just as well. Sam had already decided to arrange a private sit-down with Brad Goodrich. She had plenty of questions about his involvement with Bitsy Newsome. And about his more recent activities.

The same day they notified Vivian, she and Abdi searched Tara's bedroom. Sam was struck by how adult it seemed. Comfortable and lived-in but not the room of a teenager. No posters, no piles of laundry, no statement pillows. A sweater draped over a chair, a pair of shoes tucked under the bed. Her shelves held a wide assortment of books, fiction and nonfiction. Everything except mysteries and procedurals. A frame by Tara's bed held a picture of her with Sam at the younger woman's swearing-in ceremony.

Back at the office, they went through Tara's desk. The young deputy kept her space neat. No candy wrappers, loose receipts, stray erasers, or bent paper clips. Just one picture of her as a child in which she held hands with a much younger-looking Vivian Fence. She stored files in the bottom drawer and supplies in the top. Probably where she kept her gun while at work. Both drawers were locked.

Sam had master keys to all the desks. She didn't share that information with her staff. No need to worry anyone. She would never take advantage of her position to invade anyone's privacy except in extenuating circumstances. Like death.

The top drawer contained an assortment of pens and pencils, including a set of colored drawing tools along with a couple of lined legal pads with pages torn off. The files in the bottom concerned cases Tara had worked on, mostly truancies and domestics. One sleeve, marked EMILY UPSHAW, was empty save for a copy of the ME's report and a death notice from *Pickett County Press*.

"No notebook," Sam told Abdi. She looked up to see Kaylee staring at the two of them. The administrative assistant broke eye contact and went back to tidying up her own desk. Maybe she was afraid to offer Sam a cup of coffee. Maybe she was afraid Sam would ask her something. She was half right.

"Kaylee, can I talk with you privately? Abdi, please join us." Sam ushered them into her office, closed the door, and turned to her assistant. "I wondered if you noticed anyone by Tara's desk in the last couple of hours," she began.

"You mean, other than me?"

"Excuse me?" Sam kept her face still.

Kaylee looked at her boss, all innocence and surprise. "I straightened up a little, ran a cloth over the top. I wanted to get it nice-looking."

"Why?"

"I was gonna set up a sort of little remembrance area. Maybe put some flowers in a vase. Display the cards that are bound to come in. Give people a way to honor her memory."

"Honor her memory?" Abdi exploded. "She hasn't been gone three hours and you're setting up a shrine? We're still investigating her death, Kaylee. That desk is off-limits. What the hell is wrong with you? Are you deliberately trying to tamper with evidence?"

"Evidence?" Kaylee looked confused. "I don't understand."

"Abdi." Sam put up a hand. "Hold up, all right?" She realized that Kaylee and many others probably thought Tara Fence had been killed in a traffic accident. Sam needed to keep it that way for now.

"Kaylee, we're looking for some notes Tara may have made for a case she was working. Think a minute. Did you remove anything from the desktop or from the drawers?"

"I don't need to think, Sheriff, and I'm really surprised you'd ask me such a thing. Tara kept her desk neat as a pin. I moved her blotter maybe a quarter of an inch and dusted a little. Picked up a pencil off the floor.

That's about it. And no, I didn't go into her file drawers. They're locked."

Did she know about the locked drawers because she tried to open them? Sam let that pass. Kaylee's bottom lip quivered, suggesting tears would follow. No good would come of that.

"Kaylee, we appreciate your thoughtfulness, we really do. For now, let's agree not to touch anything else on Tara's desk or in her locker until Mrs. Fence has a chance to come in and collect her daughter's things."

Until we know how Tara died.

Ralph Cook told her that evening. Or rather, he confirmed her worst fears when he marched into her office, visibly agitated, and announced, "Someone murdered Tara Fence."

"Wait a minute, Ralph. I have the ME's preliminary report right here. Tara died of a broken neck. They found nothing in her system. Death by car crash."

"Yeah, but why did the car crash in the first place?"

"You tell me."

"Okay." Ralph stopped to compose himself. "The vehicle's been so messed with I hardly know where to begin." He looked at his notebook. "TBI will give you a formal report, but here's what I got. Airbags disabled. Brake pads soaked with oil so they wouldn't engage. Lug nuts loosened on the back two tires. Lock pin loosened on the steering column. Fuel line was punctured as well. It's a miracle the car didn't go up in flames. About the only thing we didn't find was an incendiary device. It's seven kinds of crazy, Sheriff."

Sam agreed. The sabotage read like a laundry list of plot devices. Whoever did all this couldn't have intended Tara's death to appear accidental. Even if the killer planned for the car to burn, too much evidence pointed to murder.

She considered the possibility of a "statement" act by one or more gang members. Such activity was rising in rural communities across the state, fueled by long-term unemployment. Some of the incidents had been traced to inner-city bangers that made weekend jaunts to small towns to recruit. Byrdstown had its own collection of disaffected young men who liked to make sure law officers knew who they were.

Unless Tara uncovered gang activity at the high school level, Sam couldn't make the connection. Nothing should have made her a target, except for Emily's murder.

Within an hour, word that Tara's death was no accident had circulated throughout the office. Sam doubted Ralph spilled the beans. Maybe somebody at the auto body shop did. The news didn't help department morale. It certainly hadn't helped hers.

She made a brief announcement the next morning. "We are all in on this case," she told her staff. "We can get help from TBI and the state if we need it, but we own this investigation. She was one of ours."

That evening, Vivian called. "I'd really like you to speak about Tara at the memorial service, Sheriff Tate," she said.

"Mrs. Fence—"

"I should have given you more notice."

"It's not that, Mrs. Fence. I'm honored, really I am." Sam fought a sinking feeling. "But are you sure you want me to do this? What about the minister or a teacher? A friend? Someone who knew her longer?" Sam almost said "better."

"She didn't really have friends, Sheriff. Her work was her life. I want someone to talk about the woman she became, not about the girl she used to be. I could ask Detective Issen, I suppose. He was a terrific friend to her. But she so looked up to you. If she could pick anyone in the world to speak at her service, it would be you."

Sam couldn't say no. She owed it to Tara and to the department that had served as a surrogate family. On the other hand, she couldn't think of a way to talk about the young woman who believed she'd been given a dream job, only to end up dead.

Now Sam stood in front of a grieving community on a slate-gray afternoon to speak about a life cut too short. She'd deliberately left her notes in the car. She had no idea if she could convey the essence of Tara Fence in an extemporaneous speech, but she intended to give it her very best.

"Tara loved books. I always saw her with one, usually a paperback with a page folded at the corner. History, memoir, or science fiction. Maybe a little fantasy. Just about anything, in fact, except detective novels." That earned a smattering of light laughter and Sam began to relax.

"She liked her coffee black. I believe she might have been the only one in the office who could drink it that way." A knowing chuckle rose from the back. "She liked her desk neat, too, but she wasn't otherwise fussy. If you asked anyone around the precinct, they'd describe her as enthusiastic, smart, flexible. A good listener. Observant. Intuitive." Sam almost smiled at that.

"Those are all ideal traits for a law officer, by the way. Tara, she was a good cop. She was also a good person. I didn't know her growing up, but I got the impression she had a couple of challenges as a kid. Maybe felt like an outsider. Many of us have been there. Capable, strong young women in particular don't have an easy time of it. Trust me, I know something about that."

She noticed a couple of heads bob. "Tara didn't dwell on any struggles she may have had. That wasn't her style. She celebrated her present. She looked ahead. She knew her mother loved her"—Sam looked at Vivian—"and a mother's love goes a long way."

More nods and smiles.

"Tara wasn't one to let anything hold her back. She wanted to be a law officer. She became a law officer. She wanted to go to college. She was on track to do that. Her mother tells me I influenced Tara and she admired me. Well, I admired Tara Fence, and she changed me." Sam suddenly found it hard to speak. She coughed and cleared her throat.

"She inspired me to be a better boss, a better mentor, maybe even a better friend. That is not something I take lightly. Nor is it something I will ever forget."

Sam drew a deep breath and looked at the faces that looked back at her for comfort. "Helen Keller said, 'We know the best and most beautiful things in the world cannot be seen or even touched. They must be felt with the heart.' That's hard to imagine in this instance, but we have to try. Tara is gone but not gone. She's here." Sam thumped her chest. "Remember that. She will always be with us. Always." She hastily added "glory to God" and walked off the podium.

A few parishioners called out "amen" or "she is with Jesus." Many more wiped their eyes. Vivian looked if not pleased then at least reassured. Sam moved to the back of the church to stand with the other officers. It was all she could do not to exit the building.

"You may have a future as a public speaker," Abdi whispered.

"I'd rather have a present as an effective sheriff," Sam replied with a jagged edge to her voice. "Which means I need to find the son of a bitch who did this."

WINTER

“Love never dies of a natural death. It dies because we don't know how to replenish its source, it dies of blindness and errors and betrayals. It dies of illnesses and wounds, it dies of weariness, of witherings, of tarnishings, but never of natural death.”

~ Anaïs Nin, *The Four-Chambered Heart*

Chapter 28

The days between Thanksgiving and Christmas ran on their own high-voltage energy. Holiday mania put off the lonely isolation that is winter's natural state. For a brief period of time, goodwill wrapped itself around every word, every thought, and every endeavor. Children became more compliant, pews filled on Sunday, happy shoppers and contented diners swarmed the streets. While youngsters supplied most of the season's unfiltered enthusiasm, the adults often seemed burdened by the hyped-up atmosphere.

For Sam and her deputies, the holidays meant more work: overindulgent revelers, highway accidents where alcohol factored in, a spike in domestic crime and drug use.

Misery hung over the department like the decorations Kaylee and Sallie Mae put up after Thanksgiving. As usual, Pickett County Sheriff's Office cosponsored a crafts bazaar to raise money for volunteer community services. Once again, Sam nixed the idea of a Secret Santa. She found forced giving distasteful. She wanted nothing more than an end to the killing, but she doubted any Santa, secret or otherwise, could deliver on that particular wish.

Jerry had suspended poker night indefinitely. "It's for the best," he assured Sam. "December's almost always a no-show, what with all the holiday-related activities. And this way, you won't be put in an awkward position."

Too late for that, Sam thought.

"We're still expecting you to drop by Christmas Day," Jerry added. The O'Neil family opened their house every year after church services. Sam couldn't skip an appearance no matter how much work she had. Or how much she wanted to be anywhere else.

"I'll be there."

"So, Brad Goodrich's family name is Popov?" Terry remarked during one of their calls. "And he's related to an owner of a waste management company in New Jersey? It sounds like a script for a B movie. Are you sure you're not dealing with mob involvement?"

"I don't know. That's your area of expertise. Have the Russians moved into businesses formerly managed by Italians?"

"There's been some turnover," Terry reported. "La Cosa Nostra, what we call LCN, has moved on to more sophisticated enterprises, leaving the old businesses up for grabs." She heard him typing. "Okay, I just checked our organized crime database. The last Popov we followed was Gregor, aka 'Grizzly,' and he died in 2014."

"Brad's loan may be aboveboard, but something stinks."

"The crime, if there is one, is in how the money has been used," Terry mused. "The Tennessee AG's office might be interested in whatever information you've pulled together. What would Brad gain by killing Bitsy Newsome?"

"That's what I aim to find out."

"If you're planning a personal visit, I should be there, Sam. Or you should take Darryl." Terry sounded resigned rather than insistent. He must have guessed she planned to ignore his request. He knew her so well.

"Terry, I don't want to make a federal case out of this, pardon the pun."

"Funny. At least promise me that if you talk with Goodrich, you'll proceed with discretion."

"Come on, Terry. Look who you're talking to."

"That's what I'm afraid of."

Sam reached Goodrich at his office the next day.

"Sheriff Tate. I was expecting your call."

"Really? Why is that?"

"A little birdie told me your detective has been asking around. Might be easier if you came right out and questioned me in person."

Despite what he described as his packed schedule, Goodrich found time to see her one evening two weeks before Christmas. Sam decided to come to his house instead of bringing him into her office or meeting at his. In either of those instances, he was likely to have a lawyer with him.

"Wonderful," he said once they set the date. "I've been feeling the lack of a friendly get-together this month. This is friendly, isn't it?"

"I don't see why not." She didn't want to spook him.

A few unexpected flakes of snow were falling when she pulled up to the imposing house. She saw no other cars, which meant no counsel would be standing by, legal or otherwise. Maybe Brad believed he had nothing to fear from a rural county sheriff.

Brad answered the door, casually yet impeccably dressed in a forest-green cashmere sweater and gray slacks. The Christmas tree by his front window would have put a holiday store to shame. The freshly cut and perfectly formed giant blue spruce gave off a gentle pine fragrance. Someone had dressed the tree in small silver-and-gold handcrafted ornaments and strung it with tiny white lights. A perfectly symmetrical star sat at the top.

Presents with coordinated wrapping paper circled the trunk. Sam wagered the boxes were empty. The entire display resembled an artfully designed showroom rather than a lived-in home.

Brad poured himself a Scotch from a well-stocked sidebar. He eyed her up and down. "I presume you're still on duty?"

"Yes."

"I expected as much." He took a generous swallow. "To what do I owe this visit?"

"Let me get right to it, Brad. I know you're the principal mover and shaker behind the paper-thin scheme to develop land around Dale Hollow Lake. Land you can't legally develop and aren't likely to ever own. I also know about your involvement with Bitsy, at least your professional involvement. Not sure why you pretended otherwise. Maybe you can help me understand."

Way to go, Tate, she chided herself. No finesse whatsoever. She sounded like a bad actor in a worse play. Brad reacted not with fear but with what seemed like mild delight. He chuckled and shook his head. Indulging her, as if she were an impolite child at an adult party.

"Not the best approach, Sheriff Tate, leading off with an accusation. It just puts me on my guard. Or it would if I had anything to hide. I don't, by the way. And in answering you, I'll try to demonstrate more consideration than you've managed to show me during your first five minutes in my home." He lifted his glass, a gesture of bonhomie. Cheers and good luck, he seemed to imply.

Sam kept still.

"I didn't reveal my involvement with the project at Dale Hollow Lake because I found Toby's curiosity, like yours, intrusive and out of line in a friendly setting. I don't care if he's a renowned judge. He was trafficking in gossip and I wanted no part of it. As you've since discovered, I did allow myself to be persuaded that development along Dale Hollow's shoreline was possible."

"Persuaded by Lincoln Charles?"

"You don't like him, do you, Sheriff? Probably because he moved a lot more quickly than your office did after the Emily Upshaw murder. Stole your thunder. Lincoln Charles is a politician. I'm a businessman. Regardless of who recommended what, I quickly realized this project had no legs. If you know anything about business"—his tone implied she didn't—"you would understand these kinds of proposals don't come with guarantees. Once in a while we have to fold our tents and go home. This is one of those times. My investors will be repaid."

"Including your cousin?"

His face darkened. "Aren't we being a diligent county sheriff? Yes, even my father's cousin, Oleg, who happens to be a legitimate businessman. Our transaction involved a loan between blood relations. Nothing illegal about it."

He pulled himself off the back of the sofa, his manner affable, his tone anything but. "I'm not sure what you're really after. Everything I've done has been aboveboard. If I had broken any laws, I would have heard from the attorney general's office. Not that it's any of your concern. You're out of your jurisdiction, Sheriff Tate, and possibly out of your depth."

She kept her expression pleasant. She could duplicate his style: approachable, amused, sincerely insincere. Smile as weapon.

"I expect you'll be getting a call very soon, Brad," she said. "I've already talked with someone high up in the AG's office about your project. The office has been interested in you for some time. Oh, and you can also expect involvement from the FBI. Something about money laundering or fraud; I can't remember which. It's out of my jurisdiction."

Sam mixed a couple nuggets of truth—she had called an acquaintance in the AG's office—with a whole lotta bull, as Sallie Mae would say. She didn't know whether Brad's transgressions rose to the level of an FBI investigation. She was looking for leverage, playing a long game.

He didn't balk. "I appreciate the heads up, Sheriff. I'll be sure to notify my attorney. That still doesn't explain why you're interested in my business. Or why you came all the way out here." Brad stood. Maybe to hustle her to the door. Or to hover over her chair in an attempt to intimidate her. Not a chance.

Sam rose before he got a step away from the couch. She could make five feet eight inches look a lot taller. He stopped. The two of them stood about a yard from each other like two gunslingers. The only thing missing were the guns. She'd left hers in the car.

"If you want to talk while standing up, we can do that, Brad. It seems less, how did you put it, friendly, so I recommend we sit back down."

They took their respective places. Sam didn't get comfortable.

"You're up a creek without a paddle," she began before he had a chance to draw a breath. "Even if I don't understand the details of your particular deal, it suggests something shady. For one thing, you started raising money for DHL before it legally came into existence via a non-registered DBA that conveniently disappeared the day the other company officially opened its doors. That alone warrants a second look."

Brad didn't comment.

"You also contracted for preliminary studies on the lake-adjacent property, a project not covered in your original promotional material. Is that because you knew your first project was belly-up? That you'd never get your hands on that land? How did your investors feel about that? Do all of them know yet? Do you think they'll be happy to find their money set aside for a twelve-acre development farther off the shoreline?"

"You have no right—"

"I have every right when I'm investigating a murder."

He jumped up again. "Murder?"

Sam stayed seated. She knew how fast she could react; he didn't. "Specifically, Bitsy Newsome," she continued. "You made her the face of the original proposal. She asked people for money in good faith, didn't she? Until she realized the project had no chance. What did she do? Get in your face? Accuse you of poor judgment? Threaten your reputation? At what point did you decide to shut her up?"

"You think I did something to Bitsy?"

"Or was it more personal?" Sam watched Brad react to her words like a gut punch. "That's it; you were partners and lovers. Did you expect her to leave her fiancé? Did she say no? That must have stung like a handful of nettles. Another young brunette disappointing you. The latest in a long line of twenty-somethings to break your heart and ruin your dreams."

"A long line of—holy shit. You think I'm *him*? The Wedding Crasher? Jesus Christ!"

The man turned a sickly shade of gray. His breathing was so labored that Sam feared not for her safety but for his.

"Sit down, Brad. You don't look well."

He sank into the couch. Sam grabbed a bottle of water out of the mini-fridge and threw it at him, then pulled a chair across the room and perched at the edge so she almost touched his knees. In the process, she ruined the perfect symmetry of the living room arrangement. Tough.

When his breathing and his color both returned to normal, she watched his eyes and asked her question.

"Did you kill Elizabeth Newsome?"

"No." He spoke in a subdued voice. "I cared about her. Not at first. I asked her to help me because she was a smart broker and because she knew people. She was on board with putting together a group of investors. We made up glossy brochures that pitched the quality of the shoreline and the potential revenue the proposed project would pull in. We threw investor parties."

"How did Lincoln Charles figure into the scheme?"

"Link seemed to think he could get his committee to convince the Corps to sell. We were only looking for ten or fifteen acres at the top of the lake, well away from the dam and fish hatchery. He recommended I line up the funding up front, to prove the project's legitimacy. The man expected me to ask investors for money without offering any guarantees." He shook his head. "Without using his name. When I balked, he slapped me on the back and told me we each had a role to play and his was behind the scenes. I should have pulled out right then."

"What happened between you and Bitsy?"

"We became close. I knew she was getting married. Neither of us cared. Our feelings were too intense to ignore."

He put his hand to his forehead. "Bitsy saw Charles as an opportunist, someone who'd wrapped both her fiancé and her lover around his little finger. We fought. It hurt, but I realized she was frightened more than anything. And she was right. She faulted me, yes, but she also faulted Mark and herself. Most of all, she held Link responsible for involving us all in something so dicey."

"Do you think Lincoln Charles had Bitsy killed?"

"God, no." Brad sounded shocked. "He had no skin in the game and she had no power over him. The investors could speculate that he was the friend we claimed to have in Washington, but no one knew for sure. Nothing points back to him."

"And Mark Talcott?"

"He's a slimy self-important tool." No mistaking Brad's contempt. "Like Charles, he risked nothing, contributed nothing. Bitsy's problems didn't touch him. He saw her as an acquisition, nothing more. He planned to move them both to Washington so that he could be closer to the center of power."

"Did you know he's ill? That he's in D.C. for specialized treatment that Lincoln Charles made possible?"

"You're kidding me. I had no idea. Now I understand why Bitsy wouldn't leave him." A small sob caught in his throat.

Last spring, Goodrich continued, he flew to Washington to appeal to Charles to push his committee members harder.

"Do you know what he said? 'You don't want to tell me how to do my business, Brad. The project was always a long shot. I assumed you took steps to protect yourself and your investors.' That pompous prick. After all his assurances."

Brad's naïveté astounded her. Politicians often made promises they didn't intend to keep.

"Were any of the investors angry enough to threaten you? Or Bitsy?"

Brad rubbed his jaw. "Maybe. Bitsy took most of the heat. We had a couple of small investors, people who I guess should have known better than to risk their savings in a real estate scheme."

His laughter died in his throat. "I'm not an evil person, Sam," he went on. "When I couldn't move the deal forward, I tried to return some of the money without getting my name in the papers. I expected to either develop or flip the other property and get the rest of the cash back to the investors down the line."

"I need a list of these investors, Brad. All of them, big and small."

"I'll get it." She kept an eye on him while he went to his study and returned with a folder. She expected him to ask her not to show anything to the AG without warning. Instead, he looked at her with wounded eyes.

"I loved her, Sam. Do you get it? I really loved her."

As she drove away, she caught a glimpse of him in the window of his sterile house next to his flawlessly decorated tree. She couldn't imagine an unhappier display.

Chapter 29

"What's going to happen to Goodrich?" Terry peered at Sam's image on his desktop and felt a tug at his heart. She looked tired, especially around the eyes.

"I expect he's going to have a miserable Christmas, Terry. Beyond that, I honestly don't know." She sat back in her chair and played with her hair.

He couldn't remember the last time she had worn it down like that. A wave formed an S over the right side of her face and curled the ends. Even with stress visible on her face, she looked almost glamorous, like a film star.

Terry pinched his hand as a reminder to corral his wandering attention. Sam was talking about her interaction with the attorney general's office. Brad might be looking at fines or jail time; she couldn't be sure. Without question, his reputation would be in tatters. He would be labeled a cheat or, worse, a fool.

"But not a murderer."

"You knew, Terry."

"Sam." He thought about how best to proceed. "It's easy to grab facts and make them fit into a theory. The Wedding Crasher kills brown-haired women. Brad's failed relationships are all brown-haired women. Ergo . . . well, ergo nothing in this instance. Lots of women have brown hair. They aren't all potential murder victims. A lot of guys have failed relationships. Some of them also make shady investments or lousy business decisions. That doesn't mean they're killers."

"I know."

"We also have a profile," he went on. "Sketchy, but it gives us some information. Now, I'm aware you have your doubts about profiling. Let's look at Brad, though. Is he the sort to hold a grudge? Or is he more a shrug-and-move-on kind of guy? I get the impression he doesn't often shed a tear over what he doesn't have. He keeps an eye out for the next big opportunity, the ultimate score. He's long on self-regard. What kind of man thinks he can bend Washington power brokers to his will? Even politicians like Lincoln Charles know their limits. Brad isn't likely to harbor anger about old flames. They exit his life. It's their loss."

"Except for Bitsy Newsome."

"True," Terry acknowledged. "One other thing, though. Ritual is central to what the Wedding Crasher does. The killer lavishes a lot of time and attention on each of the victims. The particulars never vary. I'm not sure Brad is big on details."

"You've got a point," Sam conceded. "I think he hires people to take care of mundane things like shopping, gift-giving, and tree decorating." She chuckled at Terry's quizzical expression. "Never mind. Scratch another suspect off the list. Damn, this case aggravates the hell out of me."

"Tell me about it. How are you otherwise doing with your investigations?"

"We're back to looking at classmates of Emily's. Male and female. It's a very touchy situation, as you can imagine. Might explain why I don't have much in the way of holiday plans." Her smile looked lopsided. "Except, of course, for the command appearance at the mayor's open house. Too much food, too much wine, lots of kids."

"You might surprise yourself and have a good time."

"Anything's possible." She shifted her gaze. "I suppose you'll be going away with Mercy over the holidays?"

"We're heading to Miami over Christmas to visit her family. Too much food, too much wine, lots of kids. The usual." He laughed. She didn't join in.

"Sounds like fun. What's going on with your sting?"

"On hold. Typical FBI operation. Start and stop. Hurry up and wait. We're dealing with a cyberstalker out of St. Pete, but I'm peripheral to that investigation. Fine by me."

"That's good." Her expression softened. "Have a lovely holiday, Terry."

"You too, Tate. Catch you in the new year."

Terry stood and looked out his window. The Tampa office building afforded a relatively pleasant view. Green grass, a mix of trees, simple gardens, and a water feature with a gurgling fountain. The cerulean sky was bordered by puffy clouds. Not a bad place to work or live.

Why did he feel so unsettled? Because he kept too many secrets. From his colleagues, who never fully understood the extent of his obsession with the Wedding Crasher. From Mercy, who didn't realize he would never marry her. From the grief counselor he stopped seeing because she seemed flummoxed by Terry's potent mix of guilt, grief, and passion. From Sam, who had stirred the pot by inadvertently adding hope to his emotional stew.

He'd booked a flight to New York on impulse, convinced an in-person meeting with Arthur Randolph's mother would yield answers. The trip was strictly off the books and out of pocket. The timing meant he would miss his office's holiday party, not to mention a fancy fundraiser Mercy expected him to attend. She would be disappointed, to say the least.

He waited to tell her until their biweekly dinner at Bern's Steak House, a popular Tampa eatery. They worked their way through Caesar salads, dry aged steak with vegetables, and most of an excellent bottle of Tempranillo. Over coffee and flan, he brought up his travel plans, striving to make them sound both off-handed and unavoidable.

"Let me get this straight," she said when he'd finished. "You're going to New York the week before Christmas on business. Is this something you've been ordered to do?"

"No one tells me how to investigate the cases I manage." He took her hand. "I'm sorry, honey. That sounded defensive. I should have said I'm at liberty to make my own decisions about how I investigate. This matter just came to my attention. I'd describe it as a time-sensitive lead I need to pursue."

He hadn't answered her question and she knew it. Mercy the girlfriend gave way to Mercy the reporter.

"This can't be about the Florida mob; Mickey Civella is from Philadelphia. Is he operating in New York as well? Or, wait, is this to do with the Wedding Crasher? Do you have a suspect? Someone located on the East Coast?"

"You know I can't talk about any of this, Mercy. Look, it's only a few days." He worked to keep the irritation out of his voice. He had no right to be short with her when he was lying through his teeth. At least lying by omission.

"Can't you contact someone in the FBI office up there? Get one of the agents to follow up, use Skype, or maybe schedule a conference call? I mean, traveling at this time of year is difficult under the best of circumstances. A two-day turnaround is insane."

He couldn't tell her his superiors knew nothing of his plans. "Look at it this way: I'll be up and back before you've noticed my absence."

She pulled her hand away and sat back. "Do whatever you want. That's usually what ends up happening, anyway."

"We'll still spend the holidays with your relatives," he said as he paid the check. "I'm looking forward to that." He smiled, trying to make it light.

"Fine," Mercy said, though it clearly wasn't. "Drop me at home. I'll see you when you get back."

That night, as he packed his overnight bag, his cell phone rang. Area code 631.

"Special Agent Sloan?" A woman's voice, older. Cultured, confident, just a hint of tears behind the refined steel. "This is Constance Randolph. You were coming to see my son tomorrow." A discreet cough. "I'm afraid there's been a development. Arthur suffered a fatal heart attack this afternoon."

Terry shook his head, as if he hadn't heard correctly. "Dead?"

"Yes. It was right after lunch. He went to his room to work on his manuscript."

"Manuscript?" Terry had been stunned into one-word answers. "I'm truly sorry for your loss, Mrs. Randolph. This is just a surprise. Arthur was relatively young, wasn't he?"

"Just forty-eight, Agent Sloan. But he'd always been . . . not exactly delicate, but unused to privation. Incarceration wore him down, as you can well imagine." Resigned rather than accusatory.

Terry recalled pictures of the man. Randolph appeared soft, almost shapeless, his face preternaturally unlined, his blond hair falling into his face like a teenager's. Life inside a psychiatric facility must have been stressful. At the same time, Terry had it on good authority that Randolph enjoyed a number of advantages not accorded to normal patients: a private room, extra sessions with the psychiatrist, more time outdoors, even phone privileges.

A heart attack at forty-eight. Possible, but also unusual. Terry's experience and training warned him to proceed with caution.

"I appreciate the call, Mrs. Randolph. I imagine this must be a difficult time for you." He needed to keep her talking even as he proceeded carefully.

"I didn't want you to make a trip for nothing, Agent Sloan. Believe it or not, Arthur was looking forward to speaking with you. He welcomed FBI involvement. Those were his words, not mine."

Terry considered his next question. "You said he was working on a manuscript?"

"Yes. He wouldn't show it to me, but from what little I gathered, he intended it as a two-pronged critique of both the state's psychiatric facilities and its judicial system."

Did the man who'd ended the lives of so many innocents believe the system had wronged him? Most people would say he got off easy, including Terry. Expressing those judgments would not serve his purpose.

"I'm curious. Did Arthur indicate how he thought the FBI could help him?"

She sighed. "My son suffered from a number of delusions, which my late husband credited to excessive pampering. Arthur was a difficult child, quick to give and take offense. He managed to be both self-conscious and self-righteous. Rejection angered him. He lashed out. It cost him. It cost everyone around him." Another sigh, filled with pain and regret. "I don't think he believed himself to be falsely accused, though. He mentioned something about being unfairly singled out."

Terry felt a tingling at the back of his neck. "Singled out? For the murders?"

"I had the impression he wanted to point fingers, share the blame. That was like Arthur." She spoke with great weariness.

"Mrs. Randolph, do you think you might get a copy of his manuscript to me? Perhaps there is something I can learn that will help."

"I don't see how anything can help poor Arthur at this point, Agent Sloan. However, if you think his writing is pertinent in any manner, I can call in a technician. Arthur's computer is password-protected, but those kinds of barriers can be subverted, I imagine. Now if you'll forgive me, I must disconnect so I can make a few more calls."

"Of course." Terry thought furiously, then added, "I imagine the funeral will be held after the autopsy."

He heard her take in a quick breath. "There will be no autopsy and no funeral, Agent Sloan. Arthur was cremated two hours ago."

Chapter 30

The white oaks looked magnificent, even in midwinter. Though sparsely dressed in dead leaves and dull red buds, they still dominated the tree line. Their upper branches reached for each other like old friends, interlacing at the highest points to form a woven arch. The midday sun glittered off the makeshift roof and sent silver slivers to the ground.

Sam stopped to admire the beauty. On a chilly Sunday afternoon in February, she had the place pretty much to herself. No campers, no hikers, not even a brave fisherman disturbed the quiet. The river looked dependably solid. She knew it to be an illusion. The ice was thin, barely able in parts to sustain a child's weight. Even so, a few youngsters dared one another onto the frozen water each year. At least one impatient skater felt compelled to test the strength of the surface. Every season sheriff's deputies assisted in pulling someone out of the frigid river. Every now and then they didn't arrive in time.

She'd been hiking a trail in Obey River Park, part of her campaign to get in better shape. She'd spent this last forgettable New Year's Eve drinking, precisely because it was forgettable. Now she limited herself to an occasional beer. One cup of coffee per day, period. More regular exercise. She'd even called Sommers to chat but backed away when the psychologist again pushed for a hypnotherapy session.

"I'm worried you're engaged in avoidance," Sommers told her.

"Well, it's working," Sam replied. "No more bad dreams." She failed to add, "that I can remember."

She sat down by the tree under which Claire Hooper's body lay almost three years ago. An unconventional place to try to calm her restive brain. On the other hand, maybe the spot would offer up some of its secrets. She planned to stay there until she jogged loose some sort of association her mind had thus far refused to make.

Crossing her legs, she pressed the thumb and second finger of each hand together and rested them on her knees. Gyan Mudra, the mudra of knowledge, was a common yoga position. According to several Eastern religions, the position served as a gateway into the mind. Hindus and Buddhists believed the mudra increased memory, sharpened the brain, and enhanced concentration. No scientific evidence existed to support its effectiveness, but its practitioners swore by it.

Something else to take on faith, she thought. As if she knew anything about that subject.

She breathed deeply and felt the frosty air against her cheeks. *Empty your cluttered mind, damn it. Think of nothing. Shut up.* That last was aimed at the cynical little voice in her head. The one that interrupted to suggest that she'd tried all this before, tried to hush the interior chatter, release the negativity, let go of the fear or the skepticism or whatever interfered with clarity.

Terry believed in the value of intuition. She wanted to believe in it as well. Because he did. Because others did. Because the human brain works on multiple levels. The beating heart and the bad mood both originate in the hominid brain. Logic could begin to sort through a million random bits of information; it wouldn't inform which pieces were most important.

"Logical thinking is methodical," Terry explained in that long-ago academy class. "It works brilliantly for long-term planning and is effective in idealized settings. Intuitive thinking, on the other hand, operates on a subconscious level. It's more rapid fire and risks being less precise. You will have to rely on both kinds of thinking in law enforcement."

"Because intuitive thinking takes place without making itself known," he went on, "those of you who value absolute control may feel frustrated." The class tittered. "However, the more experience you accumulate, the more you'll be able to trust your conclusions. Your gut feeling."

"You're not discounting evidence, are you?" a cadet demanded.

"Heaven forbid," Terry said in mock horror. "Remember, though; not every piece of data you come across is evidence. Information doesn't self-sort. You have to prioritize, decide what is important. At times, that happens consciously. We all use lists, white boards, three-by-five note cards, or whichever systems we find most comfortable. Often, though, our minds make the connections out of sight." He smiled. Even back then, Sam felt the pull of his remarkable eyes.

Daydreaming does not count as intuition, Tate, she reminded herself.

She had enough information to allow for some strongly supported determinations. She felt confident one person killed both Emily Upshaw and Tara Fence. That person also came after her outside Cora Granville's house and fired on her at the mall. She had reason to believe the killer was local. Someone much younger and less experienced than the Wedding Crasher. Someone acquainted with the two young women.

Sam didn't yet know whether this new murderer used wedding motifs to throw investigators off the trail or honor a killer he admired. She wanted to connect him to the Crasher and tie everything into one neat package. She couldn't.

She reached into the back pocket of her jeans. She still carried the yellow lined paper she'd created months ago to compare the elements of Emily's murder with the Wedding Crasher's five previous homicides. The same and not the same. Soon after, her team eliminated three prime suspects. Two of them ended up in jail for other offenses. Brad Goodrich remained free for now.

His list of investors in the failed scheme yielded few surprises. Most of them were wealthy individuals out of Nashville. Sam zeroed in on a $250,000 check from Edison Toomey, owner of Green Design, LLC, a local landscaping concern. Toomey lived in Dale Hollow Lake and employed about a dozen people, including Jeff Simpson, Kaylee's husband. Sam had no idea how lucrative the landscaping business might be. She assumed Green Design was anchored by a few established customers and otherwise seasonal. She had to guess a loss that size would impact Toomey personally, if not professionally.

Toomey, a convivial, well-fed man in his fifties, didn't seem bothered about the venture. "I had a moment when I thought I might need to lay a few people off." He told Sam. "It didn't happen, though. I spoke with Brad. He's already refunded $25,000. He'll be good for the rest. And if he isn't . . ." He chuckled. "Not that I would threaten anyone in a conversation with the county sheriff, you understand."

Not everyone took such an easygoing approach. At least one investor complained to the attorney general's office. The AG, in turn, seemed prepared to move against Goodrich. Or so Sam heard from Toby Mueller when the poker game resumed in January. The group met at Billy's house. Brad begged off, probably permanently.

As she sat on the cold ground and let her thoughts form and dissipate, an idea surfaced. She and Terry had spent months focused on the differences between Emily's ritual and that of the Wedding Crasher. The yellow dress. The younger victim. The imprecise manner of death. The time of year. All their questions dealt with what wasn't the same. But what if those were the wrong questions?

Okay, let's work though this idea, Sam's suddenly helpful inner voice counseled.

Emily had some things in common with the serial victims. She was a pretty young woman whose killer chose to ritualize her death. Perhaps she wasn't supposed to represent a broken engagement but something similar, like a botched romance. Whoever murdered her also dressed her to recall an earlier period. A nod to the Wedding Crasher's style or something else? A nod to an earlier period when women didn't toy with the affections of vulnerable men? Sam had studied enough history—and lived enough of her own—to recognize the flaws in such an assumption. Heartbreak, like war, was as old as humankind.

True, some perceived offense propelled the Wedding Crasher. The same was true of about a hundred other cases. Resentment born of thwarted love or an emotional misreading was not that unusual. The Perfume Man carried the same kind of anger.

So did Arthur Randolph. He'd died, according to her aunt, who'd heard from the lawyer. Gillian also confessed she felt relief at Randolph's demise.

"Is that a terrible way to feel?" she asked Sam.

"Not at all," Sam reassured her aunt. She didn't add that Randolph's death raised more questions than answers.

She shook her head, trying to steer her mind away from this or that tangent and onto her present dilemma. Did someone help Emily's killer? Who? Any number of adults could have impacted a young person's life. Teacher. Counselor. Minister. Family doctor. Coach. Maybe the Wedding Crasher. Maybe not.

She shook her head. She kept getting tripped up by *maybes* and the *what ifs*.

A stray brown leaf spiraled to the ground. Terry's remark about seeing the forest for the trees came back to her. Her list rested in the circle of her legs. She'd marked the words "lying under one or more white oaks." All the victims lay not just outside or in a forest somewhere but underneath a very specific species of tree belonging to a particular *genus*.

The detail was never made public. Sam wasn't sure why. Maybe no one considered white oak trees noteworthy. They were common enough. The fact that all the dead bodies ended up in their shadows might have been a fluke.

Fluke or clue?

She pulled out her phone, aware that surfing the net was not part of meditation practice. Maybe she was a lost cause, or maybe her intuition was firing up. She looked up oak trees and by chance ran into a promotional piece from Tennessee's Department of Agriculture celebrating the state's diverse woody plants. The article was entertaining and informative, particularly the section on oaks.

A mature white oak, she read, looks like a romanticized version of a tree. In works of art, it appears almost as wide as it is high, anchored by a massive network of lateral roots and shaped like a glorious crown at the top. The gray bark of the white oak contrasts with the shiny green elliptical leaves, each with seven or eight rounded protrusions, like fingers on a hand.

The Druids and the Celts considered oaks to be sacred trees. Greeks revered them as epitomizing wisdom and nobility. In contemporary culture, oaks have come to represent strength, bravery, and endurance. A number of countries, including the United States, use the oak as a national symbol. Several towns, parks, schools, and at least one band include "oak" as part of their names. Tree tattoos, especially oak trees, are popular in contemporary body art.

That piece of information caused her circuits to pulse. Instead of a languid trip towards the light of consciousness, she felt as if she'd been zapped with a taser. She saw a tattoo of a tree. The uppermost branches crawled up the side of the neck, the distinctive leaves just visible above a shirt collar. The roots peeked out the sleeves and extended towards white knuckles that grabbed the back of the pew in front of him. The tattoo belonged to someone familiar. Someone she hadn't questioned. Someone Tara had.

She scrambled to her feet and raced to her car.

Chapter 31

The next day, a visitor showed up in the office, a young girl named Sandy Iverson. Sandy, a skinny fifteen-year-old sophomore, had been part of a group at Bobcat Den last November and had seen Tara Fence.

Serendipity.

"Why did you wait so long to tell us, Sandy?" Sam tried to keep the accusation out of her voice. "You know Deputy Fence died just before Thanksgiving. It's already February."

They sat in the conference room. Sandy clutched a paper cup of coffee. Her white hands contrasted with her bright blue nails. She fidgeted, twisting her dirty blond hair around her finger, tugging at her oversized jacket—possibly an older brother's—and chewing gum like her life depended on it. Her brown eyes couldn't find a place to rest. They darted around the room as if seeking a magic opening through which she could escape.

"I dunno. I was talking about the murders the other day with my little brother and then I said I thought maybe I saw the young deputy who got killed. Then my dad kind of smacked me upside the head and asked me why I hadn't said anything before." Tears appeared at the corners of her eyes.

Sam couldn't help but react with anger, though she kept her feelings off her face. Her office dealt periodically with cases of domestic abuse, especially given the high unemployment rate among Byrdstown's men.

"Never mind, Sandy. The important thing is you came in. That's really helpful."

The praise seemed to rouse the girl.

"I remember Tara because of her bright red hair. Also, she looked a couple years older but still kind of young. I thought maybe she was trying to relive her high school days by coming back to where she used to hang out. Like she'd been working in the area and thought she'd drop in for a visit or something. Except she was looking around, too. I guess because she was being a cop. Know what I mean?"

Sam did. Tara Fence's attentiveness was one of the things she most admired about the deputy. "Good observations, Sandy. What else do you remember?"

"Only that TJ Simpson was there, too, sitting by himself. He's ahead of me in school, but I have some older friends, juniors and seniors." Sandy spoke with pride. "They said he'd gotten kind of creepy and no one wanted to have anything to do with him. That's probably why he was sitting alone."

"None of you talked with TJ?"

"No, ma'am."

"What about Deputy Fence? Did you talk with her?"

"We didn't."

"Did you notice if she spoke with TJ?"

Sandy looked as if she might start to cry. "I'm sorry. I really can't recall."

"Never mind. You've already made a big difference, Sandy."

Sam brought TJ Simpson in for questioning two days later. For good measure, she asked Abdi to team with her. She also took care to let Kaylee know exactly what was taking place. The boy had just turned eighteen and didn't require a parent present. Nevertheless, Sam wasn't about to cut out the mother if the son didn't object. She did warn Kaylee against interrupting or answering for her son.

As it turned out, Kaylee said very little. TJ took control at the outset and stayed in the driver's seat. Initially, he came across as relaxed but not disrespectful. Watchful, with what Abdi later described as a touch of cunning.

They settled in the conference room. Dana brought in cans of soda for everyone. Sam opened hers and watched to see if the young man would do the same. No such luck. TJ didn't touch the can. Instead, he sat with his hands clasped in front of him.

The boy wore a long-sleeved black shirt with a dark purple tie, black jeans, and Doc Martens. He'd washed and slicked back his hair. A single silver stud graced his left ear. No other decorations, except for the tree tattoo, just visible at his collar and cuffs.

Abdi had already questioned several teachers. According to all of them, TJ had returned to classes with renewed confidence following his stint in rehab. While he hadn't participated in any after-school activities, he'd managed to hold onto a B average, helped by excellent grades in English. He'd made up all his schoolwork and was on track to graduate on time. This past fall, his grades had slipped again and he began to cut classes.

Abdi asked TJ about his absences.

"I take a little time off to think. Commune with nature, that sort of thing. All the craziness of senior year, all the pressure. I guess it gets to me. You know how it is."

Sam noticed Kaylee frown. TJ ignored his mother.

"The death of a classmate must have been hard as well," Abdi continued.

"Sure." The boy's expression didn't change. "That, too. But I'm good now. My teachers know they don't have to worry. I may have to take a couple classes this summer. No big deal. I'll graduate." He pocketed the coin he'd been playing with and looked up with a grin.

"Then what? College?"

TJ cut his eyes to his mother. "We'll see." He shrugged.

"Were you acquainted with Emily Upshaw, TJ?"

"Acquainted? Everyone was acquainted with Emily, Detective. She was the most popular girl in school."

"Did you hang out with her?"

"Hang out? Interesting phrase. More like we shared a couple of classes when we were sophomores."

"Before you took time off."

TJ shook his head. "Come on, Detective Issen. You know I was in rehab."

"Okay, before rehab. You came back in your junior year. Were you still friends?"

"We were never friends."

"Really?"

"Really. I was behind and I had to concentrate on my work. She was in my English class. She offered to help with one assignment. We discussed it in the hall. That's about it."

"Then you didn't have feelings for her?"

"Asked and answered, Detective." Challenging.

"Did you know about her new boyfriend?"

The gray eyes blinked once. "Did she have a new boyfriend?"

"An older man. A musician from Nashville."

"Well, good for her."

Abdi glanced at his notes. "Did you ever visit the Bluebird Café in Nashville?"

"Doesn't ring a bell."

"What about Bobcat Den here in Byrdstown?"

"I used to. Not so much anymore."

"I wondered because someone recalled seeing you there last November."

"Is that a crime?"

"Not at all. Do you recall seeing a woman with red hair? Deputy Tara Fence."

"Tara Fence. Hmm, is that the deputy who was killed? That was awful." TJ affected a shocked look.

"Yes. Did you see her then? Or perhaps speak to her?"

"Honestly, Detective, I can't recall." TJ's smile stopped short of his eyes.

"I'm curious about your tattoo," Sam broke in. "Is it the whole tree or just a couple of branches and leaves?"

"You wanna see, Sheriff?"

He stood up, yanked off his tie, slid out of his shirt, and stood bare-chested. Abdi rose, his hand on his holster. Kaylee jumped to her feet. She appeared well and truly shocked.

"Tommy James Simpson, what do you think you're doing? Get dressed immediately!"

The boy grinned.

Sam remained seated with her hands in her lap. "It's all right, Abdi, Kaylee. Let's all sit down. TJ seems to want to model for us."

His was not a pumped-up physique. His chest was concave and hairless. His skin looked mottled. Sam took some time to study the elaborate tattoo. The main trunk had been etched on his chest. The roots extended down below the waistband of his pants. A few branches reached up and encircled his neck. One extended down each arm and ended in the familiar elliptical leaves with the rounded edges.

"That's pretty fancy work, TJ. How long have you had it?"

"Two years, Sheriff. Before I took my little, ah, sabbatical. Had to get it done in Nashville. Nobody around here knows what they're doing when it comes to ink."

"What's it supposed to be? An oak tree? Maybe a white oak?"

He looked at her as if she'd lost her mind. "It's supposed to be a tree, Sheriff. That's all. And since you're gonna ask why I got it, to please my dad. To honor his sacrifice, really. He had it rough, going from owning a contracting company to working for someone else's landscaping business."

"It's certainly unusual," Sam said. She kept her eyes on his.

"It's a better version of ordinary," TJ scoffed. "The guy I went to is in Nashville. He specializes in tree art. You can ask him. He probably does a dozen of these in a month, maybe more."

Slowly, as if he were performing a reverse striptease, he put his clothes back on. Then he sat down, folded his hands exactly as they'd been before, and arranged his features to look pleasantly bland.

"How else can I help you today, Sheriff?"

"Do you own a gun, TJ?"

He scoffed. "What would I do with a gun?"

Sam noted he hadn't answered the question. "What about a semiautomatic rifle?"

"Maybe my dad—"

"We have a rifle, Sheriff," Kaylee said. "For the house. It belongs to my husband. He uses it for hunting sometimes. Like just about everyone else around here. Mostly, we keep it for protection. And to scare off critters. I think Jeff might have shot at something in the backyard just the other night."

Sam nodded as if she'd been given new information. Semiautomatic rifles were a regular feature of most households. Whoever fired at her could have borrowed one from almost anyone. A neighbor, a friend, a classmate. A mentor.

"Might help if we could take a look at it, Kaylee. If you don't mind."

Kaylee stood up and rested a hand on her son's shoulder. His smirk disappeared.

"I'll talk to my husband about the rifle, Sheriff. Meanwhile, my boy here has cooperated with you, never mind his little stunt earlier. Last time I checked, being a smart-aleck teenager wasn't a crime. I'd like to get him home now so he can get to his schoolwork. If you need anything else, I'm going to have to get in touch with a lawyer."

Sam looked at Abdi. "No need, Kaylee. I think we're done here," she said.

"I'll be back soon to finish up the workday. Assuming I still have a job." She gave Sam a pointed look.

"Kaylee—"

"All right, then. Let's go, TJ." They left the conference room.

As soon as mother and son were out of earshot, Abdi turned to his boss. "That didn't go so well. I don't think I'll be drinking the coffee anytime soon."

Sam returned to her office and spent an hour looking out the window. She could have all the bad feelings about Tommy Simpson she wanted. He was a messed-up kid with an attitude problem and a weakness for drugs she guessed rehab hadn't extinguished. He was left-handed. He had a chip on his shoulder. So did Clayton Littlewood, aka the Perfume Man. And plenty of other young men. That didn't make them killers.

Kaylee returned at four thirty and stayed another hour. She kept busy at her desk. She didn't smile. She didn't offer Sam any coffee.

Sam's cell phone rang at half past five. She picked up just as the assistant knocked on the door.

"Hold on, Terry. Come in."

"I'm leaving now."

"Kaylee—"

"Good night, Sheriff."

"Trouble in paradise?" Terry asked.

"You caught that? Yeah, things are a little chilly around here. I just interviewed her son, Tommy. Who now goes by the name TJ."

"Really? Has he found a place on your suspect list?"

"You could say that. I remembered seeing TJ at Emily's memorial service and noticing bits of what might have been a tree tattoo. To top it off, TJ seems to be left-handed, or so it appeared during his little striptease." She summarized the interview.

"You're onto something, Sam. Never mind TJ's little cat-and-mouse game. You have someone who put him and Tara in the same place at the same time. He's left-handed, as was Emily's killer. The tree tattoo—"

"Is apparently common," Sam interrupted. "And lots of people are left-handed. Yes, I can put him at Bobcat

Den at the same time as Tara, thanks to a somewhat shaky witness. She didn't see them exchange a single word, though. No one ever heard him argue with Emily, either. He has no obvious motive."

"He's a troubled kid."

"Not a crime, Terry. Byrdstown has a lot of those."

"What about texts he may have sent? Or his alibi?"

Sam snorted. "Oh, right, the digital footprint that always trips up the suspects. Except everyone is smart enough to use burner phones now. As for an alibi, I suspect his mother will claim he was home with the family. I managed to cause a serious rift with her, as you can tell."

She slammed a fist on her desk. "Damn it! Every time I think I'm getting a toehold, the ground shifts beneath my feet."

"You're doing everything right. You're following both the evidence and your gut."

"I'm trying to catch a shadow with a butterfly net. My gut's not telling me a damned thing, by the way. I sat under some trees over the weekend. An idea came to me—isn't that how it's supposed to work?—and I followed it all the way out to a dead end. Now we're coming up on hunting season for the Wedding Crasher and oh, I've still got two dead local girls. Their killer might be playing me, but I can't prove it. Who cares what my gut feels?"

Nothing. *Maybe he hung up,* Sam thought. She wouldn't have blamed him.

At last he spoke. "Here's what my gut tells me, Sam. First, TJ was more interested in Emily Upshaw than he let on. Second, the tree tattoo means more than he claims it does. Emily isn't the only victim left under an oak tree. Maybe we can tie everything together after all."

Hope raised its head and then buried itself even deeper. "I can't think about that right now, Terry. My priorities are to solve the murders of two local young women. At least that's what my bosses pay me to do. I need to figure out whether TJ Simpson killed Emily and Tara. Maybe he did, maybe he didn't, maybe he knows who did. I also have to decide what his mother might know about any of it. She seemed as upset about his behavior as she did about my interview. On the other hand, she was more than willing to back up his story about being home."

"I'm about to be submerged in work. Sam, I promise you—"

"Let's not make any promises we can't keep, Terry. I've had enough of those to last a lifetime."

Chapter 32

TJ slammed his fist on the Jetta's steering wheel. Over and over until he'd raised a sizeable welt along the side of his hand. Good. Maybe the pain would sharpen his senses. He didn't want to hurt himself, but it was better than smashing someone else's skull.

None of this had to happen. Emily and he had been friends. They had a special bond. At least he thought they did, until she got too full of herself to give him the time of day. As for Tara Fence, he had nothing against her. Until she stuck her nose where it didn't belong.

Now everything had gone to shit, thanks to two, no, three bitches who thought they were better or smarter or more special. Emily's death was about righting a wrong and paying his respects to a mentor he needed to impress. Killing the deputy was about covering his ass.

As for the sheriff, he couldn't say for sure why he did what he did. Maybe he just wanted to yank her chain. He made a couple of rookie moves. Shooting at her nearly got him caught. Following her to Nashville after the service nearly got him killed. She still didn't put two and two together. She still spun her wheels while her lame detective interviewed everyone else on the planet. Until suddenly she had it all figured out.

No, not all of it. But enough to haul his ass down to the office. Then she had to go and involve his mother even though he was legally of age. And now? Now she had deputies trailing him all over the place. If they'd stopped him for speeding or picked him up for drugs, he might have shrugged it off. They didn't, because they weren't watching him for minor offenses. Which made him all the more paranoid.

FUBAR, all of it fucked up beyond all repair.

He pounded the wheel again. *Goddamn junkie,* his inner voice screamed, *can't you get anything right?*

Then another voice intruded, quieter, calmer. *It's all going to work out.*

He thought about Emily. Pretty, popular, perfect Emily. Who had a passion for poetry he didn't share until they both took Mrs. Neil's sophomore English class. The old biddy made the verses sing. Her fervent readings jump-started all his senses. He could taste air, smell death, hold desire in his hand. He could do anything, be anything. He could be friends with the most admired girl in school.

He faked his way through rehab, limiting himself to purloined marijuana he used mostly to calm his anxiety at losing so much time. When he returned to Pickett County High School, he found himself stuck between sophomore and junior years. Emily had moved on. She still stopped to talk with him in the hall, mostly out of curiosity, he suspected. Clean and sober, he nevertheless projected danger along with his newfound maturity. Some girls found him exciting. Not Emily. She made it clear she had no interest in taking their part-time friendship any further.

That spring, the Newsome woman's death dominated the conversation. The idea of a serial killer both frightened and titillated the students. Emily shrugged it off.

"I got a summer job in Nashville," she announced in late May. "I'll probably be safer there than here." Her defiant attitude surprised and excited him.

"I get to Nashville now and again," he told her. "We could meet up after you get off work."

"Nah, I'm going to be pretty tired. And it's a long ride. I'll probably just come home."

That was her first lie.

He followed her after work to the Bluebird Café and caught the tail end of a performance by a mediocre band fronted by an aging pretty boy who understood nothing about country music. He didn't know what shocked him more, that Emily knew this pretender or that she apparently liked him. In the older man's presence, she acted in a frankly sexual manner he couldn't square with the poetry-loving virgin he thought he knew.

He wondered if she planned to continue her fling into the school year. Maybe bring him around to the few local joints. That would shock her classmates, not to mention her parents. He wouldn't put it past her.

TJ kept Emily and her man under surveillance throughout the summer. Sometimes the older guy traveled up to Pickett County to meet Emily in some out-of-the-way place so they could make out. She hadn't given herself to him, he knew. Somehow, that knowledge lifted Tommy's spirits.

What Emily didn't know was that her boyfriend continued to hook up with a parade of women back in Nashville. His disloyalty insulted TJ. The younger man considered taking his rival out permanently. He decided his best ammunition was evidence of the creep's betrayal, which he collected on his cell phone.

Meanwhile, TJ found a new supplier in the city. Not the hard stuff, mostly weed. Just to keep the edge off. Maybe a little coke if he needed a push.

He tried to stay in touch, but Emily pulled away. Without the structure of school, they had little opportunity to connect. Maybe a random text here and there, mostly unanswered on her part.

He felt their friendship fade and with it, his chance for more. A relationship. Love. An ordinary life. He hated himself for wanting any of it as much as he did. What did he expect? He'd been so far from normal for so long he wouldn't know what that meant.

He arranged to run into her in Nashville one afternoon. "Oh, hey," he said, affecting a casual air. "How you been? Haven't heard from you in a while. Thought you might have decided to quit school and become a country singer."

"Nope," she said with a smile that made his heart ache with longing. "Just tired from work."

"You can tell me all about it over coffee."

She looked at him as if he had lost his mind. "Tell you about what, TJ? I go to work. I deal with snotty customers. I go home and do it all over again the next day. That's it." Emily scrutinized him. "You don't look so good. I hope you haven't slid back into your old habits."

Her words hurt and so did her lies. He didn't have to waste his time. Soon enough he'd turn eighteen and he could break free of everything—his family, his school, his past. Emily.

Still, he wanted to let her know she'd made a mistake before she made an even bigger one. Got in over her head. Regretted her choices. He convinced himself he had her best interests at heart.

Maybe he did, until the night he saw her drive off to Dark Skies Park near the end of August to give herself to the least deserving guy on the planet.

What a fool he'd been. Emily was like every other female except his mother. Self-centered and indifferent when it came to who they trampled over. So intent on their version of perfection that they paid no heed to anyone else. Not quite the undeserving bride but close enough. He knew what had to be done.

He was alone at home the next afternoon. His father had taken his brothers to see a double header, followed by pizza. His mother had gone to a mall in Livingston for what she called "hours of retail therapy."

Emily, glowing from her previous evening's debauchery, seemed willing enough to play the savior when he told her he needed help. Saint Emily. He even managed to feed her Rohypnol in a beer. But he gave her too much or maybe not enough. What did he know about anyone's drug tolerance except his own?

Then he tried to cut her throat on the sides, like he'd seen it done. Except he was shaking like a leaf and she was screaming so loudly he thought the whole neighborhood would end up in the basement with them. He hit the jugular and got caught in a fountain of blood. The area around him looked like the Red Sea. He continued to slash until Emily's throat looked like badly butchered meat. She passed out; she still didn't die.

Panicked, he called the one person he never wanted to ask for help.

The cleanup was the worst part of the afternoon, but the two of them got it done while he babbled like an idiot. They dressed the body in a high-neck dress—"Not a wedding dress, TJ. This is something a little different, okay?"—and took it back to Dark Skies at dusk.

TJ felt soothed by the ceremony that had become second nature to him. Later came the blistering lecture, his mentor incredulous over the boy's thoughtlessness, his poor planning, his reckless stupidity. Harsh, absolutely, but nothing he didn't expect or deserve.

After that, though, the mistakes seemed to feed off one another. He blamed the incident at the old lady's house on drugs and his own grief. He never intended to kill that damned sheriff. Just wanted to see if he could rattle her freaky calm. Knock her off her game, maybe divert her attention. The mall shoot-out was completely unexpected; he'd gone to observe. Carrying, sure, but only because the parts of Nashville he frequented were dangerous.

He took a couple of items from his parents' house and sold them. He had his dealer add heroin to his purchases. He used it sparingly; he had his habit under control. Sometimes his memory failed him. Even that was a blessing in disguise. He could shut his eyes without seeing Emily's blood, without feeling as if he were drowning in it.

Tara Fence messed it all up. She was all over him from the get-go that day. Staring at him, staring at his tattoo like she could read it. Maybe she could or maybe she was just psyching him out. Why the hell did he go up to her and goad her like that? She'd provoked him, coming into Bobcat Den in her uniform. Wait, was she in uniform? He couldn't remember. It didn't matter. She was acting all Sherlock Holmes, playing at being a detective.

He acted on instinct; his impulse was to end Tara. He tried to be smart about it. A crash wouldn't tie back to the ritual. Accidents happen. Only he overdid it. Again. How was he supposed to know how much damage he needed to inflict on the car? How could he have made things worse?

TJ thumped the steering wheel again. Worse was his dealer pressing him for payment. Worse was his mother ready to send him back to rehab. Worse was the one girl he might have loved lying in a months-old grave. Worse was the young police officer he'd killed. Worse was his mentor's fury, barely contained by a paper-thin layer of charity. Worse was the damned sheriff and her damned sidekick.

"No more," he said aloud. He'd been paying his dues to the living and the dead for years. Time for a change. He needed his own life, far away from here. Spring was coming. He would play his part in one more ritual. Then he'd be gone.

Chapter 33

In February, Terry learned he'd be running phase two of the Civella sting. The FBI wanted to target key players within Civella's organization and turn them into assets. The venture required several agents to go undercover and more to provide surveillance 24/7 and, if necessary, backup.

Terry welcomed the assignment. Though he spent most of his time behind a desk, he preferred fieldwork. He wouldn't be undercover, but he'd be in charge, supervising those who were. A successful resolution to this phase of the operation would bring him notice, maybe more opportunities.

To do what, Sloan?

"Do you have to be involved every step of the way?" Mercy asked him one night as they lay in bed.

"You know I do, honey. This sting could turn into a coup for the FBI and a stepping stone for me. I'll only be tied up three or four weeks. Bored half the time. Missing you all of the time."

Partly true, he thought, thankful that Mercy couldn't read his expression in the dark.

Terry tapped Agent George Sanchez, a rising star in the Tampa office, to play a smooth-talking human trafficker from Cuba named Jorge Diaz. A handsome, urbane man in his early thirties, Sanchez made a believable criminal, one with a legitimate veneer.

The agent spent ten days in Miami establishing his backstory. He made himself visible to the appropriate people in all the appropriate places and made his interest in meeting with Mickey Civella known. No one believed

Civella would meet with a prospective partner without first sending an intermediary. On day seven, one materialized.

The man Sanchez met in Miami appeared as innocuous as his name, Walter Sands. Five foot ten, maybe 165 pounds, thinning flaxen hair, dusty hazel eyes. He came across as deliberately, if expensively, nondescript, right down to his tailored beige suit, his watery lemon tie, and his plain gold wedding band. No one doubted he was as ruthless as anyone working for Civella.

"Walter Sands is actually William Sorrel," one of Terry's agents told him. "A licensed attorney in three states with an MBA from Wharton. Lives with his wife and two kids in West Chester, an upscale suburb outside Philadelphia. Nice house. Crime must pay."

During their initial meeting over drinks at a Miami Beach café, "Sands" and "Diaz" chatted about their spouses and children. Civella's man admitted he both indulged and overprotected his fifteen-year-old daughter.

"That's his weak spot," Terry announced to his team.

Sorrel invited his new friend to Tampa to discuss business. They met in a serviceable minisuite in a generic downtown hotel chain. Each man brought a two-person security detail. Sorrel's men swept the room and swiped a scanner over the undercover agent.

"Can't be too careful," he observed.

"Of course not," Sanchez agreed. He straightened his blazer and brushed off an invisible speck of lint. Then he patted Sorrel on the shoulder as if to say "no hard feelings" and deposited a miniscule listening device on the other man's collar.

As the bodyguards cooled their heels in the hall, the two men sat down to discuss business.

"Explain again why Mr. Civella might take an interest in your enterprise," Sorrel began.

"Of course," Sanchez replied. "First, because it's become quite profitable. Second, because I assume most of the risk. Third, because I have experience. I already operate in several regions around the world. Now I wish to expand and Florida is a good place to establish a, what do you call it, a beachhead. I've been told Mr. Civella is the man to make that happen. If I may."

The undercover agent powered up a laptop and turned the screen to face Sorrel. "We are, as I explained, online wholesalers. Think Amazon but more specialized. Our product is human."

"You provide slaves to interested buyers."

"I wouldn't say—"

Sorrel waved away the other man's concerns. "I'm not making a judgment, Diaz. I'm providing clarity. Please go on."

"Very well, then. There is a high demand for domestic labor. Whole families are especially desirable. The category we call 'companion' remains by far our most popular category. I'd like to show you—"

"I don't need to see—" Sorrel protested.

"—how we've cataloged the available stock according to gender, physical attributes, and age. Under teenage girls, for instance . . ." He brought up an image of a pretty girl with long blond hair and a bright smile. She wore the pleated skirt and blazer of a school uniform.

"What the hell?" Sorrel leapt from his chair, his eyes on the screen. "That's a picture of my daughter! You bastard! If you think—"

"I think you will want to play along, Mr. Sorrel," Sanchez replied. "Let's not upset your people." He stood and threw an arm around the older man's shoulders just as the four men flung themselves into the room, weapons drawn.

"Hey, guys." Sanchez-as-Diaz projected easygoing charm. "Sorry for the outburst. Mr. Sands got excited about the product line. Let's put the guns away, eh? Everything is good. Maybe you can go for coffee or something."

"It's fine," Sorrel told his men. "Go."

As soon as they left, Terry and two other agents entered from the next room through a connecting door.

"FBI," Sorrell sneered, eyeing their jackets. "I should have known. Are you borrowing dirty tricks from the CIA now?"

"If we were, you'd be in a dark hole somewhere and your daughter's picture would be live on a popular human trafficking site," Terry replied. "That can still be arranged, Mr. Sorrel."

"What do you want?"

"Let's call it an arrangement. You supply us with information on Mickey Civella's criminal activities. You're a lawyer; you know exactly what that means. What are his plans for South/Central Florida? Who are his partners? What meetings is he taking? What promises is he making? We need names, dates, physical or digital evidence. Anything we can use in court, along with your testimony. In return for which—"

Sorrel's rolling laugh surprised them. "You'll what? Protect me and my family? From La Cosa Nostra? Pardon my skepticism, but you can't even seem to protect innocent women from getting butchered and dressed up like brides. Yes, I know who you are, Agent Sloan. Your reputation precedes you."

Terry refused to take the bait. "I was going to say, in return for which we'll keep you out of jail and your daughter's picture off the dark websites and out of the hands of traffickers."

Sorrel looked incredulous. "That's it? I'll need far more if I'm going to risk my life, Agent Sloan."

"Not my department, Sorrel," Terry said. "You can hammer out the details with the next people you meet." He looked at his watch, nodded at his agents. "These gentlemen will escort you out. You don't want to be late."

"Agent Sloan—"

"You have something to say, Mr. Sorrel?"

Sorrel offered a chilling smile. "A little perspective to offer. Mickey Civella and I are simply well-placed cogs in an efficient machine, albeit he is higher up the food chain. Blood still counts for something. Don't kid yourself, though. LCN isn't the old Mafia. No more infighting or family feuds. We have many friends and alliances. We operate in boardrooms, courtrooms, Silicon Valley, even on Capitol Hill. And in more remote locations. Long Island. North-/Central Tennessee."

Terry fought against his impulse to grab Sorrel by his tie and choke him. "What's that supposed to mean?" he demanded.

"Not my department, Special Agent Sloan. I leave it to you to connect the dots."

* * *

At the office the following day, Terry waded through several rounds of hand-pumping and back-slapping. Champagne glasses appeared and toasts were made, along with offers of more substantial after-work celebrations. Applebaum called to congratulate Terry, as did his old boss in D.C.

"People here notice victories, Terry," he said. "You close your other major case, you can write your own ticket."

His other case. As if he needed reminding. Anxiety over Sorrel's words coupled with his sense that he was in a race against the calendar. The sting had eaten up half of March.

Terry spent most of his week off at the office pouring over everything connected with the Wedding Crasher murders. Mercy left on vacation. She viewed his work-related activities as a betrayal. She had a point.

He held off calling Sam. Better to have something to bring to the table, something that helped move at least one of the investigations. He certainly couldn't tell her about his interest (or anyone else's) in a twenty-five-year-old case. Not yet. First, he had to help her catch a killer, or two, operating in the here and now.

He reviewed the case files from the beginning. What connections between the five victims had he missed? The women seemed to be randomly selected. The geography suggested convenience. The appearance suggested a type. The circumstances suggested a motive. All of the women were engaged to be married. Logic suggested they were versions of a bride who missed her wedding.

Terry and his colleagues originally considered the possibility that someone in the killer's past provided the motive for the killings. A girlfriend or maybe even a relative who preceded the victims but didn't become one herself. A young woman whose spring wedding was derailed because of injury, illness, death. Or a change of heart. Someone whose absence had inadvertently triggered a ritual.

Terry wasn't prepared to hunt a phantom until he'd exhausted every other possibility.

The same and not the same. A way Sam had of deciding what Emily Upshaw's murder had in common with the Wedding Crasher deaths. Most everyone connected with those cases saw only what connected the victims to each other. The ritual never varied. The killings always took place in April. The women were all in their twenties, all brown-haired, all engaged to be married. All the same.

Yet one was not the same, was it?

He considered Janet Barnes. Pretty and popular, she'd served on the student council and maintained an A– average. No creepy stalkers or angry exes. Everyone admired Janet. The fiancé, Sean Finnegan, had been devastated. His alibi for the time of her murder held.

The same. Except she came first. First is never the same. The first victim could be a convenient start for an obsession or the catalyst. If catalyst, not the same.

Detectives interviewed roommates, classmates, and boyfriends past and present. Just before Finnegan, Janet had dated a football player named Dan King. According to Janet's roommate, the relationship quickly became lopsided.

"Nice guy but needy," she told the detective. "After about two months, they went out of sync, you know? Like he had 'forever' on his brain and she'd moved on. Then she met Sean and everything changed. She was so happy."

The rejected suitor goes after the girl who hurt him. Classic setup for a volatile situation. However, King died nine months before Janet's death in what appeared to be an unintentional opioid overdose. Legitimate prescription improperly administered. Maybe self-treating an injury; football can be rough on young bodies.

So can unrequited love, Terry thought.

He brought up the reports on Daniel King. Not much there. The same class as Janet. Only child of devoted older parents from St. Petersburg who came to all his games. They'd accepted the ruling of death by accidental overdose. The visit by investigators inquiring about Janet Barnes just a few months later perplexed them.

"We didn't know the girl," Jack was quoted as saying. "Dan never brought her home. Maybe we met her when we visited campus, but I can't be sure."

According to Teresa King, "they only dated two or three months, but Dan was certain she was his 'soul mate.' He fell in love pretty easily. Got his heart beat up more than once."

No accident, but suicide. In which case . . .

One note, thrown in almost haphazardly, jumped out and hit Terry like a slap across the face. What the hell? Had anyone followed up on that? Clearly not. And neither had he, though he must have looked at the case file dozens of times. He could engage in self-recrimination later. He had some legwork to do.

He ran a quick check and learned that the Kings had moved just down the coast to Bradenton. Close enough. He decided to pay them a visit.

SPRING

"Will people understand that love, not hate, guided me? I may never know. I'm not sure I care. I don't work as hard as I do in order to win admirers or score points. My actions have never been about anyone else's acceptance or entertainment. I simply do what needs to be done. To all of you. For all of us."

~ The Wedding Crasher

Chapter 34

The spring thaw that reached Tennessee in mid-March didn't extend to relations between Sam and her administrative assistant. Kaylee remained polite but distant. She came in, did her work, and left at five. She continued to keep her desktop neat as a pin but didn't touch anything in Sam's office. She limited her interactions with her boss. No more offers to fill Sam's mug. No more teasing the sheriff about her habits. No more advice, unsolicited or otherwise.

"At least you'll avoid death by coffee," Abdi observed.

"Very funny, Abdi. I happen to consider this a serious problem. The last thing I need or want is workplace tension."

"I reckon that ship has sailed. People around here are fixin' to jump out of their skin." He saw Sam's expression and immediately added, "That's not a bad thing. Some of us feel we might have a break in the case. That's got people motivated."

"I just hope we can all stay that way, Abdi. Surveilling TJ is a time-consuming and expensive proposition. That boy is covering a lot of territory."

Sam had assigned two deputies to watch Kaylee's son day and night. Abdi covered the weekends. "I want to know where he goes, who he meets, if he has any friends, all of it," she ordered. "Never engage, and I mean never. Take notes, take pictures, report. Period."

He went out every night, always out of town. Sometimes he ended up in a bar in Cookeville; other times he drove the one hundred twenty miles to Nashville. As often as not, he met up with another man on Broadway, the epicenter of the city's music and drug scene. TJ never bothered to be subtle about either the meeting or the exchange of money and product. His was one of half a dozen such interactions at any given moment.

"He's outside our jurisdiction," Abdi told Sam. "If he realizes we're watching him, he's giving us the finger."

"I suspect he's aware of our presence all right. He's also figured out we're not really interested in his drug habit."

She wondered if she'd erred by bringing him in for questioning. She had nothing she could use against him. She knew it and he knew it. The killer left no clues, no usable DNA or fingerprints. No eyewitnesses stepped forward with accounts of a young man fitting TJ's description anywhere near the park where Emily's body had been found. Or in the vicinity of Tara's car.

On a hunch, Sam had Abdi show the boy's picture around the Bluebird Café. Some of the younger patrons recognized him. No one could say how often he came in, only that he always seemed to be alone.

She wanted to search his room, search the entire Simpson property. She'd carefully broached the subject to a local judge, only to receive a stern talking-to about overreach. Bottom line, she couldn't turn her gut feeling into probable cause.

Every so often, she caught herself opening her desk drawer and staring at the bourbon she still kept stashed there. Other times she fought the urge to run out the door, up Main Street to where the road petered out, across the patchwork of small farms and groves of trees, and into Kentucky. How nice it would be to disappear. Or at least find another small town where a yoga-loving, poker-playing ex–law officer could hide out for a while.

Her nightmares made an appearance nearly every night now, populated by figures in dark hoodies or opaque wedding veils. The girl in the rose dress popped up from time to time to warn or advise or simply stand and point. Sam called Dr. Sommers, only to reach a recorded message explaining that the psychiatrist was on "an extended sabbatical." The message included a phone number of a colleague for MNPD employees who required counseling. Sam wasn't an employee, but she did put in a call to see when the doctor planned to return. No one had that information.

Work kept her from losing her mind. Her office spent the back half of February and into March caught up in a regional operation aimed at busting up an active drug ring. Deputies from Pickett, Fentress, Overton, and Clay Counties partnered with TBI to nab gang leaders operating across the four counties. She welcomed the distraction.

Meanwhile, she collected résumés to fill Tara's position, even though her heart wasn't in it. Ralph and Dana caught a driver wanted for vehicular manslaughter. Pickett County High School announced a date for the prom. Jerry scheduled another poker game for the beginning of April. Life went on as usual. If "usual" meant that people looked over their shoulders, barred their doors, and stayed in at night.

Abdi knocked on Sam's door on the first official day of spring and entered to find his boss sewing a button on a spare shirt.

"I found this in Tara's desk." He opened his hand to reveal a thin silver necklace with a single delicate charm.

"That doesn't look like something Tara would wear. Who knows, though? I'll get it to her mother." Something tugged at her, a recollection, an image. She pushed it aside.

Abdi dropped the necklace into a small plastic bag, which he placed on her desk. "I didn't expect to find you doing needlework, Sheriff," he said.

"Everybody in the army learns how to sew a button, Abdi. The military is equal opportunity that way." She looked up. "You probably had your sewing done for you, what with all those sisters."

Abdi pretended to be offended. "I know how to sew, at least enough to do basic work. My sisters taught me. I used to practice on their projects. Always someplace my mistakes wouldn't show."

Sam sat up straight, her mending forgotten. "My mother did the same thing with me. She told me I'd learn to be more careful if I worked on clothing I might have to wear." Her eyes widened. "Abdi Issen, you're a genius."

He blushed. "What convinced you?"

She told him.

Two days later, Sam met Nate Fillmore at TBI's Nashville Crime Lab. A modern brick-and-glass facility, the Crime Lab also boasted its own vault for evidence collected by the Criminal Investigative Division. Whatever investigators had collected from the Hooper and Newsome murder scenes still resided here.

"Let me get this straight," Nate began after they shook hands in the lobby. "You want to look at the bridal dress worn by the Newsome woman. Even though our experts already checked it for trace evidence."

"I'm not looking for trace evidence," Sam replied. "Actually, I'm not looking at all. I brought my own expert."

"And where is this expert?"

"Yoo-hoo. Here I am, ready to go."

The clarion greeting was followed by the voice's owner. Hattie McCoy emerged from the main-floor ladies' room, a revelation in living color. She wore an avocado-green dress accompanied by a voluminous scarf of cantaloupe, lemon, raspberry, and grape. The hues brought to mind a fruit basket. She'd wound the scarf around her neck and tied it so it appeared to bloom at one shoulder. Her shiny russet hair tumbled to her shoulders. Iridescent earrings dangled from each lobe, and a beaded bracelet of glass or gemstone twinkled on her right wrist.

Nate Fillmore stood stock-still, apparently dumbstruck by the vision before him. Sam coughed and thumped her chest to stifle her laughter.

"Thank you so much for allowing me that tiny respite, Sheriff," Hattie trilled. "The ride from Livingston is rather long, though the company delightful." She extended her manicured hand to Nate. "You must be Agent Fillmore. What an interesting job you have."

"Ms. McCoy—Hattie—sells vintage wedding dresses," Sam explained. "She knows as much about what goes into creating and altering a gown as anyone I can think of."

"I'm sure she does." Nate had recovered himself. He took the woman's hand and put his own on top of hers. "Thank you for coming, Ms. McCoy. And thank you for bringing your version of a beautiful spring day inside this dreary building. May I say you've done more to brighten up this place in a few minutes than anyone I can remember meeting in my twenty-year career."

Hattie blushed like a ripe strawberry. "I'm all about spreading a little cheer, Agent Fillmore."

"Shall we?" Nate asked as he offered the woman his arm.

Sam found herself smiling. She couldn't tell who was having more fun, Nate or Hattie.

The TBI agent pushed open a door off the main lobby and led them down a corridor to a windowless room. The dress in which Bitsy Newsome had been found was laid out on the table.

"This is what we call the 'triage room,' which is where we do a lot of detailed inspection," Nate explained. "You'll need to wear these." He offered a box of disposable gloves to Hattie, who carefully pulled on a pair, and to Sam, who shook her head.

"I'm only here to observe."

Once she donned the gloves and a pair of glasses, Hattie was all business. "If you could give me a little space, Agent Fillmore," she said politely but firmly. Nate stepped back.

"Now, the sheriff has asked me to assess the alterations and share my observations." Hattie spoke as if she were delivering a lecture. "I saw a photo of this dress several months ago. At that time, I suggested this was an older dress with an altered neckline that utterly destroyed its appeal. Some of my reaction might have stemmed from my proprietary interest in the piece, which I believed came from my store. I'm afraid I still can't be certain it is one of my dresses, and the sheriff's office hasn't tied my client list to this particular gown. I suppose that's fortunate." She fanned herself, then lifted one of the lace sleeves.

"While the recent changes have betrayed the designer's intent, which is, in my view, unforgiveable, the workmanship is beyond reproach. Although, hold on." Hattie bent over the dress until her nose almost touched the table. "Fascinating."

Sam felt her heart rate accelerate. She'd been careful on the drive over not to talk specifics or lead Hattie toward any conclusions. Whatever the woman might discover, she would do so without coaching.

"What is it?" Nate asked. He looked understandably skeptical. His forensics team had been over the dress more than once.

"You do realize two different people altered the dress, don't you?"

Nate appeared flummoxed. "I, uh—"

"Most of the handwork was done by an experienced sewer. However, someone else finished the hem at the bottom of the left sleeve. The stitches are larger, clumsier. Made by a less-experienced hand. Almost as if the principal seamstress turned over a tiny bit of piecework to an apprentice."

An apprentice. Sam bit her lip.

"One other thing. A running stitch, which is used to bind two pieces of material together, can give you some information. A hemming stitch, also known as a slip stitch, reveals a lot more. The stitches in a hand-sewn hem are directional, usually right to left. Take a look." She pointed to the hem of the gown. Nate leaned in, his attention riveted.

"Here is an admirable example of a whipstitch," Hattie continued. "The same work can be found on the right sleeve hem. However, the hem at the left sleeve is different. Not simply because the stitching is crooked. It also travels left to right. Which strongly suggests that someone else helped finish this gown. Someone inexperienced and likely left-handed."

Hattie looked sideways at Sam. "I hope this information proves useful."

"Son of a—gun," Nate said, catching himself at the last second. "Ms. McCoy—Hattie—you could teach a forensics class."

Hattie McCoy favored the agent with her most charming smile. "Why thank you, Agent Fillmore. I believe I'd enjoy that."

As for Sam, she fought the urge to throw her arms around Hattie McCoy. Instead, she leaned forward to tap the woman on the shoulder. "I can't begin to tell you how valuable your input has been today."

Hattie's joyous laugh filled the tiny room. "Well then, the trip was more than worth it."

On the drive back home, Sam half-listened to her companion's happy chatter and smiled or commented where suitable. Mostly she thought about the ties that bind. Between a sheriff and an FBI agent. Between a serial killer and a novice. Between family members.

Sam regretfully declined Hattie's invitation to lunch. She was hungry; she was also eager to share her news. As soon as she dropped the proprietress back at the shop, she dialed Terry.

"I'm glad you picked up. I've got something that connects the cases together."

"No kidding. I've got something that blows the cases apart. Where are you?"

The question surprised her. "Livingston, headed back to Byrdstown. About twenty minutes out. I just dropped off Hattie McCoy."

"Interesting. I'll see you when you get to the office."

"What? Where are you?" she yelled, but he'd disconnected.

Chapter 35

Sam hit the accelerator. She was prepared to use her siren, her horn, even her loudspeaker. Fortunately, traffic was light. Twenty minutes later, she pulled into the parking lot, saw the rental car, and sprinted for the door. She slowed herself down just as she reached for the handle.

Easy does it, Tate.

"What, you can't Skype or FaceTime like everybody else?" she said to Terry, who stood by Kaylee's desk, cup in hand. Kaylee was smiling up at Terry like a schoolgirl with a crush.

"I just got here. I'm on my way up to Chicago. Since I pass through Nashville, I thought I'd take a detour, grab a very late lunch or very early dinner with my favorite county sheriff. And grab a cup of Pickett County's finest coffee, of course." He toasted Kaylee, who tittered.

Sam fought to keep from rolling her eyes. She tried to match his over-the-top bonhomie.

"We're always glad to see you, Special Agent Sloan. Come on in." She waved Terry into her office. "Could you hold my calls, Kaylee?"

"Of course, Sheriff." Polite, formal.

Terry stepped into her office and locked the door behind him. His cheerful mien disappeared, as if the sun had dropped behind a cloud bank.

"How soundproof is your office, Sam?"

"Our conversation should be private as long as we don't shout."

"Fine, but I want to be careful."

"What's going on, Terry? I call you to tell you about a promising development and find you camped on my doorstep. I'm not buying your 'on-the-way-to-Chicago' story."

He threw his jacket on a chair and dropped his briefcase next to it. As an afterthought, he pried open the window and dumped his mug.

"As soon as I got the paperwork in hand, I hopped the first flight I could get. Between my badge and my flashers, I made record time. Passed right through security in Tampa and jumped to the head of the car rental line in Nashville."

Sam leaned against her desk, suddenly dizzy. "I'm sorry, I'm not following. Paperwork? Last-minute trips? What are you talking about?"

Instead of answering, he said, "Kaylee mentioned you were in Nashville. Too bad I didn't hitch a ride."

"That's why I called." She described her morning with Hattie and Nate. "I've got an inexperienced left-handed killer who had help with at least one of his victims. An inexperienced left-handed apprentice who helped hem the dress worn by the latest Wedding Crasher victim. This is not a coincidence, Terry. I've got all the pieces; I just have to put them together."

"I can help with that."

Sam pushed herself off the desk. "How?"

"I had to go back to the beginning, Sam. To Janet. She wasn't simply the first in a series of random victims chosen by a ritualistic killer. She was the very reason the killing began. The catalyst."

"Didn't you go down that road when you inherited the case files? What did Janet do? Who did she do it to? No one turned up any vengeful friends or relatives."

"Try this on for size. What if Dan King, the boy she dated before her engagement, didn't die of an overdose? What if he killed himself?"

Sam put a hand to her forehead. "And someone killed Janet to avenge Dan? And created an annual killing ritual? Who? His parents? Cousins? Friends? An ex-girlfriend? And why didn't the local authorities follow through with all this?"

"Remember, his death was ruled an accident, not a suicide or a homicide. No one back then delved into King's background. Which is why we all missed two crucial details."

"Which are?"

He popped the briefcase locks and withdrew a set of documents. She read through them twice, stopping the second time to absorb the full meaning of what she held in her hands.

"You've got to be kidding," she exclaimed. "Dan King was adopted?"

"Yes."

"And his birthday is in April."

"Right."

"Who was—?"

"Keep reading. Florida requires a court order to access sealed records. I managed to move things along. Lucky for me, the FBI has close relationships with at least a few Florida Family Court judges."

Sam looked down again at the legal papers and blinked. Terry had supplied her with the last piece of the puzzle. The entire ugly picture came into view. "Holy shit," she half-whispered. "It's not like that's a common name."

"I've got one more tidbit. Wait until you hear what Dan King—"

Terry stopped mid-sentence. The doorknob to Sam's office rotated, the movement nearly imperceptible. Then it rattled. A second or two of silence followed. Then they heard a sharp rapping.

"Someone wants in," Terry said.

Sam yanked open the door, nearly sending Kaylee to the floor with a full pot of steaming coffee. Remarkably, she managed not to spill even a drop as she tripped into the office.

"I keep forgetting you lock your doors now, Sheriff Tate. If I didn't know better, I'd guess you were napping. Or plotting in secret." She tilted her head as if she expected an apology or an explanation.

"How about some coffee?" Terry held out his mug. Kaylee pretended not to notice. She walked over to Sam's desk to fill her cup. She put down the pot, began to straighten a couple of folders Sam left there, plainly marked with the names of the last three homicides.

"How was your trip to Nashville, Sheriff? Did you find what you were looking for?"

Sam opened her mouth, glanced at Terry, and shut it. Kaylee had gone from standoffish to being as chatty as a magpie.

"I'll take some of that coffee, Kaylee." Terry stuck his mug right under her nose, breaking her sightline to the folders. She poured and watched him as he sipped. He drank it without grimacing.

"Thanks, Kaylee. I don't know how Sheriff Tate ever managed without you."

"She's never had to, Agent Sloan, at least not since she's become sheriff. I don't think she likes my coffee, though." She approximated a chuckle.

"You've been here, what, three years?" Terry continued as if picking up a conversational thread.

"I have indeed, Agent Sloan."

"And before that, you were down south somewhere. Georgia, wasn't it?"

"That's right."

"Moving. That's gotta be a strain on the family."

"We did all right."

"I imagine you could have gotten a health-care job up here. You trained as a nurse, didn't you? Yet you chose to work in the sheriff's office. Maybe the hours are better. Pay's not as good, though. That matters when you have three boys to feed. It is three, isn't it?"

"My goodness, Agent Sloan. I guess you think you know just about everything there is to know about me and my family." Kaylee's blue eyes darkened. "The thing is, plans don't always work out the way we intend. Careers change. Locations change. Lives change. Sheriff Jackson gave me this job and I was glad to get it. Sheriff Tate invited me to stay on. I have no complaints." Her restrained expression suggested otherwise. "Now if you'll both excuse me, I have work to do."

"How's TJ?" Sam asked in what she hoped was a relaxed tone.

The assistant sighed. "He was a little shook up, to tell the truth. Beneath his tough-guy exterior, he's really very sensitive. You know how kids are. No, I guess you wouldn't."

Sam overlooked the barb. "Kaylee, I hope you understand—"

"That you were doing your job? I do, Sheriff Tate, I honestly do. Water under the bridge, so to speak. TJ—oh gosh, that's hard to remember; I keep wanting to call him Tommy—has almost made up his schoolwork. He's on track to graduate the end of the coming summer. And then, well, we'll see. College, I expect." Kaylee beamed.

"Glad to hear it. By the way, I noticed you looking at the folders on the desk."

"Not really, Sheriff. I just—"

"You might be interested to know we found a connection between all the murders."

Terry moved to the window. He stared through the glass as if he found something fascinating outside. A streetlamp, a car, a patch of grass, a bud on a tree branch.

"You don't say? Good for you, Sheriff. I'll just be—"

"What threw us were the differences between Emily's murder and the earlier ones. No bridal outfit, no missing finger, different manner of death. Yet one odd detail matched. The Wedding Crasher's victims all ended up lying under white oak trees. A particular detail not made public but known by Emily's murderer as well."

"Is that why you brought TJ in?" Kaylee sighed with relief. "You thought his tree tattoo meant something? Please. He's going through a phase."

"So, trees don't hold any significance for him? Or you?"

"What on earth are you talking about?"

"I noticed you wear an oak leaf on a chain. Every day for as long as I can remember."

Kaylee, caught off guard, brought her free hand to her neck. "This? It's just a trinket. I can't even remember where I got it."

"You sure about that? Looks brand-new. Maybe you bought a replacement for the one you lost over by Deputy Fence's desk." Sam opened her hand to reveal a tiny silver leaf just like the one Kaylee wore.

"I can't imagine what you think—"

"I think you were trying to help TJ," Sam interrupted. "I think you found a way to get into Tara's locked desk and remove anything she jotted down about the Upshaw murder, including notes about her meeting with TJ at Bobcat Den. I think you provided the alibis to get him off the hook for the two murders. Maybe you even asked him to stand down after he shot at me. Twice."

"He's just a boy," Kaylee whispered.

Terry spoke up. "He's the same age you were when you gave up your first child."

Kaylee fixed him with an icy stare. "You're confused, Agent. TJ is my eldest."

"I mean the child you had at seventeen. The one you put up for adoption. Not that you had a choice. You were an unwed teenaged mother, just like your mother had been. That's why she encouraged you to give up the child. Tough situation."

"I—"

"Florida law is strict about adoptions," Terry went on. "You couldn't have contacted the boy until he turned twenty-one. But you located him, didn't you? Then you watched his life unfold from the sidelines."

Terry had acquired an edge to his voice. "Dan King. The boy who wanted to become a forest ranger. The boy who chose a school where he could major in dendrology, the study of woody plants. The reliable football player whose teammates called him White Oak. A questionable nickname, but these things happen in college. The student who never made it to his twenty-first birthday. The hopeless romantic who got his heart busted, thanks to Janet Barnes."

Kaylee stood like a statue, white knuckling the carafe. Sam desperately wanted her to say something, do something. Start talking. Stop lying. Put down the damned coffee pot.

"Why did you involve TJ, Kaylee?" she asked. "Do you wonder he turned to drugs after what you put him through? Or that he became a murderer?" She tapped her head. "What were you thinking, making him your apprentice? What were you trying to teach your boy?"

"What do you think she taught him?" Terry broke in angrily. "That murder is acceptable? Or butchery is honorable? How about this: Girls that look like girls who hurt your feelings deserve to die."

"You don't know what it's been like," Kaylee protested.

"Oh, we do, Kaylee," Sam corrected her. "We know about heartbreak, about pain. About the courage it takes to move on, about the futility of staying in the past." She glanced at Terry.

"You're not parents. You can't understand, either of you."

"Reality check, Kaylee," Terry said. "Killing five innocent young women doesn't make you a caring mother. It makes you a vengeful bitch. Enlisting your son to help you doesn't make you a good parent. It makes you a monster."

Kaylee howled, a primitive sound that mixed grief, fear, and rage. She hurled the coffeepot at Terry's head and fled through the door. Sam jumped in the air, half receiver, half ballerina, and caught the carafe midair as

Terry moved forward. The two of them went crashing to the floor. Sam landed on top of Terry, drenched in coffee but still holding the carafe more or less upright.

"Shit!" Sam yelled as she struggled to her feet.

Terry grabbed her by the elbows. "Are you hurt?" he demanded.

"Only my pride. What about you?"

"I'm fine. We gotta move."

Chapter 36

They almost bowled over Abdi and Dana on the way out. The near misses were piling up.

"What the hell, Sheriff?" Abdi exclaimed. "Kaylee just bolted out of here like a jackrabbit."

"Did you see where she went?" Sam got out the front door in time to see the Mazda SUV race south on Main Street. Terry tugged on her sleeve. She realized she must look like a madwoman to her staff, dripping coffee and screaming like a banshee.

Breathe, Tate.

She turned to the staff and spoke as calmly as she could. "We have a situation, people," she said. "Kaylee Simpson is the prime suspect in the Wedding Crasher murders. She's on the run. Her son TJ is an accomplice and is also a suspect in the deaths of Emily Upshaw and Tara Fence. If he's not with her already, he will be."

She read the shock in their faces.

"I know this is a lot to process. Right now, we have some coordinating to do." Sam pointed to the dispatcher who'd joined the group in the main room. "Rosie, send out a BOLO. 'Suspect is a blond Caucasian female, mid-forties, highly agitated. She may be armed. Approach with caution.' Make sure this reaches the sheriffs in the five surrounding counties, the Highway Patrol, TBI, and the FBI field office. Any questions come back to you, run them by Special Agent Sloan."

She looked at Terry for confirmation. He was already on the phone, probably to Darryl.

"Cob," she continued, "call the school and have them pull TJ out of class. Then go pick up the boy and bring him here. Take someone with you."

Terry hung up. "Darryl's on his way over. We need to launch a coordinated manhunt. Local, state, federal. You okay with having your office serve as command central?"

"Good a place as any."

"Sheriff." Cob had his hand over the phone receiver. "The school says TJ Simpson got a text in class and took off like a bat out of hell."

"Okay. Get hold of Jeff Simpson. Tell him to pull his other two kids out of school and come to the station. No details. If he asks if he needs a lawyer, tell him it's his decision. Rosie, update the BOLO to include an eighteen-year-old male, possibly armed." She turned to Terry. "I've got to call the mayor, the commissioners, the district attorney general . . ."

"In a minute. Go change."

She looked down at her coffee-soaked shirt. "You're right." She dashed back into her office, pulling on a dry shirt and removing the wet one in one move.

"Neat trick. You learn that in the army?"

"No, backstage at a dozen small Nashville dives." She jerked her head up. "We gotta send someone to Kaylee's house. What if—?"

"She won't be there," Terry declared. "But you might find evidence that will tell us where she is. Go. Take backup."

"What do you want the rest of us to do, Sheriff?" one of the deputies asked.

"Clear your desks, check your weapons, and hang tight. Agent Sloan is running point on the manhunt. All of you will be involved one way or the other. Abdi, Ralph, gear up and come with me."

The men grabbed their guns and their vests.

It took just six minutes for them to reach the Simpson home, a relatively new two-story brick house just outside the town limits. Two-car garage, open and empty.

"Probable cause?" she asked Abdi.

"Place is wide open."

Sam signaled Ralph to circle the house. She and Abdi entered with guns drawn, startling a calico cat. The place was tidy and plain vanilla enlivened with embroidered pillows, a hand-knit throw, a wall tapestry, a bouquet of papier-mâché flowers in a glass vase with clear beads.

They quickly cleared the rooms on the first and second floors. Nothing appeared out of place.

"I found a workshop out back," Ralph reported. "Standard collection of tools, no knives or cleavers. An empty box of rifle ammo. No rifle." He held up a metal crowbar. "I borrowed this just in case."

In the kitchen they found a wooden door fixed with a wraparound keyless lock. Sam turned in a circle, pointed.

"The utilities are over there. Washer/dryer is on the second floor. So, what's downstairs and why does it need protection?" She pushed at the door; it swung away from her.

"Another unlocked door," Abdi observed. "Someone was in a hurry."

They drew their weapons and tiptoed single file down the stairs. Sam strained to hear anything. Voices. Footsteps. An intake of breath.

A flip of the wall switch revealed what looked like a partially finished room with two lamps and a hooked rug on the floor. The space was neatly appointed, comfortable and almost homey. Several satin pillows were piled next to a box of candles. A wooden spool-holder shared space with a deep bowl filled with ribbons. A long white dress hung in a makeshift closet. Shelves were neatly stacked with fabric, mostly remnants. A pair of ripped jeans, a man's flannel shirt, and a kitchen towel perched on the edge of an ironing board next to a late-model sewing machine. Neat as a pin, except for an open trunk, its contents tossed, and a hanger lying on the floor.

"Off-limits to the Simpson men, I'd guess," Abdi said.

"Except maybe Tommy," Sam replied. "Gloves on, people."

A laptop, a Rolodex, and a box with business cards sat at one corner of a small wooden desk. Abdi plucked out a card. "Says here she's an 'expert seamstress specializing in formal wear.' Handy if you're into postmortem tailoring."

Sam pulled at the desk drawers until she found the locked one. Ralph smashed the handle.

"Let's hope you don't find a container full of fingers," Abdi muttered.

"Nope." She held up an empty box with the image of a falcon printed on the side.

Ralph whistled. "Kestrel. That's about the lightest knife made. Aerospace-grade titanium and top-quality stainless steel. Carves through just about anything."

"Including unconscious people." Sam pulled out a bottle of small white pills.

"You think she killed them here?" Abdi asked.

"No. Not with her family upstairs. I'm guessing she met them somewhere, maybe at their homes, knocked them unconscious, had Tommy meet her, drove to an unknown place—a parking lot or an abandoned building—and slit their throats. Then it's off to the woods. And this"—Sam reached on a top shelf and pulled down a roll of plastic sheeting—"helped keep the staging area clean."

"What do you want to do now?"

"You and I are headed back, Abdi. Ralph, this house is now a crime scene. I need you to seal it off and wait for the forensic investigators to go over it with a fine-tooth comb."

"Yes, ma'am." If Ralph was disappointed not to be part of the manhunt, he kept it to himself.

When they got back, they found the conference room crammed with deputies, investigators, and agents. Nate Fillmore and Darryl Cutler hovered over a map of Tennessee spread on the table. A state trooper stood at the whiteboard. Jeff Simpson and his younger sons waited in Sam's office looking dazed and exhausted.

"We're almost up to speed," Terry told her. "I gather you didn't find our suspects?"

"Just enough evidence to put them away." She didn't add, "if we catch them." She didn't need to.

He rested a hand lightly on Sam's arm. "We will resolve this." He nodded towards the office. "You need a word, I'd guess."

Sam sent the two boys off with Dana. She told Jeff Simpson as much as she could in as straightforward a manner as possible.

"I don't understand, Sheriff. You think my wife is the Wedding Crasher? And my son is an accomplice? How? Why?" The man's despair lay just beneath his thin mask of composure.

"We're piecing together the how based on evidence we found in the basement of your house, Mr. Simpson. As for why, I can only say she clearly felt the need to"—she searched for the right word—"mark the death of her eldest child. You knew she had a son out of wedlock?"

"I—yes, she told me. She was just a kid. She had a lot of regrets and some perhaps unrealistic expectations that she could meet him when he turned twenty-one. That would have been seven or eight years ago. When I asked her back then, she said it didn't matter anymore."

"The boy, Daniel, was already dead at that point."

"What? She wouldn't have murdered him!"

"No, Dan King killed himself. Kaylee allegedly murdered the girl she held responsible for his suicide. Then she apparently kept on killing young women who looked like the first one, even as your family moved from Florida to Georgia and up here. One each spring, except when TJ was in rehab."

Simpson remained superficially calm. He's in shock, Sam decided.

"And you believe my son helped her with this—ritual—over seven years?"

"Yes."

He gulped and swallowed several times before he could continue. "What about the Upshaw girl?"

"Emily Upshaw and Tara Fence were both killed by TJ. We believe Kaylee stepped in to help in the first instance. Tara died because her suspicions alarmed TJ. He also shot at me with a rifle near my home and again near a shopping mall in Nashville. He used a gun that time."

"I don't even own a gun."

"Mr. Simpson—"

"Do you know where they are now? Kaylee and Tommy?" The man had gone white.

"No. We think they may be planning another ritual."

"Another murder."

"We're about to launch a manhunt."

"God almighty." The façade cracked. Jeff Simpson covered his eyes, lowered his head, and wept with his whole body.

Sam slipped outside and closed the door. His younger sons were playing a video game.

Dana looked up from her desk and came over. "What do you need me to do, Sheriff?" she asked.

"Give the father a moment, then let the kids back into the room. They all need to be together. I'm gonna want you to call around, see if you can find Mr. Simpson and his family a place to stay. I don't know if they have friends they can trust."

"Somebody will help," Dana said with absolute conviction.

Terry met her at the conference room door as the meeting began to break up.

"We've got six teams headed to check state parks within a hundred miles of Byrdstown. Other agents are coordinating with the National Park Service to comb Big South Fork. It's a large area, but we want to cover all the bases. We'll have at least one chopper at our disposal, which may cut our time." He looked at his watch. "We've got maybe three hours of daylight left. Oh, and I've asked the Highway Patrol to watch the southern routes out of the state in case mother and son decided to head back to Florida."

"They didn't."

His eyes searched hers. "What did you figure out?"

"Is Dale Hollow Lake State Park on your list?"

He glanced at his notebook. "Yeah, why?"

"That's where we'll find them."

"Do you want to pull everyone else off?"

"Not yet. I'm operating on an informed hunch."

"Those are the best kind."

Cars sped off in all directions, a kaleidoscope of flashing lights and screaming sirens. Sam pointed at two deputies and a state trooper. "You, you, and you. Follow us," she ordered.

Sam, Terry, Abdi, and Darryl piled into Sam's vehicle. Terry drove while Sam punched in the GPS coordinates.

"What makes you think they're headed to Dale Hollow?" Darryl asked.

Sam pivoted in her seat to face him. "*Pickett County Press* ran a story last week about a stand of oak trees on the east side of the lake that might be the oldest in the state. That's a big deal in Tennessee. The Landmark and Historic Tree Registry sent some people out to look. Kaylee had the article up on her computer."

Darryl nodded. "The symbolism is important to her."

"I don't know how she's going to pull off another ritual, though. Unless she already had another victim in mind. Do you think she's grabbed some brunette along the way?"

"Not this time." Terry answered.

"How do you figure?"

Terry gripped the steering wheel more tightly. "I don't think she needs anyone else. I think this is her final ritual."

Chapter 37

They sped along the winding back road that led to the eastern shore of Dale Hollow Lake. Sam didn't bother to calm her racing heart. She wanted to feel the adrenaline. The more, the better.

She brought up the *Pickett County Press* article on her phone. "I need to get in touch with Connor Jefferson," she told the others. "He's the forester with the Department of Agriculture who's quoted in the story. I really hope he's not on vacation."

She reached Jefferson, who sounded both puzzled and delighted to hear from her. "I had no idea the sheriff's office shared our excitement about protecting the state's old trees," he said.

"It's more than that, I'm afraid. Your old trees might be the setting for a serious crime. I need to know precisely where they're located."

"Well, that was not what I expected to hear. Okay, meet me at the Star Point Resort and I'll get you to the site."

The resort was a collection of rental cabins that squatted along the lake. A narrow access road led to a small parking area. All seven officers slid out of the two cars with vests on and weapons at the ready. They stayed close to the vehicles and low to the ground.

"Over there." Sam pointed. Kaylee's Mazda was parked in the far corner next to the beater Tommy sometimes drove.

A state vehicle drove into the area and a tall man in uniform jumped out with a hearty wave. Connor Jefferson.

Sam fumbled for her phone and called him. "Ranger Jefferson, could you get back in your vehicle, please?"

"Don't need to tell me twice," he responded and popped back inside like a reverse jack-in-the-box.

Abdi, Darryl, and Terry moved into position by Kaylee's car. The others eased up to the driver's side of the blue Mazda. Hand signals sent them to rush the doors.

Unlocked. And empty.

Sam knocked on Jefferson's window. The ranger opened the door and unfolded himself. He was probably six foot five, with smooth walnut skin and abundant white hair. His glasses lent him a scholarly look.

"Sheriff Tate," he said with a broad smile. "Looks like we're hitting the ground running. I gather those cars belong to the people you're tracking down."

Sam shook his proffered hand, then made quick introductions. "Our suspects are here. At least I presume they are." She looked down at the ground. "No sign anyone's driven out of the lot recently."

"This is where most people might leave their vehicles," Jefferson said. "I've got a way to get us a little closer."

"You can direct us to the location and stay behind, if you'd rather."

"And miss all the excitement, Sheriff Tate? Not a chance." Jefferson reached back into his car's glove compartment and pulled out a Sig Sauer P365. He offered a grim smile in response to Sam's surprised expression. "Rangers these days tend to follow the Boy Scout motto," he said. "You know; be prepared."

They piled back into two cars and drove along a finger of land on a road that finally petered out. Jefferson called a halt. "At this point, the only way in is on foot," he told the group.

They crept single file along a little-used trail for about a quarter mile. Jefferson stayed up front, apparently comfortable with taking the lead and taking a chance they were walking into an ambush. Sam followed close behind, then Terry, and Darryl. The deputies and the state trooper brought up the rear.

Pickett County enjoyed a flawless spring day of moderate temperatures and low humidity. Soft breezes stirred the new leaves, birdsong filled the air, dappled sunlight lit their path. A profusion of early wildflowers dotted the landscape to each side. Sam made a conscious effort to slow her breathing. As much as she wanted to yell "let's go!" and sprint ahead of the others, she held herself back. The situation demanded caution.

They finally came to a hillock adjacent to the shore. Five oaks stood just visible over the rise, their branches intertwined like friends around a campfire. Broad and tall, they dominated the little mound of land. Most of the trees were in early bloom, their pale gray bark healthy, their young leaves a deep glossy green. The limbs formed a protective canopy much like the one she'd sat beneath last winter. This time of year, the foliage filtered the sunlight, causing patches of light and dark.

Connor Jefferson stood and pointed, as stately and prepossessing as one of his beloved trees. His white hair glinted in a shaft of sunlight. Sam was just thinking he made a perfect target when staccato rifle fire pierced the relative quiet. The sound bounced off the nearby water. Sam counted four shots. Jefferson toppled like timber.

"Everybody down!" Terry roared.

Sam and Abdi scrambled to the fallen ranger, who struggled to a seated position, his hand to his head. Blood leaked through his fingers.

"I'm okay," he gasped. "It's just a graze from a single bullet. Height has certain disadvantages. However, it seems your suspect isn't a particularly good shot." His words tumbled over one another.

"Detective," he continued, "if you reach into the small bag strapped around my waist, you'll find some antibiotic cream and a gauze bandage. I realize triage under fire is not optimal."

"You really are prepared," Abdi said with a touch of admiration.

"Take care of him, Abdi," Sam told her second. Then she stood, both arms in the air. "Kaylee," she called out. "Stop shooting and talk to me."

"Sam!" Terry barked.

She ignored him. She took a couple of steps off the path and up a moderate incline. "Kaylee, please," she said again. "Tell me what I can do to help."

"Help, Sheriff?" Kaylee still wasn't visible, but she sounded calm, almost relaxed. "How? Do you want a part in my ritual? Probably not. You're more an observer than a participant. Or do you think you can pull some strings and keep me out of jail? I'm sorry, I don't believe you have that kind of clout. Wait, maybe you think you can help me with my pain or my guilt or whatever Agent Sloan's profilers have decided is driving me. That's a bit of a reach, don't you think? Given your own issues."

"Kaylee, I just want to—" Sam took a step.

"Do not move, Sheriff Tate." Kaylee's voice hardened. "Not one damned inch or I'll blow your head off. Good. Now, let me ask you this: Do you think you can help bring back either of my two sons? Can you do that? Are you that special?"

"Two sons? Kaylee, what are you talking about?"

Sam strode to the crest, praying she could avoid a bullet to the head, and stopped short.

Kaylee Simpson stood over the body of her son, a shotgun pointed at Sam's chest. The young man, in black slacks and a jacket, lay with his hands crossed one over the other. Coppery blood covered the upper half of his body and pooled on the ground, yet his face appeared untouched. Even in death, TJ Simpson wore a faint scowl.

Kaylee was dressed in a knee-length, elbow-sleeved toffee-colored silk dress. Other than a discreet red spray across the hemline and a single drop on her matching *peau de soie* shoes, she'd managed to avoid getting splattered by her son's blood. Instead, she looked for all the world like a cocktail party hostess who had suddenly decided to take everyone hostage.

"Oh, Kaylee."

"Sorry I didn't have a chance to clean up, Sheriff Tate. I was a bit pressed for time. Goodness, don't look so upset. It's for the best. TJ got himself up here, even took his own drugs. Made it easier. He was troubled, you know. Both my boys were troubled. But they were good boys."

She shook her head; her face cleared and her mood lightened, almost as if she were channeling a different Kaylee.

"By the way, I'm dying to ask you, girl to girl, what do you think of my outfit? I've had this for nearly eight years and this is the first time I've ever had a chance to wear it. You look surprised. I bet Special Agent Sloan wouldn't be surprised, though. Let's bring him on up here. I'd love to get his opinion. He can at least pretend to like my dress. He's quite good at pretending, I've come to realize."

Behind her, Sam sensed rather than saw Terry walk up beside her, his gun trained on Kaylee. The others took up positions just behind them.

"Here I am, Kaylee, and I'm not gonna pretend," he said. "Your situation is not good. You're responsible for six murders. That is hard time in a federal penitentiary. On the other hand, it doesn't have to be a death sentence."

Kaylee gave a jagged laugh. "That's a lie, Agent Sloan. We both know it. I don't care, though. I don't plan on going to jail. I won't do that to Jeff and my other boys."

"What do you want, Kaylee?" Sam asked.

"I want to complete my ritual."

"Can you do that? It's not April. You don't have a bride." *Jesus, I hope she doesn't think I'm going to volunteer.*

"I don't need it to be April, Sheriff, and I don't need a bride. The ritual is a means to an end. I created it, and I can change the specifics. You still haven't figured that out, have you? You're so stupid. You're all so damned stupid."

She swung the rifle left to right without firing, sending Sam and the others into a crouch.

"What matters," Kaylee continued, "is the intention."

"Why don't you tell us what you mean, Kaylee," Terry asked. Trying to keep her talking. "What is the intention?"

Kaylee smiled, a slow expression that spread across her face and lit it from within.

"To honor the dead, Agent Sloan. That's what you and your profilers never understood. That's all that matters. That, and finishing what I started."

Kaylee cradled the rifle in one arm but kept her finger on the trigger. She reached into her belt and pulled out a knife.

"Rifle or knife? Obviously, I prefer the latter. It's messy, though, and I hate to leave a mess. On the other hand, it will become your mess. Yours and Agent Sloan's. I think that's fitting, don't you?"

She raised her knife to the left side of her neck and executed a deep cut, then managed to slice the right side, though not as deeply. She dropped the gun and sank to her knees as the blood arced from the two wounds like a fountain.

"I . . . just need a little more . . . time . . ." she said and fell over.

Terry shot forward, Sam on his heels. Kaylee lay at a right angle to her son, a smile on her face. She still clutched the knife. A deadly, efficient-looking instrument, equal parts blade and handle. Sam kicked it away as the hand that held it began to relax.

"Hang on, Kaylee," Terry said. He knelt in the blood and dirt, barely avoiding the copious spray, and put a hand on each wound. "If I can just slow this down . . ."

Kaylee raised an arm and batted away his hands. "No."

They went back and forth for precious seconds, Terry trying to staunch the flow and Kaylee struggling against him, even as her strength ebbed. Finally, she got hold of his wrist. "Let me go," she said, her voice soft but clear.

Sam put a hand on his arm. "Do what she says."

Terry sat back on his haunches. The fountain of blood became a stream, then a trickle. Kaylee took a deep, shuddering breath and mouthed the words "thank you." Then she turned her head to the trees she revered and died.

"Abdi," Sam said, "call Nate and Doc Holloway. Unless"—she looked at Darryl—"you want to call in your people."

"Nate's closer," Darryl said. Sam had never seen him look so shaken.

She stared at the dead woman. Three years she'd sat outside Sam's office, giggling, flirting, making silly jokes and bad coffee for the staff. All that time and for years before, the woman had harbored deep resentments, assuaged only by the annual performance of a scripted ritual that ultimately claimed the lives of nine people.

Terry stood up and wiped bloodied hands on saturated jeans to little effect. "I'm guessing forensics will want my clothes."

"Hold on," Sam told him. "They'll be here soon."

"Speaking of clothes, what's she wearing?" asked one of the deputies, nodding at the still figure in the beige dress. "That's no bridal gown."

"No," Terry replied. "She's dressed as the mother of the groom."

Chapter 38

Jeff Simpson asked Dana to clear out Kaylee's desk and throw the contents in the trash. Then, in short order, he quit his job, packed up his house, put it on the market, pulled his two boys out of school, and left town. No one knew exactly when he departed or where he went.

Several days after Sam drove by the empty house, she got a call from a Harlan Joist, who identified himself as director of Silas Crematorium in Nashville.

"Your name was left with us by Mr. Jeffrey Simpson as a responsible party," he informed her.

"Responsible party?"

Joist covered his discomfort with an apologetic cough. "Yes, well, this is a bit awkward. Mr. Simpson arranged to have his wife and son cremated after their remains were, ah, released from the medical examiner's office. However, he seems to have left the decision as to disposal of the ashes with you."

"With me."

Another cough. "We can take care of it here for a small fee, you understand. Unfortunately, Mr. Simpson's payment didn't cover that cost."

"I'll come get them."

Sam drove to Nashville the next day, picked up two plain urns (included free of charge), and headed from there directly to the Obey River Recreation Area. She scattered the ashes under the same trees she'd sat beneath last winter. She couldn't have explained why she needed to do what she did. It occurred to her she might be breaking an ordinance or two. She reckoned no one would question the county sheriff.

The Wedding Crasher story dominated the news for several weeks. Sam spent as much time as possible in the office. A providential bout of laryngitis allowed her to croak her way through a single press conference. Sallie Mae Davenport, Sam's new administrative assistant, directed most inquiries either to Calvin Jakes or to the mayor's office. Terry handled the bulk of the interviews, while Abdi ably represented Pickett County Sheriff's Office as needed. Becky Rattle once again stood sentry at the front door.

The arrangement worked. The FBI welcomed the positive publicity attached to catching a notorious serial killer. Jerry O'Neil assumed bragging rights on behalf of "one of the finest groups of law officers this side of the Mississippi." Billy Owens endorsed Abdi as Sam's choice of spokesperson. "Makes us look forward-thinking, if you catch my drift," he chortled. "I tell you what, Sam. You should be very pleased."

She didn't feel pleased, not in the least. She felt the burden of the five deaths, including Kaylee and TJ, that had occurred on her watch. Worse, the woman responsible had worked in Sam's department while her equally murderous offspring attended the local school. Her staff remained shell-shocked. A pall hung over the office. Sam suspected many of the deputies questioned their judgment. Questioned hers as well, which they had every right to do.

One morning, she called an impromptu meeting in the main room. "It's gonna take us time to recover," she told the assemblage. "Expect to feel grief and a fair amount of confusion. But know this. You performed to capacity, each and every one of you. I am as proud to serve with you as I have ever been to serve with anyone."

Her speech had the desired effect. Chins lifted and shoulders squared.

"Your talk definitely helped," Abdi told her afterwards. He let a beat go by. "She fooled us all. But we caught her."

Sam opened her mouth to object. Her trusted second put his hand up, exactly as she always did. "We caught her, Sheriff Tate. That's what's important here."

She had another dream, one she managed to remember. In it, she played both hunter and hunted. Dressed in a robe of rose silk, she stalked a version of Kaylee Simpson and finally cornered the woman in a tree. The tree morphed into the warehouse where she'd saved her partner with a precision kill shot four years earlier. This time when Sam fired, Kaylee disappeared behind a curtain of tulle and organza.

"You missed," she heard a child whisper.

"Missed what?" she asked just before she woke up.

Efforts to reach Dr. Sommers again proved fruitless. "My friends downtown tell me she's on some sort of extended leave," Eddie Gould reported. "Nobody can say why or for how long. Who knows? Maybe she's in witness protection." He laughed; Sam didn't join in. The doctor's mysterious disappearance worried her, and not because she needed a shrink.

The media circus finally packed up and left town. So did Terry. She tried and failed to ignore the hurt in her heart. It wasn't like she could ask him to stay in Pickett County indefinitely. His vague assurances that he would be in touch soon did nothing to assuage her anxiety over his departure.

Emily Upshaw's class prepared for graduation. The family announced a scholarship in the girl's name. The school decided to rename a reading room in Tara's memory. Sam was asked to attend both ceremonies.

The newest department hire, Michelle Tyler, continued to adjust well. The Memphis native had more experience and training than Sam usually saw in new recruits. She'd followed her cop father into police work, met her life partner, and adopted a baby girl. When Sam asked Michelle why she'd abandoned city life to move her family to such an unsophisticated burg, the woman answered with a straight face, "I like to fish."

Aunt Gillian telephoned just before Memorial weekend. "Congratulations," she told her niece. "You've caught not one killer but two. Are they going to make you mayor?"

"They're going to let me keep my job," Sam laughed. "And before you ask, yes, I am coming to visit. I've just got to clear my desk a little."

"That's nice, dear. Only—" Her aunt faltered; her voice cracked. "Can you make it sooner rather than later?"

"Gillian, you don't sound right. What's wrong. Is it Ma?"

"Your mother is okay. I'm afraid I'm not. I didn't want to bother you."

"Stop. Where are you?"

"In the hospital. My cousin Karen flew in three days ago. But I'm going home because, well, everything seems to be moving faster than expected."

Sam was on a plane the next day. Ten days later, she found herself in the front row of the Presbyterian Church of Dover, sandwiched between Cousin Karen and Uncle Vernon in a black stretch dress she picked up at Target.

In front of her, a younger Gillian smiled from a photo perched on an easel near the altar.

One week. That's all she had with the woman who'd raised her from the time she was a traumatized nine-year-old until she fled her adopted home to become a student, a singer, a soldier, and finally a cop. The cancer had progressed rapidly, as if eager to devour its host and move on to other hapless victims.

The ghost in the bed, with its wispy hair and skeletal body, looked nothing like her beautiful aunt. The mind, though, remained sharp as a tack through the fog of pain. They held hands and exchanged stories. Gillian joked about not living long enough to collect Social Security. Sam sang to her aunt in a clear low voice.

Gone, just like that.

The church filled to near capacity. *Who are all these people?* Sam wondered. Not relatives; only a handful survived. She recognized a few faces: Gillian's colleagues from the university, local friends and neighbors, members of the congregation. People Gillian and Kevin added to the support structure they'd built from scratch. People they'd touched.

Sam shook her head and bit back tears. *You were loved, Gillian,* she told the smiling image. *So were you, my dear,* she imagined her aunt saying.

She stayed in Dover two more days, then caught an early-morning flight back. She splurged on an Uber to Byrdstown instead of requesting a pickup. She wanted a couple of hours to decompress. She tried to reach Terry, suddenly anxious to talk with him. The call went to voice mail.

Abdi poked his head into her office that afternoon. "I'm sorry about your aunt."

“Thanks. Can you come in a minute? Shut the door and pull up a chair.”

She told him as much about the defining incident of her childhood as she could as quickly as she could. A summary, almost like a police report, that covered the dry facts about who did what to whom and what happened afterwards: who took care of the two surviving family members, how Sophie Russo of Queens, New York, became Sophie Walsh of Dover, Delaware, before insisting on a new name entirely once she turned eighteen. How the gunman named Arthur Randolph lived and surprised everyone by dying. She briefly addressed her nagging concerns that the past wasn’t completely buried. She even mentioned her dreams without going into detail.

Abdi struggled to remain composed. “Damn,” he finally blurted out. “I can see

why you’re not a fan of weddings.”

Sam couldn’t help it; she burst out laughing and felt her chest loosen. She wiped her eyes with both hands. “Thank you for making this easier, Abdi.”

“Anytime. Although—you don’t have more to share, do you?”

“Nope, you’re all caught up.” She laughed again. “For now, let’s keep this between us. Eventually, it won’t matter.”

“I can keep a secret, Sheriff.”

She smiled. “Call me Sam.”

Chapter 39

Two days later, Terry showed up at her office at six P.M. No notice.

"We gotta stop meeting like this, Agent Sloan," Sam told him.

"I was in Cookeville to wrap things up," he protested. "Scout's honor. Ask Sallie Mae."

Sallie Mae blushed like a primrose. "That's what he told me, Sheriff."

"Well, all right. Step into my office."

He entered behind her. The door shut and locked behind him. He looked over his shoulder, startled.

"I just had it installed," Sam told him. "Now all I have to do is remember to keep a set of keys with me if I head to the ladies' room."

"I heard about Gillian, Sam. I can't tell you how sorry I am. Why didn't you call?"

"Everything happened so fast. I had a week. Besides, it's not like you were going to fly up to Delaware and hold my hand." She exhaled. "Sorry, I haven't been able to process any of it. I'll have to go back, of course. To make arrangements."

"Your mother—"

"My mother doesn't walk, doesn't talk, doesn't read. Probably doesn't remember she once had a husband or a son and still has a daughter. She may not know if it's Tuesday or Christmas, if she lives in Delaware or Denmark, if she's eating creamed corn or cake. But she's my mother. She has needs, which Gillian took care of for years." She swallowed a sob. "I can't shirk my responsibility anymore. I don't want to."

"What are you going to do?"

Sam gulped. She'd decided, hadn't she? Even if she hadn't admitted it. Or said anything to anyone.

"I'm moving back." There it was.

Terry watched her carefully. He seemed to be working out what to say to her.

"To Delaware?"

"Not necessarily. It's not home for me anymore. I just need to be closer than a plane ride. Somewhere on the East Coast within two hours of her facility."

"Couldn't you move her closer to you?"

"I thought about it, believe me. The thing is, she's comfortable where she is, Terry. She's got a routine. They know her. Everything is paid for in perpetuity, thanks to an agreement extracted years ago by a clever lawyer. How can I upend her life?"

"Yet you're willing to upend yours."

"My life? I live in a rented room in a house away from town. I have acquaintances and subordinates rather than friends. My social life consists of church picnics and holiday parties. I also enjoy yoga, bourbon, and the occasional nightmare. I'll always be the new sheriff in town, even though I sit at the poker table with the big boys. At least I hired an administrative assistant who knits instead of killing brunettes. Coffee's better, too."

"Sam."

"I've been running away my entire adult life, Terry. Time for me to plant a flag. Just not in Tennessee."

She swiped a hand at her face, realized she had tears running down her cheeks. "I'll be fine. I've been working on my résumé. Someone will want a former sheriff with a couple of high-profile cases under her belt, right?" She looked at him more closely. "Terry, what's going on? I swear you've tried on about a dozen expressions in the last thirty seconds. Is this about my sad story or your news?"

Terry ducked his head. "Hang on while I try out my enigmatic expression. There." He took a couple of deep breaths. "I have three news items. To start with, I've been promoted."

"Well, that's exciting. Will you be running the field office in Tampa?"

"Nope. I'm headed back to D.C. to rejoin the Criminal Investigative Division. Next week, if you can believe it. I'll keep my special agent status with a pay bump. Take on selected field assignments while I study for a master's degree. Then, just about when my knees give out, I'll become a supervisor."

He stopped, looked at her. "Well, you've sure got the inscrutable thing down pat. I didn't expect a parade, but maybe a show of happiness."

In truth, she felt trapped between elation and dread. Would she never be free of this man? "Sorry, you caught me by surprise. Congratulations, Terry. D.C. is the big time. Should be a real career booster for Mercy as well."

"What? Never mind. Let's get back to you a minute. If you're determined to move back to the mid-Atlantic region, I can help. Make a few calls, call in a few markers. Not that you need my help. With your résumé, you could easily find a job within driving distance of your mother. Small town or major cities like Philadelphia, Annapolis, or Baltimore. Washington would be ideal. We'd see more of each other." He grinned.

"Ideal? Are you serious? Look, maybe you and Mercy are going to be D.C.'s newest power couple, but if you think I'm going to be hanging out with you two, you're wrong."

"Hang out?" Terry looked surprised, then angry. He strode over to Sam, grabbed her by the arms. "What the hell is wrong with you? There is no Mercy. I mean, she's not coming with me. If you'd let me finish—"

"She—what?" Sam broke away from him. "You didn't say anything—"

"She isn't coming. I've been working my way around to telling you that. I didn't want my situation to affect any decision you made. Not that it would, mind you. Obviously, I want you to move closer to me, but only if it works for you."

"If what works for me?"

"Jesus, Tate, why are you being so obtuse?" Terry yelled.

"You're not exactly making yourself clear, Sloan!" She matched his volume.

They froze at the discreet knock at the door. Sallie Mae.

"Sheriff? Everything all right in there? I thought I'd take off."

"Go ahead, Sallie Mae. We're good here. Have a nice night."

They listened for the receding footsteps. Terry released her arms and stepped back.

"Mercy's not coming because we're not together anymore," he said quietly. "I had to own up to not loving her the way she needed me to. First to myself, then to her."

Sam found it difficult to breathe. "I'll bet that was hard for you both."

"I hurt her, Sam. That's the worst part." He looked pained. "She accused me of using her to rebound from my wife's death."

"She wasn't the rebound, Terry. Maybe I was."

His eyes flashed. "No, Tate. You were the one that got away."

Sam swayed on her feet. "How'd you let that happen, Sloan?"

He reached for her and took her in his arms. Gently, so she could pull away if she wanted. She had no interest in pulling away.

"I don't know, but it's not going to happen twice."

He kissed her. Slowly, then with greater urgency. She answered in kind. She felt as if she'd been pumped full of oxygen. Or plugged into an outlet and switched on. As if she'd been tossed off a high cliff or lifted into the air. As if she'd been brought back from the dead.

They broke off for a couple of seconds, then dove back in for more. All at once, Terry leaned back an inch. His expression hovered between hunger and concern.

"Too much?" he asked. "Too fast? Should we go out to dinner? Wait until we have someplace classy to go? By which I don't mean either the Sportsman Lodge or your rented room."

Her green eyes twinkled. "We have another option, Agent Sloan. I have a comfortable couch." Sam inclined her head to the leather sofa against one wall. "Complete with removable back cushions."

"Ah, the perks of being a sheriff," he replied as he unbuttoned her pressed white shirt.

* * *

Afterwards, they rested in a tangle of arms and legs.

"We fit," Terry said.

"How so?" Sam murmured.

"I mean we fit together. I'd forgotten how well."

She propped herself up on one elbow. "Are you suggesting I'm forgettable?"

"Anything but." He pulled her to him and began to nibble her ear. She giggled with pleasure.

"That tickles."

"How about if I move down a bit?"

She pushed lightly against his chest. "Much as I like that idea, we have some talking to do."

"About what just happened? About us?"

"Hell, no. I mean, yes. Of course. It's just that a lot has happened. Is happening. I don't know how much I can handle at one time."

"I get it; no declarations. Except—" Doubt filled his eyes. "I know we're going through some big changes. We'll both be starting new jobs—"

"Assuming I get one."

He kissed her. "You will. What I'm trying to say in my clumsy way is I want you in my new life. I want us to work."

"Me, too, Terry."

His sigh of relief melted her heart. "Okay, then. Where were we?" He nuzzled her neck.

"Hold on, fella. Wasn't there a third piece of news you had to share?"

"Way to kill a mood, Tate." Terry pulled himself up to sit at the edge of the couch. He ran a hand through his hair. "I don't know if this qualifies as news. More like an informed hunch."

She sat up next to him. "What is it?"

"I don't believe Arthur Randolph died of natural causes."

Sam stared at him. "Suicide? No, you think he was murdered."

"Yes." Terry filled her in on his discussion with Randolph's mother and her subsequent discovery that her son's computer had been wiped. He also told her about the exchange with William Sorrel.

"I should have told you all this months ago, Sam. What with the Wedding Crasher—" He shook his head. "Maybe I thought I was shielding you. Doesn't matter. No excuse."

Her anger flared, then dissipated.

"Never mind, Terry. Something's off about the Randolph death. We always assumed he acted alone. Does his missing manuscript say different? Sorrel's words are cryptic, to say the least. He's implying mob interest in Randolph and in me. Why? My family was never connected to organized crime. Who cares about the long-ago recollections of a traumatized little girl?"

Terry looked off. "I can think of one person. An MNPD psychiatrist who evaluated a new recruit for the Nashville police and continued a professional relationship with her. Dr. Jayne Sommers."

"My former shrink. Who, by the way, has conveniently disappeared."

Epilogue

Jayne Sommers balanced her purchases in one arm and unlocked the door to her second-floor "studio suite." That's how the seedy rent-by-the-week motel she'd lived in for two months referred to the four-hundred-square-foot space. The kitchen area featured a two-burner stove and half refrigerator. The adjacent alcove held a wobbly little table and two chairs. The main area boasted a ratty couch and a lumpy bed with a scarred dresser.

At least the common walls were joined at the kitchen and bathroom. The configuration muffled the sounds of squeaky mattresses and stage-worthy groans from the adjacent occupants. The place was a destination for the professionals who brought their marks or low-rent sugar daddies who thought they were showing their women a good time. Afternoon flings and one-night stands were the norm. The cast of characters changed. Only she and the taciturn clerk at the front desk provided continuity.

Jayne stumbled from blistering sunlight into near darkness. The blackout curtains added a layer of privacy and gave a boost to the ancient air conditioner. She had no reason to look out to the gravel parking lot or the barren landscape just beyond, unrelieved save for a series of sagging wires strung between brown poles. She had every reason not to want anyone to look in.

She assumed she'd be safe in this desolate stretch of desert in southwest Arizona. She was close to the border yet far from much of anything else. She reminded herself daily she would move on when enough time had passed. Three months tops. Then San Diego for a while. Hawaii after that. She had a plan.

The isolation, the desolation, the boredom of her life weighed on her. Logic dictated she be patient. Sanity pushed her to move. How long would the man with the menacing voice look for her? How much effort would he or his cohorts expend? She didn't understand why he considered Samantha Tate's recollection of the massacre so important. She only understood her failure to fully unlock those memories had disappointed her one-time benefactor. He'd let her know as much in no uncertain terms. After their last conversation, she'd fled.

She knew the Wedding Crasher had been captured. The headlines jumped at her from newspapers and televisions wherever she went. The story dominated national news for a week. Images of the arresting officers shared space with a grainy image of the killer and her son.

How she'd wanted to call Sam to offer congratulations and a warning. She didn't dare. She had no computer, no phone. Once, at the beginning of her stay, she'd visited an Internet café and logged onto the web to check for messages. After ten minutes, she logged off in a panic. Outside, she stomped on her phone and tossed it into the sewer.

Keep yourself in the present, she ordered herself. *Unpack the groceries, take a shower.* She headed for the bathroom, peeling her clothes off and dropping them on the floor. She couldn't get used to the dry heat; she felt caked in dust and sucked of moisture. Showering helped her feel half human, notwithstanding the unpredictable water pressure.

Today the shower proved satisfying, the water flow steady and warm. Afterwards, she wrapped herself in the heavy bath sheet she'd bought at a local big-box store.

The small luxury always afforded her a modicum of comfort.

She swiped at the fogged mirror and saw a woman she scarcely recognized. Her pitch-black hair reached almost to her shoulders. Her cheekbones pushed against skin that looked like parchment paper. The wire-rim glasses she wore were from years earlier, the prescription serviceable though out of date. She was someone else. Jayne Sommers was gone, perhaps forever.

The room phone by the bed rang. Probably the front desk, although she couldn't imagine why. Maybe the owner had decided to raise the room rent. Why not? He certainly had a captive audience.

"Please forgive the intrusion, Dr. Sommers," said the caller.

Jayne stopped breathing. One or two seconds. Then her heart began to race, faster and faster until her chest hurt. She broke out in a cold sweat. Light-headed, she leaned against the wall and pulled the towel more tightly around her.

"I hope I didn't catch you at an inopportune time," he continued. The voice mesmerized her. His was an instrument that could soothe or menace, inspire or terrorize.

"A bit inconvenient," she managed to say. "Perhaps I can call you back?"

His chortle unnerved her. "I think not, Dr. Sommers. However, I will hold while you make yourself more comfortable."

"I'll be just a minute, then." She lay the receiver facedown on the bed and whipped her head around. He can't see me, she reminded herself. Or can he? She yanked on a T-shirt and a pair of sweatpants from the closet. Then she circled to the kitchen for a bottle of wine before returning to the bedside.

"Sorry to keep you waiting." She spoke in her most professional manner. "How can I help you, Mr. . . . I don't believe I ever got your name."

"Jones will do. Tell me, how do you like southern Arizona?"

She put a hand to her throat. How did he find her? She wouldn't ask. "It's temporary," she replied, and could have kicked herself.

"Of course. No doubt you'll then head to the coast or beyond. Do your colleagues know you're not returning? Do your patients? You've made a point of staying out of touch, Dr. Sommers. Virtually no communication with anyone. Very much below the radar, so to speak. Not good for business."

"Mr. Jones," she managed to say. "I don't know how or why my life is any of your concern. As for our professional dealings, I clearly did not meet your expectations. I made an error in judgment in taking payment from you. That was tantamount to accepting a bribe. I told you as much during our last conversation." She said nothing about his threats against her daughter.

"I regret I may have misled you into believing I could pull twenty-five-year-old memories out of Samantha Tate," she went on. "Perhaps I could have done so but only with her permission. I couldn't very well put her under without consent, could I? As I explained to you, I can repay the money. I only need an address or an account number—"

"Stop." The single word, softly uttered, chilled her blood.

"Dr. Sommers," he continued, "you don't know who you're dealing with. Or why. The second is related to the first. Let me enlighten you. On the face of it, I'm a wealthy and successful businessman, as well as the scion of a powerful and well-connected family. I have education, skill, money as well as other forms of capital, and a flexible set of ethics. In other words, I'm in a position to run for political office at a high level, maybe even the highest." He chuckled.

"I don't need to hear this."

"Allow me to finish. My family has worked very hard to stay both visible and invisible. It's a balancing act, believe me. To operate in the light of day and the middle of the night, metaphorically speaking. In front of and behind the scenes."

"Legally and illegally," she said. She'd begun to compose herself. She'd dealt with all manner of criminals. He was just another thug.

"You catch on quickly. To move an entire organization from questionable practices into legitimate businesses with access to mainstream levers of power took patience and several generations. Although some of us made that journey within a single lifetime."

She felt a twinge of impatience mix with her fear. Good, she was regaining control. "I don't know what you expect from me at this point," she said.

"What I *expected,* Dr. Sommers, was information on what the grown-up version of the little girl in a rose-colored dress remembered about the wedding that destroyed her family. Specifically, did she recall the man in a brown suit? Where he sat? What kind of gun he had? Where he pointed it? What he looked like?"

"Memories are tricky, Mr. Jones. I can't say if Samantha Tate will ever fully recall the face of the man in a brown suit with a gun." She took a deep breath. "Or if she'll recognize him twenty-five years later when he becomes a candidate for political office. She is a detective, however, and a very good one."

"As are you, Dr. Sommers."

She stuck the receiver between her shoulder and her ear, reached under the bed, and pulled out two pieces of luggage. Still holding the phone, she moved around the room, opening drawers and cabinets, grabbing items, throwing them into the open bags.

"I'm sorry I can't be of further assistance, Mr. Jones." She kept her tone even. "If you will provide an address, I will get you your money. Otherwise, I believe our business is finished." She waited.

"Very well, Dr. Sommers." The caller disconnected.

Ten minutes later, Dr. Jayne Sommers tossed a wad of cash on the bed and left her miserable room with a suitcase and a knapsack. She opened the trunk of her rental car, threw her luggage inside, and stood a moment by the driver's side to look around. *I won't miss this place, not at all,* she thought. Then the side of her head exploded. She was dead before she hit the asphalt.

--END--

About the Author

Thanks for reading *The Wedding Crasher*. I hope you'll take a minute to review it wherever you bought it or heard about it. The reviews help readers find me and they help me enormously.

About me: I'm the author of four books, including *Hope in Small Doses* which was both an Eric Hoffer medal finalist and a BookList book of the week, and *The Former Assassin*, a suspense thriller and Kindle Review category finalist for 2018. My essays have appeared in *The New York Times, USA Today, Newsweek,* and *Humanist Magazine*, as well as three anthologies. I've also published a number of short stories and co-authored the interactive murder mystery musicals that make up the *Café Noir* series, published by Samuel French. I'm a member of Mystery Writers of America, Sisters in Crime, and the Independent Book Publishers Association (IBPA).

The Wedding Crasher is the first in a planned series of mystery books about Samantha Tate. The second, *Bird in Hand*, will be published in 2020. You can read more at https://nikkistern.com. While you're there, why not subscribe? You can get a heads up on events, activities, and new work. You can also follow me on Facebook (Nikki Stern, Author), on Twitter and Instagram (@realnikkistern), where I post pictures of art, nature, and my dog.

Made in the USA
Middletown, DE
24 April 2019